DESCENSION
KNIGHTS OF THE SERAPHIM
Copyright 2023 © Olivia Boothe
https://oliviaboothe.com

Book cover design:
TrifBookDesign
https://trifbookdesign.com/

Internal layout:
Lunar Morrigan Arts
Giulia Calligola
https://www.lunarmorriganarts.com/

DESCENSION
KNIGHTS OF THE SERAPHIM

OLIVIA BOOTHE

*For those who believe
there is more beyond the veil.*

AUTHOR'S NOTE

Descension: Knights of the Seraphim is a dark apocalyptic fantasy romance. Triggers include: graphic violence, explicit sexual content, and other mature situations. For a more comprehensive content/trigger list, visit www.oliviaboothe.com

This is book two in the Hell's Angel series and cannot be read as a standalone novel. For the full reading experience please check out:

Afterworld: Losing Salvation 0.5
a short prequel (not required reading)
AVAILABLE FOR FREE

Afterworld: Road to Redemption
book one in the series (required reading)
AVAILABLE ON KU

Reader Discretion is Advised

Then war broke out in heaven. Michael and his angels
fought against the dragon, and the dragon and his angels
fought back. But he was not strong enough, and they
lost their place in heaven. The great dragon was hurled
down—that ancient serpent called the devil, or Satan,
who leads the whole world astray. He was hurled down,
and his angels with him.

REFELATION 12:7-9

CHAPTER 1

JAX

I could tolerate being hungry, but cold *and* hungry? This shit was getting old. Five months after winning the battle against my mother and the New York City Devil's Army sect, and we were still out here in search of the damn sanctuary, gaunt and exhausted. Food was scarce and with about two dozen hungry mouths to feed, things were looking grim.

It was late March and a high noon sun shone brilliantly above us, but a frigid breeze blew through my hair as a small crew of scavengers and I crept through another abandoned town in bumfuck New York, hunting for resources. The brutal winter we'd had refused to retract her frosty claws from the Northeast, not to mention that we were still recovering from the late winter storm we'd had a couple of weeks ago—which dumped over two feet of snow.

Dirty, frozen chunks still clung to the shadowed parts of this town where the sun seldom hit and the landscape was a depressing canvass of leafless trees and brown, cracked earth. Spring flowers were nowhere near budding, let alone blooming.

A cold shiver slithered down my back as the cold wind hit my face. "I'd give my left nut for some sixty-degree weather. I don't know how much more of this I can take."

"I'd give *my* left nut for some hot coffee right about now," Chaz said next to me as he pointed his rifle at the unmistakable green Starbucks sign about a hundred yards ahead.

"It wouldn't even have to be good coffee," I said.

Liling and Camila giggled behind us, whispering together as I led the scavenging group toward the coffeehouse's parking lot. At least they could still find the humor in things, even when we'd been out here for hours with only a can of corn to our name.

"I doubt there's anything edible left in here, but we should still take a look," I said as we approached Starbuck's entrance. Pushing the butt of my rifle against the already broken glass door, I cleared all the jagged pieces until I could reach inside and open the lock.

With slow and steady steps, we eased through, shards of glass softly crunching under our feet as we listened for the telltale signs of any damned scavenging for their own meal.

Nothing rushed out of the shop.

Brown wooden tables sat hidden under a thick layer of dust. A large 'hiring' sign still hung from the counter. A stale stench wafted from the direction of the now-inoperable open-air cooler that had once displayed their pre-made sandwiches and snacks. Whatever wasn't gone was black and unrecognizable, and I cringed at the sight.

"Perhaps they have sealed coffee beans in the back," Chaz whispered. He hopped over the service counter and nudged the back door with his gun. A collective silence overtook the space as we all held our breath, waiting to see if something had been asleep back there. The eerie *creak* the door made shot the hairs on my neck straight up, and I raised my rifle out of reflex, pointing it toward the opening. Nothing but silence leaked from the back room, but we remained hushed and alert.

"Taco Bell is empty," Clint announced as he walked into the Starbucks, startling us. "Too bad. I was hoping to find a few cans of refried beans." Clint looked around the musty interior of the café. "What are we hoping to find here?"

We all released the breath we'd been holding as we shook our heads. Good thing no damned had been lurking in that back room.

"What does it look like, dumbass? Coffee," Camila said with a smirk.

He leaned against an exposed brick column. "Seriously?"

I shrugged. "Worth a shot."

Chaz disappeared into the back room, and I took another look around behind the counters before following him in. "You three stay out here and keep watch while Chaz and I inspect the storage area." It was never easy taking my eyes off them when out scavenging for resources, but they were hardened by the harshness of our new world and were damn good at taking care of themselves. Clint had survived through the worst of the disease that overtook New York City. Liling had literally escaped from the bowels of the Horsemen's lair, and Camila had stayed strong in her faith, regardless of the atrocities she'd witnessed.

Still, I couldn't forget they were all just kids. Keeping them safe was my responsibility—I owed that much to Father Ortega and Jian. I would've preferred if they'd stayed at our camp in Stockbridge with the rest of the survivors, but Clint was our best tracker and trying to reason with two hard-headed teenage girls when they were bored out of their minds was pointless.

A bit of sunshine filtered through the broken blind, lighting up the small back room. The instant my eyes landed on the shelving unit lining the adjacent wall, I lowered my weapon and smiled, unable to hold back the whistle that burst from my lips.

Jackpot.

"Salted Almond Chocolate Bites." I read the label on one of the packaged items sitting on the shelf. "I mean, it's not coffee, but it sounds amazing." Whoever raided the supermarket must've overlooked Starbucks. "Got anything good?" I asked Chaz.

He huffed as he rummaged through a cupboard on the other side of the room. "Paper cups, stainless-steel thermoses, and mugs. We can fill the thermoses with water from the creek before heading back to camp."

I checked the next package on the shelf. "Woo-wee. Dark Chocolate-Covered Espresso Beans. Now, *that's* what I'm talking about, baby. There's a bunch of 'em, too."

Chaz looked up from his search, an eyebrow hiked way up.

"Caramel waffles… some oatmeal," I went on as I pulled my bag off my shoulders. If Hank had been with us, he would have been giving me puppy eyes, drooling at the find. Not that he would've left Kate's side, even if I'd tried to lure him away with the promise of snacks. Ever since he sensed the baby growing inside her, he'd turned into a bit of a ferocious protector, even more than before. They were literally attached at the hip.

Which made spending any time alone with my baby mama a bit of a project.

"Find anything good?" Clint asked from the door, startling me and dissolving all thoughts of Kate's warm body wrapped in mine.

"Fuck, kid. Didn't I say to stay outside with the girls?"

"They can handle themselves. Plus, we haven't seen a walking corpse in forever."

Both girls peeked their heads through the door. "What's everyone talking about?" Liling asked.

"Jax's a bit paranoid about me leaving you out there all alone…" he mocked.

"Why? Is it because we're *girls*?" she asked, her eyes rolling.

"I never said that," I crooned back.

"Yeah, Jax," Camila added with similar flair, trying to echo Liling's irritated tone. "Plus, it's not like we've seen a whole bunch of zombies around."

Clint crossed his arms, a satisfied grin creasing his lips. "See. That's what I said."

I shook my head. While hardened by this deadly world, in the end, Clint, Liling, and Camila were still just kids. And the fact we hadn't seen any d'shiad or damned wasn't exactly a good sign. Grunting, I went back to packing my bags. "Just keep an eye on the front door, will ya? There are worse things than zombies or demons out there."

"Yeah, like what?" Camila asked.

"*People.* Now go."

"Fuck this," Chaz said, giving up his search. "Liling, you get in here; I'll go keep watch with Camila and Clint."

In true teenage fashion, her shoulders slumped as she reluctantly accepted her new task.

"You didn't think you were just coming for the tour, did you?" I teased.

She stuck her tongue out at me.

"Come on, the quicker we get this done, the faster we can get back to camp. Just see if you can find anything else useful."

"Is coffee useful?" she asked.

My ears perked up, and I nearly choked on the chocolate bean I'd stuffed inside my mouth. "Don't mess with me, Liling…" I warned as I finished stuffing my bag.

"We *are* in a coffee shop," Liling said matter-of-factly.

I dropped my duffle and rose to my feet. Before her, a cabinet full of packaged coffees stared back at me. An insane craving bubbled in my gut, and I practically drooled. "Oh yeah, definitely useful. I can fit a few in my bag. Give me the ground stuff; we can't do much with whole beans without a grinder."

Loading four packs of coffee into my duffle, I was so euphoric, I almost didn't hear the scream that erupted from outside. It wasn't until it sounded again, louder this time, that Liling and I stared at each other, instantly recognizing the voice.

Camila...

"Shit. Time to go." I hauled my bag over my shoulder and grabbed my rifle from where I'd left it. I ran out of the back room and nearly slammed into Clint, who was already on his way out, his rifle drawn. Through the broken glass door, I caught sight of Chaz and Camila in the parking lot. The girl cowered behind the big guy while the Marine pointed his rifle at something I couldn't see from my position.

"Liling, stay back," I ordered as I dropped my duffle and pushed through the broken front door. "Clint, with me."

Growling like a d'shiad, but looking nothing like a hellhound, a lumbering monstrosity creeped across the parking lot on all fours. Spikes protruded from its spine, its slimy, black leathery skin steamed, burning by the sunlight. When it opened its mouth, rows of too many sharp teeth dripped with saliva. Though longer-limbed, it held the swagger of a croc. Given the sun's damage to its skin, this beast was clearly Hell-born, which meant desperation had brought it out during daylight hours, giving us the advantage.

I hoped.

"Haven't seen that type before," Chaz called out when I approached the beast from the opposite side, while Clint circled around to block it from behind. "Do you think they come in packs like the hounds?"

"No clue," I muttered, but I knew what he was getting at. If there were any more of them around, gunfire could lure them to us. Even slowed down by the sun, we couldn't take on a horde of demons.

Cursing under my breath, I lowered my rifle and reached for the army knife strapped to my thigh. Clint shot me a raised brow, but Chaz kept his eyes focused on the beast as it made its way toward him and Camila. He'd seen me do hand to hand combat with a giant scorpion before, so going up against a giant lizard thing wasn't a shocker. Granted, back then, I'd also been nearly invincible with Astaroth tied to my soul. With the demon gone and my ability to heal from mortal wounds non-existent, the knife shook slightly in my hand. I gripped the handle tighter and rushed at the beast, silencing all thoughts on how this could go wrong and hoping not to lose my nerve—or a limb.

I'd done this before, and I was fucking good at it. I didn't need a Horseman fused to my soul to take down one of hell's minions. Or, at least, that's what I tried to sell myself.

As I got about two feet from the monster, it belted an ear-splitting shriek that stopped me in my tracks. Literally. Some unseen force froze my body, limb by limb, muscle fiber by muscle fiber.

Balancing on one foot mid-run, I stood suspended like a fucking ballerina about to break into a pirouette. The knife slipped from my stone-still fingers. No part of my body budged, no matter how hard I begged my muscles to move.

The skull-crushing shriek that had escaped the beast still echoed in my brain. Its scaly lips peeled back in a snarl, and it looked like it was grinning with malice. Even as its flesh blistered from the sunlight, and strips of the black leather-like skin peeled off and evaporated into smoke, the demon didn't flinch, as if the sun was a mere nuisance.

From the corner of my eye, I noted Chaz was stuck in a similar frozen position. His rifle lay propped up on his massive shoulder, ready to fire, but if he was having the same trouble moving as I did, his finger couldn't pull the trigger. Clint fared no better on the other side of the monster.

We were royally fucked.

The lizard-thing continued its calculated stroll toward Chaz and Camila. It sniffed the air, licking its chops as if savoring something tasty, drool dripping at the corners of its cracked lips. Each drop sizzled as it hit the asphalt.

I couldn't quite figure out how it could smell anything aside from the stench of its own burning flesh.

Suddenly, a smoky substance spewed from its mouth, constricting my airways as it reached my nose. My lungs struggled for oxygen, and the lump in my throat had no way of escaping through my forced-shut lips. I couldn't make out what this new substance was, but it was suffocating. My vision blurred, and I was about to lose consciousness when shots rang out and the beast inhaled the smoke into its body.

More shots blasted and somehow, through the corner of my eye, I was able to make out Liling's form. Aiming her gun, she fired another round, and whatever power had imprisoned me loosened its hold on my body, finally enabling my muscles to move, but the relief was short-lived. I tried taking a few steps toward the beast, but walking felt like wading through waist-deep mud.

Camila and Chaz both unfroze as well, and the marine wasted no time spraying the beast with bullets. What did it matter now? Liling had already fired her weapon, might as well shred the son-of-a-bitch.

The demon shrieked and that otherworldly feeling of being paralyzed by some unseen force took a hold of us again. Chaz couldn't fire anymore. For some reason, though, Liling wasn't affected by the demon's strange ability to control us with its shriek. Perhaps she wasn't close enough for it to reach? She kept firing. Unfortunately, she still needed some target practice, and most of her bullets bounced off the asphalt—it's a miracle she didn't shoot one of us. But whenever she did manage to hit the demon, I felt the hold on me lessen.

I waited for a chip in the armor and managed to grab my army knife off the ground and lurched toward the beast.

Pitiful human... a voice hissed in my head, the words spoken in Latin. I looked around to see if anybody else had heard it too, but everyone seemed oblivious.

Your soul reeks of hellfire ... the voice spoke again, and this time, the lizard-like beast cocked its head slightly, his dark gaze penetrating mine. And that's when I knew the voice was coming from *it*. **You're a child of the darkness, but you've sold yourself back to these vermin.**

My body tensed. Last time I was able to hear demon thoughts was because I had one of the Horsemen fused to my soul. I couldn't understand how this was even possible. Astaroth had been completely wiped from existence, stabbed with empyrean steel. I knew because I'd died with him before Gavri'el breathed life back into me. I was certain no trace of him had remained.

Then again... I shook my head, refusing to allow the idea to take root in my mind.

The beast chuckled in my head. **You are forever bound to our realm, mortal. I can smell him in you. His essence is entwined with yours. But you know this. Deep down you know, even though you try to hide it, try to deny his existence. You feel his shadow, feel the pull of his power tugging at the fringes of your reality.**

"Shut the fuck up, you slimy shit." The whole crew turned in my direction, confused about who I was talking to. Only seconds had passed between unfreezing and now, yet it seemed like more time had elapsed. This demon was playing with my head. It appeared its power worked like that of a siren of some sort, and I needed its voice out of my head ASAP.

The demon growled, haunches raised as if ready to launch itself at me, but I roared in defense and rushed him, dodging its mouth and aiming my knife at its jaw. "Say *hello* to my little friend, motherfucker," I gritted, my knife cutting through flesh, pushing all the way through to the demon's skull. The lizard fell dead at my feet, and I pulled my blade free. Black ooze covered my arm up to my elbow, but other than the putrid stink emanating from its wound, it didn't seem to pose a threat any longer.

Shaking the blood off my arm, I said, "Never seen anything like it, but seems to be some type of lizard-like siren."

"More like a banshee if you ask me," Chaz grunted, rolling his shoulders and stretching his neck. "And that's some nasty ass funk coming off its dead body."

Clint nudged the corpse with his gun. It disintegrated at the touch, leaving a pile of black ash that soon got swooped away by the wind. "Earplugs might help. Maybe some filtered masks for the black shit that it spewed into the air. Let's hope we don't run into any more of these banshee lizard demons, though. Not being able to move at all was terrifying, and I've seen some terrifying shit since the world got fucked. Not to mention, the thing kept moving even after Chaz emptied a clip into the fucker." His eyes shifted to Liling. "You weren't affected at all?"

Sweat dripped down the side of her face as she holstered her gun back onto her belt. "I think I was too far," she said, her voice shaking. "Jax, I'm sorry for wasting so many bullets, but it was hard to distinguish the beast from that weird smoke. I didn't know what else to do." She pressed her lips into a tight line, trying to hold back tears.

I placed a hand on her shoulder. "You did well, Liling. You saved our asses."

We hadn't given Camila a gun as we hadn't encountered demons in quite some time, but after today, I probably wouldn't be comfortable taking her out with us anymore. She was barely thirteen, and I was not about to let the padre down by allowing his niece to get mauled by one of these nasties.

We'd become efficient at taking out infected, but demons were a different ball game, especially if they were now braving the sun. Thankfully, no one had gotten hurt, but I couldn't be sure more banshees weren't out there.

I'd had enough excitement on this scavenging mission. "Let's head back. I don't want to get caught after dark out here. Eyes peeled and stay close. We don't know if there aren't any more surprises lurking in this town."

Clint pulled out a map from his backpack, which he'd managed to confiscate weeks ago out of a trashed car. Thank God. Thing had come in very handy when navigating the area. Kid was not only a great scavenger, but a human GPS. He pointed to some spot on the map and started rambling off directions like he'd lived here his whole life. "If we head east down this road, we can hit up a couple of gas stations and maybe even a few extra shops before taking a right at this intersection and looping back up to camp. It's about thirty minutes out of the way, but we really need to find some gas or we ain't getting the buses back on the road anytime soon."

"Kid's right," Chaz said. "We're running out of food, Cap. And we got a lot of mouths to feed. We need to get those wheels back on the road and toward that sanctuary or we're fucked out here."

After some consideration, I agreed. We hit the lottery about a half a mile down the four-lane road when we reached the two broken-down gas stations, one on each side of the road. Not sure how it was possible, but inside one of the garages, we found two beat-up vehicles. Both had almost-full tanks of gas, which we siphoned into two red portable gas containers. In the other station, we found a fully operable van. It looked like it had been plucked from six decades ago, but I couldn't give two fucks.

After hot wiring the metal box, we jumped in and drove past a funeral home and toward the center of town, Chaz in the driver's seat, with me next to him, and the rest of the crew bounced around in the seatless back. We didn't see any more demons braving the sunlight, which eased the tension that had built up in my chest since we'd left Starbucks.

No one seemed to have noticed the exchange between the demon and me, which was a relief. I had no way of explaining why I could hear it speak in my head. Not to mention the things it said rattled something I'd tried to ignore for the last few months since the attack at the cathedral.

A sharp sting shot through my heart, causing my breath to catch. I rubbed at my chest as I adjusted myself on the seat. Chaz looked over, but I shrugged his concern away. It wasn't the first time I'd felt it. Kind of like a phantom pain that, every once in a while, reminded me I should be dead.

That's where Kate had stabbed me after Astaroth had taken full possession of my body. It was the only way to kill the son of a bitch, but in doing so, she'd killed me, too. Gavri'el had healed me back to life. Apparently, my job here on Earth wasn't done yet, but a part of me couldn't shake the feeling that a piece of my soul had stayed tethered to that demon or hell or to some darkness I couldn't quite define.

And now that fucking lizard-banshee had confirmed my fear, or maybe it had exploited it. Who the fuck knew, but sooner or later, I was going to need to come clean to Kate. It wasn't just the pain inside my chest, or the nudge at the back of my mind; I'd been having nightmares, too. She deserved the truth, especially if more of those demons were lurking around. If there was even a microscopic chance those beasts could use me against her or the baby, I'd slash my own throat. No second thoughts.

When we finally arrived in the center of town, we parked in front of a small gift shop next to the town's welcome center. Even though I wished for us to stay as a group, it was faster to go through the restaurants on Main Street in groups of two.

While Chaz and Camila walked into Salmon Run Fish House, and Clint led Liling into Prado's Café, I was left guarding the street.

I should've kept my eyes on either of the two restaurants, but as I leaned my ass against the passenger door of the van, I couldn't help but peer inside the gift shop. Its white-framed glass facade seemed undisturbed by the devastation around it. While many of the small shops showed signs of break-ins, this one was spared.

Guess nobody had any use for wedding gifts and random home decor these days. The display of dried flowers behind one of the windows was the only indication this store, too, had been affected by the passage of time. It wasn't the flowers or the unbroken glass that truly caught my attention, though. On the front window display, a stuffed teddy bear lay nestled next to a onesie, and I couldn't tear my eyes away from it.

Pushing off from the van, I peeked deeper into the shop. The baby section was just beyond the cashier, close enough to the windows where, if I decided to go in, I'd still be able to see if there was any trouble out on the street. After scanning the streets one last time, I abandoned my post and tried turning the knob. To my surprise, the door simply creaked open.

In a couple of strides, I closed the distance to the baby display. Above the toys, baby clothes in pink and blue hung from a clothes rack. I touched one, and the softness of the fabric took me by surprise as it catapulted me through time, back to before the world ended. A time not marred by all this grim darkness and death. I was unable to help the smile curling the corners of my lips.

The only clues we had that we were expecting a boy were Mikha'el's word and Kate's vision. I didn't trust Mikha'el; he'd promised to return and here we were, five months later, and there was no sign of him. A mother's instinct carried more weight in my eyes. I grabbed two blue onesies and a teddy bear, hiding them inside my jacket before I took up my post outside once more.

Chaz and Camila returned first. I eyed their approach, but neither of their faces let on if their search was successful. Chaz dropped his bag on the passenger side of the car and it landed with a heavy *thud*.

"What did you find?" I asked.

"Take a look," the big guy said with a shrug.

I unzipped his bag, revealing filled water bottles and two fermented sausages. That was it. Water, while extremely important, didn't fill stomachs. It was a good find, but we needed a proper meal.

"It's for the coffee," Camila chirped when my only response was a nod.

I offered her a gentle smile. At least we had coffee. "I guess we're all good, then."

Clint and Liling scored some pickled olives, a couple jars of marinara sauce, and four boxes of expired whole wheat pasta. Better than nothing.

Before the sun began to fade, we were back on the road, en route to our camp. Before the gates opened, Stockbridge, Massachusetts, would have been a lovely place to visit. With a golf club and a wildlife park, botanical garden, several museums, and what used to be cozy inns, this small town must have been a popular vacation spot.

The museums held nothing of interest for us now, though. Artwork and historic estates held little value these days, and we were in no mindset to explore the memorabilia when we arrived. The wildlife park seemed interesting at first, but all we ever saw were squirrels, birds, and the occasional rabbit— which made for a nice meaty snack once in a while.

We'd arrived a month ago, short on gas and supplies. The plan hadn't been to stay much longer than a few days to gather more supplies and rest. But after several weeks, we hadn't been able to find enough gas to get the two buses back on the road. We hoped that now, after the new gas haul, we could fill up the tanks enough to take us farther north toward Albany in search of the sanctuary. Kate was certain the boat people we'd met back when she and I were rushing to get Hank across the Hudson had been heading there.

It was a strong hunch, but a hunch, nonetheless. We had two dozen people with us, the majority of them the young girls we'd rescued from my mother's clutches. These people depended on us—on us finding them a safe place to live and wait.

Wait for what? Fuck if I knew. All we had was some cryptic message from an angel who promised us help was on the way and that our son was the key to salvation. Perhaps a cure to the disease that had killed off more than half the population before turning them into zombies. That was five months ago, and the angels had been MIA and we were still miles from Albany.

But what if we never found the sanctuary? What the hell were we supposed to do with all these people? With all the promises we'd made them—the lies we'd told them just to keep people sane. It was a possibility Kate refused to entertain. Maybe because she had renewed faith; perhaps she had a connection to Micha'el that kept her hope intact. Or maybe she was just lying to herself like we all were. Because we had nothing else to hold on to.

We should've never stayed in this town this long to begin with. We would've been better off packing up what we could carry and kept going on foot. But the peacefulness of Pine Street was hard to come by these days, and when we found not only an episcopal church, but also St. Joseph's Catholic church just a short walk away from a cemetery, we knew this was a place we could regroup. The hallowed ground offered us protection in the event of a demon attack.

After clearing the area of any Damned, we were able to settle in. The Red Lion Inn offered all the comforts you'd wish for after sleeping mostly in bus seats for two months. Getting stuck in a snowstorm a couple of weeks back had been the worst of it, but I hoped we were ready to move out now that the days were getting longer and warmer. Even in its peacefulness, Stockbridge wasn't sustainable—we needed stable food, not just shelter.

We slowly pulled into the parking lot of the inn, calling out to the two male Guardians standing on the porch, keeping watch to ensure they didn't mistake us for pillagers. After handing over our haul, I strapped my rifle over my shoulder and ambled inside.

Before I reached the hallway, Kate ambushed me in the lounge, and Hank was right behind her. Hair up in a high ponytail, a few strands hung loosely, framing her face. Cheeks rosy, she glowed, either from the pregnancy or because she was still peeved with me for not letting her tag along this morning.

Either way, the blush suited her well. She was as stunning as ever. Her round belly was accentuated by the too-small pants she wore. Her long sweater did very little to hide that the top button of her pants was open. She was growing out of clothes faster than we could find new ones, but I knew that wasn't what furrowed her brow.

She hated being idle, and this pregnancy had been progressing faster than we'd expected. At five months, she looked like she was two weeks past-due—at least, from what I'd heard the other women say. I'd not dared make that assessment on my own for fear of being fed to Hank in small chunks.

Still, it had taken a toll on her body. She would be a serious liability out on runs. I'd rather suffer her wrath than let her put herself at risk because she felt she had something to prove.

We all knew she was a badass. And right now, we needed her safe so she could birth this baby and keep kicking demon ass afterward.

"It's nearly sundown, Jax. We spoke about this," she said, sticking her index finger in my chest.

"Ow, have you gotten stronger since this morning?"

"Stop changing the subject. We agreed, no runs after dark."

"We're back before dark."

"*Barely.* You had Camila and Liling with you. I've been a nervous wreck."

"The girls can handle themselves. And we made it back, baby. We're safe."

She crossed her arms and huffed. Hank followed suit with his own huff, like the shadow he was.

My eyes narrowed over him. "I know. You'll always side with her. I've got something that will cheer you up, angel," I said, giving her a kiss on the cheek.

Her arms remained crossed above her belly, those eyes brimming with mock anger. "What?" she asked, her lips pouty. God, she was fucking adorable.

Pulling out the teddy bear and onesies from under my jacket, I said, "Gifts for the little dude."

CHAPTER 2
KATE

All my anger melted away the instant Jax's blue eyes twinkled when he showed me the onesies and teddy bear he'd found.

A nervous laugh twitched at the corners of his lips and he ran a hand through his sweaty hair. "When I saw the cute dog on the front of one of the onesies, I immediately thought of Hank and how he's gonna go bonkers over the baby." He nodded toward my belly and something deeper than love shone in his eyes. Rubbing the back of his neck, he sighed, deep and heavy. "So, I took them off the rack. Had to bring them home, you know?"

Only Jax was capable of making me want to punch and kiss him at the same time. He could be a pain in my ass at times, but mostly, he worshiped the ground I walked on. And these little tender moments when he showed me he'd been thinking of our baby as if I wasn't carrying humanity's human/angel/demon-hybrid savior, but just our son, reminded me how much I truly loved this man.

Of how much I never expected to find happiness again amongst all the darkness and death.

I rushed toward him, wanting to rope my arms around his neck but barely able to due to the beach ball in my belly. I burst into tears when he kissed my forehead and placed a hand on my baby bump. "Home?" I asked. "How do you even know where that is these days?"

Tipping my chin up, he kissed my lips. "Angel, *you're* my home. No matter where in this fucking shithole of a planet we end up, you will always be the only place I'll ever call home. You, the baby, and Hank."

More tears streamed from my eyes and I wiped at them furiously, whimpering and laughing at the same time. I wanted to blame it all on the hormones, but truth be told, I'd been an utter mess all day. Not because I was hormonal, but because every day I was reminded about how frail our lives were.

One minute we could all be here, and the next, someone could be gone. I'd lost so much to this war that I was beyond petrified of losing the people I loved all over again. Rules kept us alive; it was the pact we'd established before leaving New York City. I'd been so furious when I found out he'd taken the girls with him against my wishes, I wanted to wring his neck. And when it was approaching sundown and they still hadn't showed up, I swore I was going to go into labor.

I hadn't told Jax because I didn't want to worry him, but I'd been experiencing contractions for the last few days. I'd figured they were Braxton Hicks from the pregnancy book, *What to Expect When You're Expecting*, Clint had scavenged from a library a couple of weeks back. That kid was always thinking about the things none of us ever did. Our minds were always on the essentials: food, water, shelter. He'd found me a body pillow for which I would be forever grateful, plus a jar of pickled olives—my secret pregnancy craving.

The contractions had intensified, though they weren't consistent, which meant I wasn't in active labor. Difference was, I was not pregnant with a typical baby. At twenty weeks,

I should've just recently started to sport my baby bump, but in reality, I looked to be at term. It was worrying since none of the survivors in our party were medical professionals. We didn't even have a nurse in our ranks.

All I had was a guide published decades ago, but nothing about this pregnancy was normal, and the expectations regarding birthing a human/angel/demon baby could not be found in any book. Not a day went by where I didn't worry about the mechanics of giving birth during the apocalypse. It was back to the Middle Ages for me—no pain meds, no hospital.

What if the baby was presented in a breech position? What if I needed an emergency cesarean? What if he came too early? What if the baby needed oxygen or an incubator? What if I developed an infection?

And even if delivery went without a hitch, then what? Clint and the scavenger groups were always on the lookout for baby items, but the stash of supplies I had were meager and wouldn't last long. I'd begun to make cloth diapers from sheets, and I'd secretly prayed to any being who would listen to please ensure I could breastfeed this baby, because finding baby formula that was not expired had been near to impossible. So, what would happen if I had no milk? How the heck was I supposed to nourish my baby?

Perhaps it was the stress of pregnancy, plus seeing how unsettled the group had become that the weight of it all took a toll on my body. We were a bunch of starving, sitting ducks, camped out inside this broken-down abandoned historic inn, at risk of a potential demon or zombie attack—all because some person who I'd briefly met months ago had told me there was a sanctuary somewhere in Albany.

These people chose to follow me blindly because they witnessed a miracle the night Gavri'el showed up with her wings spread wide and glowing like the sun. She'd brought Jax back from the dead, giving them hope that God had not forsaken us. She gave them something to believe in, and now they looked to me for guidance, for answers.

Because they believed I carried their salvation—that my son was the chosen one.

But the chosen one for what? I couldn't deny there were days I felt like Sara Connor fighting against the machines—fighting to find that glimmer of hope. I had no idea what fate awaited my baby, but lately, one phrase kept ringing inside my head: *There's no fate but what we make.* Such a stupid movie line, but heaven-fall if it didn't ring true in my heart. I couldn't sit idle and wait for shit to happen; I couldn't rely on an angel's prophetic words when that angel had spread her wings once more and left, never to return.

It's why I'd suggested we bring the survivors to Albany. I grew tired of waiting for Mikha'el to show up. Things had worsened in the city with daily demon attacks. Death was out there, amassing his army, and I couldn't risk him coming for me and the baby.

But after weeks on the road, having to detour because of impassable roads or bridges, losing precious time and resources, I'd begun to doubt my resolve. We lucked out when we found this abandoned town with minimal damage and a very small infestation of infected. But we'd drained it of all that had been left behind by the people who'd once lived here, and I'd started to recognize that lost look in people's eyes—the cloud of desperation hovering over them because they too had probably started to lose their faith in this mission.

The most upsetting part was the fact that I had no clue what we would do if we didn't find the sanctuary. What was I supposed to tell these people? To turn around and head back to the city with zero gas and food? Rebuild? Adapt and learn to share this world with demons and zombies? Create our own sanctuary? Where? How?

My head hurt from all the unanswered questions.

"Hey, what's the matter?" Jax asked. "We don't have to keep the onesies if you don't like them."

I smiled and wiped at the stupid tears bubbling at the corners of my eyes. "No, silly. It's not that. I love them and the teddy. I'm just growing restless… everyone is. We can't stay in this town. We have to keep moving."

"Here, why don't you sit down?" He took me by the hand and guided me into the inn's main dining room. From the antique pictures hung on the walls, it was easy to tell it was once a lovely, quaint space surrounded by now-dusty and opaque crystal chandeliers, antique china, and colonial pewter. Now it was our makeshift mess hall. All the square tables had been reorganized into one long table, with no fancy tablecloths or centerpieces, and certainly no elaborate meals.

With a hand on my back, I slowly lowered onto a wooden chair. Doing anything these days required so much energy. Jax took the chair across from me and spun it around, straddling it and placing his forearms on the backrest. "I think we have enough gas now to get back on the road."

"Are you serious?"

"Yup. Clint took us through some back roads, and we ended up in this tiny little village where we were able to score about six jugs of gasoline. According to Clint's map, Albany is about fifty miles northwest—an hour trip max—even if we take the local roads to avoid the broken-down vehicle blockades on the highway."

"Will six jugs be enough?"

"The gasoline has likely degraded considerably, but I think it should be enough to get us there."

"Provided we don't run into a horde of Devoured or demons or other survivors." These days, the living were more dangerous than the dead.

Jax stood and walked over, crouching down to be at eye level. "Those variables never change, angel. We're gonna get through this, okay? We're going to find that sanctuary."

I sighed into my palms. "But what if we don't? What am I supposed to say to all these people?"

He peeled my hands away. "This is not you, Kate. You're a fighter. You don't give up."

"I don't know, maybe it's this place. I just don't feel right here."

He straightened. "Did something happen while I was gone?"

My tailbone hurt, so I stood as well. "No. It's this town." I lowered my voice, as I didn't want to alarm anybody lingering in the hallway. "Have you ever wondered why there were no survivors here? Why we only found practically a handful of infected. Why was this place still so full of resources, even almost two years after the gates opened?"

"What are you saying?"

"I'm saying that ever since we arrived, I've had this strange sensation at the back of my neck, like something wasn't right here, and it's only worsened in the last few weeks."

His gaze dropped as if contemplating his words. "Not gonna say I didn't find it odd too, but after being on the road for so long, it felt good to just have a place to crash for a while." He grabbed my elbow and leaned in closer to my ear. "But now that you mention it, there's something I need to tell you. Today, while scavenging, we—"

"Hey, Miss Katie," Clint called out, smiling ear to ear as he strolled in from the inn's kitchen, interrupting whatever Jax was about to say. My lungs deflated a little. I really wanted to know what Jax planned to tell me, but the kid was always so kind and sweet, I couldn't help but smile back.

Every time I looked at him, my heart cracked a tiny bit. The kid was only eighteen, but the apocalypse had hardened him into a man. Shaggy brown hair, weathered green eyes, and skin that looked like it had spent too much time in the sun. If I didn't know better, I'd think he was in his late twenties.

Still, as hard as he had to fight to survive, he took each day in stride, always smiling, always looking for ways to help out. The kid seldom talked about his life before the gates opened. Guess he wasn't much different from the rest of us. That world no longer existed, and sometimes it was best not to touch those memories. All we knew was that he was alone, and now he considered our crew his family.

He rubbed Hank between the ears before plopping his ass on top of the dining table and popping what looked like a chocolate nugget into his mouth.

"What are you eating?" I asked, suspiciously eyeing the small snack bag in his hand.

Clint flashed me a crooked grin, reminding me that underneath all the grime, there still existed a very handsome young man who would've had all the girls pining for his attention—probably still did from the way I always caught the girls giggling whenever he was around. He gestured toward Jax. "Your man here raided a Starbucks."

I turned toward Jax. "Is that so?"

"We didn't find much in terms of real food, but we now have enough coffee to last us until the next apocalypse. Oh, and loads of chocolate treats."

Suddenly, I felt a jab inside my belly. "Ow," I said, placing a hand on my stomach. "Please don't joke about another apocalypse. You've upset the baby."

"Wait, what?" Jax asked, his body going rigid.

"The baby… he just kicked. Really hard."

Hank whined and paced back and forth—always the worried pooch.

"I'm okay," I told him with a wink.

Clint laughed. "Maybe the baby wants some of this chocolate."

"Or maybe he's telling his momma she needs to rest," Jax added, looking a bit concerned. "Tell her, Hank; you're the only one she'll listen to."

I rolled my eyes. Neither of these men knew anything about pregnancy.

Clint jumped off the table. "Well, I didn't mean to interrupt. Just came to tell you Liling and Camila are in the kitchen, helping the other girls unpack our haul in case you were looking for them." He grinned and added, "There's a little jar of your favorite stuff, too."

"Oh my God, I could kiss you right now."

"Hey now," Jax said, crossing his arms.

Clint laughed and pulled something else out of his pants pocket. "Gonna grab a smoke before dinner, if that's okay?"

Jax took a couple of steps toward Clint, hands on his waist. "Wait, you scored cigarettes and didn't tell me?"

Wiggling the half-empty pack in the air, Clint ambled toward the front door. "Finders keepers. Your words, man."

"Dinner is at eight," I shouted after him as he exited the door.

"Can't believe the kid has been holding out on me."

"That shit's not good for you, anyway." I jabbed at his arm. After a short, shared laugh, I said, "So, what was it you were gonna tell me before Clint showed up?"

He sat down on one of the dining chairs, patting Hank on the neck as he looked up at me. "We, ah…" He paused, biting down on his bottom lip. "You know what? It can wait until after dinner. Right now, I'd rather freshen up before we eat."

"The guys brought in buckets of fresh water from the creek. They left a couple in our bathroom."

He stood and drew me in close, palming my cheek. "How about I give you a rubdown later tonight… help ease some of that stress?"

"That sounds divine."

Kissing me, long and deep, the warmth of his breath ignited desire in my core. He caressed my jaw, drawing a moan from my lips. "I've missed you, angel."

"I've missed you, too."

Our gazes locked, and I reached up to cup his bearded face. He'd grown it back out and I loved how rugged it made him look. "How about we do more than just a rubdown?" I asked, raising my brows, a hint of mischief in my voice.

He laughed, that deep rumble vibrating through my body and touching me in all the right places. "You sure it's okay, though? You know, with the baby and all? Plus, you said you've been achy…"

"Hush. If I say I'm okay to fuck, then I'm okay to fuck."

His eyes widened. "Damn. I love it when you talk dirty to me." He leaned in for another kiss, but I rushed him off to get cleaned up while Hank and I wobbled over to the kitchen to see what we could scrounge up for dinner.

Dinner was a sad meal of expired whole wheat pasta and marinara sauce cooked over an open fire. We were so hungry, we practically ate in silence, except for the clinking of metal spoons against porcelain china. By the time the roaring flames inside the large fireplace burned out, not a single morsel was left on anyone's plate.

The adults topped off the night with a cup of dark roast coffee Jax had brewed the old-fashioned way. I had a cup of the decaffeinated variety—which tasted like a crappy Manhattan sidewalk-bought cup of joe on a busy morning commute on the way to the station.

Literal heaven.

Would've tasted even better with a little milk and sugar, but beggars couldn't be choosers.

To preserve firewood, batteries, and candles, bedtime was early. Made no sense to stay up when we could just rise with the sun and do everything we needed to do without wasting resources. I said goodnight to the girls while Jax walked around the perimeter of the inn, making sure our night watch was secure.

I'd finished rinsing my teeth when Jax walked into our room, a small lit candle in his hand. Sprawled on our king-sized bed, Hank lifted his head, ears perked as he watched Jax approach the bathroom. Jax placed the candle on the sink's countertop, then leaned his shoulder against the doorframe. Crossing his arms, he took a deep breath. The flickering flames of the candle reflected in his blue eyes.

"You look exhausted," I said.

"It's been a long day."

"Are we set for tomorrow?"

"We start packing up at the crack of dawn. Should be on the road by noon."

I wrapped my arms around his neck as best as I could and buried my nose in his chest, inhaling the comforting scent of his warm skin. He smelled like caffeine, smoke, and something more, something uniquely him. I never felt safer than when I was encased in his chest. Even with my big belly protruding, he was still able to encircle his arms around me.

I sighed and sagged into his embrace. "As much as this place gives me the creeps, I am going to miss having our own little room. Who knows what the sanctuary will actually be like. If we'll have privacy. If they'll even take us in."

Jax gently pulled away and caressed my jaw. "That's a problem for another day, angel. How about that back rub I promised you instead?"

I smiled and nodded, letting him guide me toward the large canopy bed. Hank reluctantly hopped off and trotted toward the sitting area of our suite, then jumped up onto one of the sofas.

During the day, the vibrant green rug dominated the space, along with the paisley wallpaper. The room's Colonial decor wasn't necessarily my taste, but after several weeks of sleeping here, I'd grown fond of the old-world charm. In the shadows, though, my entire focus was on the man standing before me.

Jax and I stood on the side of the bed as he slowly lifted my T-shirt over my head, revealing my naked breasts and enormous belly. Spring had only just started, and the temperature had dropped drastically after dusk. Without the heat of the fireplace, the room felt extremely cold and a profound chill rattled my bones. I rushed to cover myself with my arms, but Jax lowered my hands. "You're so fucking beautiful, Kate. Don't you dare hide your body from me."

"I don't feel very sexy right now, not to mention, it's so chilly."

"Maybe you can't see it, but your pregnant body is gorgeous," he said, eyes roaming every inch of my upper body. "Everything about you is the epitome of feminine beauty."

My body shivered again.

"Don't worry," he added, rubbing my arms. "I'll raise your body temperature soon enough."

I laughed and jokingly slapped his arm. "You're so fucking cocky."

He leaned down to kiss me, swallowing my shaky breath. "Oh, you have no idea…" The feel of his tongue electrified every nerve ending in my body. Sweet warmth coiled in all the right places, and I gasped into his mouth. He smirked, the bastard. The man knew exactly how to turn me on, and he relished it. "I feel it too, baby," he said as he took my hand and guided it over his cock. God help me, he was so hard,

I practically drooled, remembering how good he felt rocking inside me.

Trailing kisses down my neck, he ignited a stampede of goosebumps all over my skin. My breasts felt heavy and eager for his touch—for his devilish tongue—and I let my head fall back as he took my nipples into his mouth. Heavens above, I wasn't sure if it was the pregnancy hormones or what, but everything felt hypersensitive in the best possible way. He hadn't touched me between my legs, but I knew I was already soaked. I moaned, letting him know I needed no foreplay.

I felt his lips stretch over my breasts, and I could only imagine the massive grin that was plastered on his face as he feasted on me. He gently bit each nipple until they were hard and throbbing. "Jax, please…"

"Say it."

"I want you."

"Say exactly what you want me to do to your body."

"I need you inside me."

"You mean, you want my cock buried inside that sweet little pussy?"

"Fuck yes. Please."

"I love it when you ask nicely. But it's going to have to wait. I still owe you a back rub." He drew close to my ear and whispered, "Turn around and lean over the mattress."

To hell with the back rub. But as I was about to protest, he placed a finger over my lips. "My game. Now, do as I say."

Heaving a couple of pouty breaths, I did as he instructed, my body literally in flames. I waited as he lowered my oversized jeans and very unsexy underpants. I could've been wearing the worst pair of granny panties and he wouldn't have cared. My ass was naked before him in a matter of seconds.

The man had been serious about his promise, though, and used his fingers to apply just the right amount of pressure over my lower back and hips, summoning different types of moans from me.

"That's it, angel," he said as I swayed back and forth, savoring the much-needed relaxation. But I wanted more than just pain relief; I needed release, needed to forget about the weight that had been placed on my shoulders. I wanted pure abandonment for tonight. Pushing my backside up against his pelvis, I gasped as I felt his length strain under his pants.

"You're a bit overdressed," I whispered breathlessly.

He chuckled. "Is that right?"

"Strip, Jax. I don't know how much longer I can wait."

He didn't fight me, which meant he was growing just as eager. "Spread your legs a little."

I did as he asked, and I almost melted when I felt the warmth of his hard cock slide between my legs and against my folds. He didn't go inside me, he just teased the outer lips, soaking himself with my wetness.

The deep moan that slipped from his lungs echoed through me as the tip of his dick rubbed against my clit. I thought I was going to die if he didn't get inside me soon. He reached for my dangling breasts and squeezed with just enough pressure, fueling his need as he slid between my legs even faster.

"Fuck me, please," I begged.

Instead, he dropped to his knees and buried his tongue between my legs. He licked my entire slit, front to back, over and over until my knees quivered. I didn't know how I managed, but I spread my legs wider for him, demanding he use the tip of that tongue right on my needy clit.

And he didn't disappoint. The instant he brushed it, my world went nuclear. I came in his mouth, my entire body rippling with shock wave after shock wave of mind-melding release. I was trembling with ecstasy when he finally pushed inside me.

At this angle, I could feel every inch of him. It was pleasure and pain all mixed into one, and I couldn't get enough. I met him, thrust for thrust, chasing a second orgasm as he knocked against my g-spot.

I screamed his name into the mattress as I came again, harder this time, begging him to come inside me, to fill me. He twisted his fingers in my hair and yanked, gently but with enough force to make my scalp tingle as he chased his release. Devil be damned, he rammed into me hard and fast, skin slapping against skin, our lungs battling for oxygen until, with one final push, he gave me what I'd been craving, until he filled me to the brim. With all of him. His need. His lust. His love.

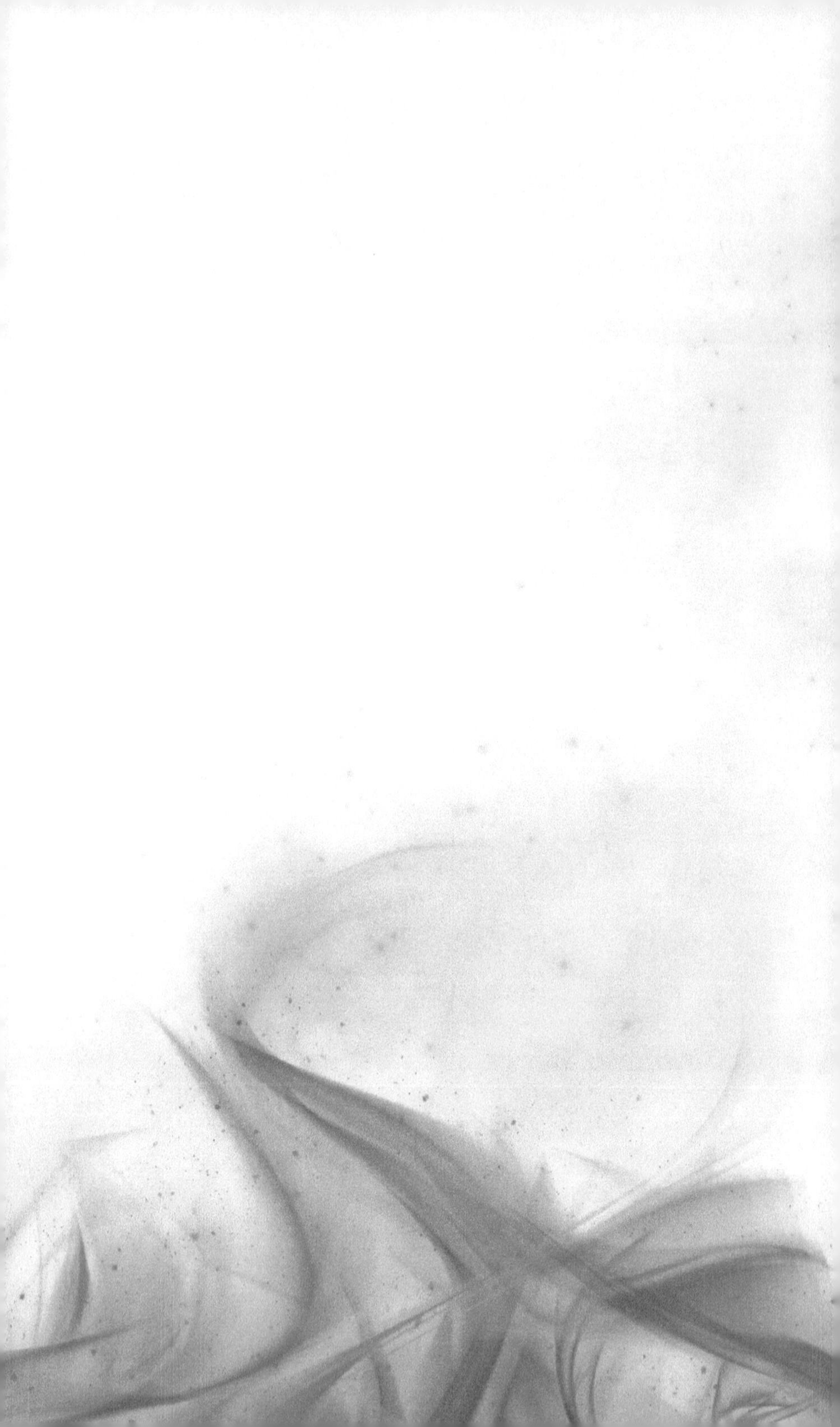

CHAPTER 3

KATE

I was woken up by a growl a few hours later. Eyes still at half mast, I lifted my head off the pillow and saw Hank pacing in the middle of the room. "What's going on, bud? You need to potty?"

He whined, and it was the sort of whine he made when danger was near. I tapped Jax's arm, which was draped over my waist, resting on my belly. "Jax, wake up. Something's wrong."

He groaned in protest. The man was not one to sleep like the dead, but I guessed after such a long hiatus without sex, he'd been worn out. I tapped his arm harder and when he still didn't rise, I went to slide out from under the covers, but a loud *boom,* followed by an orange flash outside our window, startled me in place. This time, Jax finally woke up. "What the hell was that?" he asked, sitting up abruptly in bed.

"Sounded like an explosion."

Jax jumped out of bed in his boxers and immediately switched into warrior mode. He dressed in less than ten seconds and was grabbing his pistol when frantic knocks rasped at our door. "Jax, Kate. Open up," Clint shouted, his voice loaded with panic.

Jax turned to me to make sure I was decent, but I simply nodded in a hurry as I slipped on my pants. When he finally opened the door, the screams echoing down the hall of the inn filled our room.

"What the hell is going on?" Jax asked as he peered down the hallway.

"Those fucking banshees," Clint said.

Jax's back muscles stiffened. "The demons?"

"They are all over the place. Dozens of them, if not more."

"Fuck."

"What are you two talking about?" I asked as I joined them by the door.

Clint turned to Jax, his eyebrows raised. "You didn't tell her?"

Dread scaled down my back. "Tell me what?"

When Jax simply stared at me as if he'd forgotten how to speak, Clint added, "We were attacked by a demon during our run. Nasty looking lizard thing."

"Jax?" I said more firmly. "Why the hell didn't you say anything?"

"I meant to tell you, but then…" He nodded toward the bed.

I rolled my eyes and huffed. "Really?" He knew that was a lame excuse, but we didn't have time to deal with that right now.

He looked away sheepishly.

"Tell me everything," I said to both of them. "Why do you call them banshees?"

Jax loosened a long breath, seemingly thankful I didn't dwell on the issue. "They let out this shrill," he started, "type of high-pitched sound that somehow paralyzes you."

"What?"

Clint's eyes flashed. "We don't really know how it works, either, but the shrill only seems to affect you if you're close enough to them."

I took a step closer. "Okay, so get our snipers on the fucking roof and shoot the damn things."

"They're already trying, but the banshees are staying back," the kid said.

My brows dipped. "That doesn't make sense. If they need to be close, how are they supposed to control us if they are staying back?"

"It doesn't seem like they are interested in controlling us. They are controlling the infected."

Jax snapped his neck toward Clint. "Come again?"

"We don't know where they came from, but there's a horde attacking the inn. But these aren't the typical mindless creatures we're used to seeing. These fucks are acting like a coordinated group."

Jax and I shared a look. The missing town's people… They'd been turned into mind-controlled infected?

Another set of screams erupted from inside the inn. My heart dropped into the pit of my stomach. "Camila and Liling…" They were one floor below us.

Jax reached for the rifle he kept resting beside the door. "I'll go check on the girls. You stay here. Clint, watch after Kate."

"The hell with that," I said, strapping on my pistol and grabbing my empyrean sword.

Jax put a strong hand on my shoulder. "Kate, please. Just stay put. Remember what we're fighting to protect." His gaze dropped to my belly.

The severe look of desperation in his eyes rooted my feet to the ground. I nodded, but the fire in my veins burned. The heavenly sword in my hand and the angelic power surging in my blood had sharpened me into a blade. I held the only weapon able to kill demons, not just send them back to hell, and my heightened strength and rapid healing abilities made me an asset in battle.

He mouthed 'I love you' before rushing into the madness, my chest thundering as his body disappeared from view. I knew he was an experienced fighter, but without his healing powers, he was as vulnerable as any human. "Be careful," I shouted after him, but Clint closed the door before I could hear a reply.

Hank paced. He was equally anxious to kick demon ass, and being ordered to stay back went against the grain as much for him as it did for me.

Another round of explosions rocked the foundation and lit up the sky outside my third-story window. I ran to look, pulling the blinds completely open. Out in the courtyard, the first person I spotted was Chaz running away from the inn's pool—now overgrown with vegetation. He must have used one of his homemade explosives to set a small cluster of the devoured ablaze. Charred arms flared as the infected spun disoriented, wails echoing through the courtyard as their bodies burned.

These things weren't your movie zombies. The human souls who had once inhabited those bodies were gone, but their vessels were filled with the essence of something primal and grotesque. Ancient and cold. They weren't entirely dead, which made them more frightening.

Guardians fired off round after round of fire power, taking out as many devoured as they could, but more kept spilling in from the shadows. Suddenly, Hank began to whine again, drawing my attention away from the bloody chaos to where he cowered in a corner.

"What's the matter, buddy?"

"It's probably the banshees," Clint said, grabbing me by the elbow and pulling me away from the window. "We're too far to be affected, but we can't take any chances. Unfortunately, Hank can probably still hear them."

More screams echoed outside my door, accompanied by the high-pitched shrills and squawks the devoured made. "They are too close, Clint. I can't stay here doing nothing while people are dying out there."

He shook his head as he stood like a statue blocking the door, rifle strapped across his chest. My heart swelled watching his determination. The kid would do anything Jax asked of him, for our sake and the sake of everyone in our crew. I appreciated his efforts, but they were in vain. With my angelic abilities, I could easily overpower him, even pregnant.

"Clint, I'm going out. You can either fight me or fight with me, but either way, I am not letting those monsters slaughter our people."

Clint's eyes flickered. He knew I wouldn't back down. "Fuck. Jax is going to kill me for this."

"I'll deal with Jax. Now, how do we protect our ears from those fucking banshee lizards?"

In a matter of minutes, we took some toilet paper—a find the whole crew had celebrated as if we'd hit gold when we searched the basement level of the inn—and used it to stuff our ears, which we then secured with some masking tape. Flimsy, but it was better than nothing. Thankfully, Hank had been a police dog, and when his owner perished, he left the shepherd's tactical gear intact. My fur ball not only had a bulletproof vest, but he had protective goggles and an earmuff hoodie to protect his ears. I could only pray they would work well to shield him from the banshee screeches.

With a couple of hand signals, I ordered Hank to stay close to my heel as we exited the room. Clint covered the rear while I led the way down the dark hallway, sword ready to slice through demon and devoured meat alike. The only light came from the moon shining through the skylight, bathing the walls with grim shadows. Farther down, near the stairwell, claws scraped against wood as something tried pushing through the door. Hank's hearing was muffled, but his sense of smell and sight were still intact. He positioned himself between my legs, matching my careful steps as we drew nearer. His entire body was aimed like an arrow as he prepared for a command to attack.

Suddenly, a dark figure crashed through the door. The familiar squawks the devoured made reached my ears like muffled tones, but they still made my skin crawl. Another loud crack erupted from behind us. Clint fired at whatever had burst through the stairwell door down the other end.

Hank and I moved in on the devoured that ran toward us. Heat pulsed through my palms as I raised my weapon and swung at the creature, severing its head just as it reached its clawed hand at me. The golden-lit angelic symbols on my hands flashed brightly as more beasts came barreling through. A few doors down, another devoured crashed through a bedroom door and screams erupted from inside.

Hank and I ran as fast as we could, my heart pounding, fear racing up my throat as I pictured the creature tearing into the young girls I knew were staying in that room. Relief welled inside me when I entered the room and saw the beast clawing at the bathroom door. The girls had locked themselves inside, but that door wouldn't hold for much longer. In a split second, I cut across the room and slashed the monster, stabbing it straight through its skull.

From behind, a devoured lunged for my neck, but Hank managed to jump on its back and bite down on its shoulder, yanking it off me, but not before the infected creature took a bite of my forearm. I hollered in agony as the sting raced up my arm. Rage barreled through me, and I spun toward the wretched creature, fueled by the angelic power coursing through my veins. I hacked its head off, followed by several more blows to the body, until all that remained was a heap of mangled flesh and black blood spatter all over me.

Clint ran into the room just as another infected entered, looking for a meal. He finished it off with a bullet to the head.

"Hallway's cleared. That's the last of 'em… for this floor, at least."

"Was anybody hurt?" I asked.

He shook his head, lowering his gaze. "They were about to pounce on the girls at the end of the hallway. Carly and Johanna."

Heavens. They were only twelve and fourteen.

When he looked back up at me, a shadow of guilt draped over his face. "If we hadn't come out to help, they would've been…"

"But we did, and they didn't."

"I'm sorry for trying to hold you back, Kate. I was only trying to do the right thing."

"Don't worry about it, kid. You *did* do the right thing, and now those girls are alive because of you."

One of the girls we'd rescued from the Horsemen's lair peeked her head through the hole the beast had managed to tear into the door.

"Stay inside, and don't come out until we say it's safe," I told her.

The girl nodded, and Clint helped me barricade the bathroom door with one of the sofas in the room.

Gunfire and screams echoed from the lower floors. "Fight's not over," I said. "Let's go." We continued toward the stairwell until we made it to the second-floor landing—the floor where Camila and Liling were staying. In the chaos, I heard Jax's voice, but I couldn't make out what he was saying. I was about to open the door to the hallway when it blew off its hinges, knocking into the three of us.

We fell backward from the blast, a rain of wood shards falling over us.

Shaking off the debris, I stood, ready to fight off whatever had barged through the door, but my breath was stolen from my lungs. An angel towered before me, his iridescent wings glimmering in the stairwell, lighting it up as if it were broad daylight.

Covered in a glorious silver-plated armor, his eyes glowed with a platinum flame as he stared down at me. A mane of ashen-colored hair fell to his shoulders, with strands sweeping over his brow. He looked magnificent, as if cut straight from moonlight.

Had Mikha'el finally returned with his army? This had to be one of his warriors. It had to. As furious as I was with Mikha'el for abandoning me—abandoning all of us—I was grateful to see one of his kind had come to our aid. "Well, better late than never," I said as I smiled up at him.

A grin carved his chiseled cheekbones, but the smile lacked warmth. Ice crusted over my bones as Hank's hackles rose, a growl rumbling in the back of his throat. The symbols on my arms and hands flared to life and an uncomfortable weight sank into my gut. This couldn't be good. Not good at all.

"You bear Zadkiel's markings," he said with wonder, eyeing the sword in my hand. "And his weapon." The silver in his eyes churned like liquid metal as he focused on my pregnant belly. "The prophecy is real, then. You carry the child meant for Samael."

I slid a protective hand over my bump and aimed the sword at the angel. "My son is not meant for anyone but me and Jax."

His cold gaze assessed my threat for a heartbeat, his brow scrunching. Something in the way he looked at me sent Hank into a frenzy of aggressive barks, froth foaming with every snarl. I'd never seen Hank like this before. He was in full-blown protective mode, and I had a feeling he would fight this angel to the death for me. I tried holding him back, but he lunged at the divine creature. The angel grabbed Hank by the neck and held him at arm's length like he was a vile animal.

I screamed, remembering when Beleth had held Hank like that. "Let him go!"

Holding him up higher, he looked at Hank as if staring at some oddity. Hank growled and whimpered. "Admirable loyalty from such a simple life form."

I took a step closer, and gritted, "I said, let him go."

From behind me, Clint raised his rifle and aimed for the angel's head. "You heard the lady."

I'd seen Mikha'el in battle, seen him square off against the Horsemen. Clint stood no chance against a warrior angel, and for a second, a thread of fear weaved around my heart. I wasn't sure I could fight him, either. The angel cocked his head and peered over at Clint, examining the young man with curiosity. But what I saw behind that gaze spoke of ancient cunning and deathly coldness.

"Clint, lower your weapon," I warned in a low voice.

"No, ma'am. I promised Jax I'd look after you. I'm not scared of no zombie or demon, and I'm not going to cower to an angel, either."

"Daughter of Eve, you are coming with me," the angel said, ignoring Clint's rifle, his voice a tenor that shook the walls. When I took too long to respond, he reached behind his back and pulled out a monstrous crossbow that looked to be made of pure gold, its surface glinting from the shimmer of his iridescent wings.

He dropped Hank to the ground like a bag of rocks and aimed the crossbow at Clint's chest. I didn't even have a chance to blink before the creature released the arrow. Clint was flung backward as the arrow pierced his torso, and he tumbled down a flight of stairs. I screamed so loud, I swore I cracked my eardrum.

My blood surged with vibrating energy and I gripped the hilt of my sword with an iron fist, swinging at the angelic beast with every ounce of strength I possessed. But the heavenly warrior was too fast, too strong, and he blocked every blow with his gauntlets. He never once tried to strike me, which infuriated me even more because I knew what he wanted.

"You. Are. Not. Taking. My. Baby," I growled with every swing as I pushed him back into the second-floor hallway, where another battle raged on between Jax and a swarm of infected.

"Kate?" Jax hollered several feet from me as he shot a devoured in the temple, then shoved his body away with a kick to the gut. "Who the fuck is that?"

But I couldn't answer; I was too enraged. All I wanted was to kill the angel who'd just killed Clint.

Then, as if tired of a pestering fly, the angel used his crossbow to knock my sword out of my hand, then he gripped me by the neck, lifting me off the ground. "You fight with honor, human, but your efforts are in vain. Your fate has been chosen. Samael will be king."

I tried prying his fingers off my neck, but it was useless—he was stronger than granite. Somewhere in the background, I heard Jax scream, his voice muffled by the fucking toilet paper still stuck in my damn ears. Tears bubbled at the corners of my eyes from the strain on my neck. "Let go of—" but I wasn't able to finish my sentence. A loud *crash* exploded from above as something fell through the roof.

The hold around my neck loosened and I dropped hard on my ass. When I looked back up, all I saw was a flash of silver metal and white-as-snow hair, then the angel's severed head fell to the ground, the heavenly creature turning into pixie dust before my eyes until it completely disintegrated, vanishing from existence. The crossbow landed on the ground with a loud *thud*.

What the hell…? A large, feminine hand extended toward me. "Katherine, are you okay?"

For a brief moment, my muscles wouldn't respond. I almost couldn't believe it. "Gavri'el?" I asked softly, unsure if what I was seeing was real.

"It is good to see you," she said, her voice sweet and flute-like, despite the fact she'd just hacked off an angel's head. Finally able to move my limbs, I accepted her hand and stood. I wanted to ask her the obvious question, but my attention was dragged toward the ear-splitting squeal of a devoured as it rushed toward us.

I instinctively put my arms up to block the attack, but the creature never made it another step. A large sword skewered it from behind before slicing upward and carving the thing in half, revealing the figure behind it.

My breath halted. Heaven's mightiest warrior stood like a pillar of lethal power and beautiful grace. Eyes glowing like molten gold, Mikha'el lowered his weapon, blackened blood dripping from Emrandael, his legendary sword. He was dressed in black leather armor, trimmed in red and gold. His brass-colored wings were tucked and his raven hair hung loosely over his brow. I wanted to run to him, fling my arms around his neck, but when his golden gaze met mine, I felt the world collapse beneath me and the weight of everything that had transpired forced me to my knees.

"Kate!" Jax's voice cut through the chaos still raging outside the inn as he ran around the archangel to reach me. "Are you hurt?" he asked, kneeling beside me. The feel of Hank's wet tongue on my face and Jax's hand on my belly gave me the strength I needed to look into his eyes, to confess what I'd done.

"I'm sorry. I'm so sorry," I said as tears streamed down my face.

"Kate, please tell me if you're hurt. Is the baby okay?"

"I should have listened to you. I should've stayed in my room."

Taking my face in his hands, he wiped at the tears. "What happened?"

"If I'd stayed, Clint…"

Jax's eyes widened and he looked around the hallway. "Where's the kid, Kate?"

"The angel… he took Hank. Demanded I go with him, but Clint tried to stop him and… and…"

"Shhh," he said softly, trying to calm me.

"He's dead because of me, Jax. I did this."

"Hey, hey. Look at me. You can't blame yourself for that. He was only trying to protect you. We all knew the risks."

"But if I stayed… If I'd listened for once…"

Jax caressed my jaw, his voice low as he gently peeled off the stupid tape and toilet paper from my ears. "Angel, we both know you weren't really going to listen to me. When do you ever? It's kinda what I love about you, as annoying as it is. You're not the kind of person to sit on your ass when others are dying."

"But Clint…" I whimpered, remembering it was his idea to use the toilet paper to protect our ears. He'd looked so silly, but there'd been no time to smile. "He was just a kid. He didn't need to die."

Jax swallowed hard, the muscles in his jaws clenching. The glossiness in his eyes told me he was holding back what I couldn't. "I know, baby. I know," he said, his voice almost cracking. After spending the last five months on the road, scavenging together—not to mention all the time back in New York they spent trading resources—losing Clint must've felt like losing a younger brother for him. I knew Jax was holding it together for me, but inside, he was probably breaking apart from hearing the news.

The archangel stepped closer. "Katherine, Jax, we need to go," Mikha'el said, voice grave and impending, completely disregarding the fact that someone had just died. That someone we cared about had lost their life because of me—again.

With Jax's help, I was able to stand, but I quickly swatted his hand away and stalked toward the archangel. "You've been gone for months, and now you want to start barking orders at me? You have some goddamn nerve." My chest heaved from all the emotions churning in my heart. I didn't care that he and Gavri'el had just saved our asses—he should have returned months ago. None of this would've happened if he'd kept his promise to return. "Explain yourself."

He took two steps back, but I got right up in his space anyway and impaled him with a flaming stare. Eyes softening over me, he said, "I will, but right now we don't have much time. More are coming, and we need to get you someplace safe."

"More of *what* are coming?" I spat.

"Sicarii. Holy assassins."

Taken aback, my shoulders tensed. "Holy assassins? You mean to tell me Heaven has its own cadre of murdering angels?"

"Doesn't killing humans go against your nature? You're supposed to be our protectors," Jax said. "Why are angels being sent to kill Kate?"

Mikha'el's wings fluttered slightly before his angelic abilities hid them from view. "The Powers of the Second Sphere were never created to kill humans. Their job has always been to watch over kingdoms and governments, to carry out missions against demonic forces, not humans. They didn't send that sicarius to kill you, Kate. He came to capture you and bring you to Samael."

I pointed toward the stairwell, the sigils on my hands sparking to life. "They don't kill humans, hmm? He killed Clint!"

Mikha'el secured his sword over his back. "I said they weren't *created* for that purpose, but that doesn't mean they won't kill. His job was to carry out his mission, no matter what. It's why the sicarii were chosen by the Powers to come after you. Once they are given an assignment, they are sworn to complete it. He did what he thought necessary to ensure he captured you… including killing a man."

Bile rose up my esophagus. "You're defending him?"

He drew closer to me, a storm of golden light dancing in his eyes. He went to reach for a rogue strand of my hair, but stopped himself. "Of course not. Never. What he did was reprehensible, and Gavri'el did right in vanquishing him. He paid for his sin with his life. The rules have changed, for our world and yours, Kate. This new war it's unlike anything we've ever faced. It's why it is so important we protect you and your child."

"Why the hell do the Powers want to hand me over to Samael?"

"There's much I need to tell you, Kate. In short, a war broke out in heaven. I was imprisoned, along with Gavri'el and several of my top lieutenants. Legions have sided with Samael, and they've sent our top assassins after you. When news broke out of their plan, several of those still fighting on my side mounted a rescue mission. The protection shield I put over you should have been enough to conceal you, but something must have tipped them off on your location. Luckily, I was able to find you just in time."

"Fuck," Jax uttered next to me, putting a fist to his forehead. "The goddamn banshee."

I turned to him. "What do you mean?"

"During yesterday's scavenging trip, when we ran into the lizard-looking demon, it spoke to me after it paralyzed me with its song—spoke to me as if it already knew me. Then it searched my mind." He locked gazes with me. "It saw… you. Us."

"Zamharee," Mikha'el uttered, his voice vexed.

Both Jax and I turned to look at him, eyebrows raised.

"You're describing sirens," he went on. "And that could be how they found you. *Zamharee* not only lure you with their demon song to paralyze you—"

"More like a demon screech," Jax said, crossing his arms. "And we prefer to call them banshees."

Mikha'el narrowed his gaze. "*Zamharee* can get inside your head. You probably led them to this camp and they, in turn, alerted Samael's lieutenants."

Jax lowered his gaze and shook his head. "I'm so sorry, angel. I should have told you about that encounter earlier. We might have been better prepared."

"So, what now?" I asked Mikha'el, ignoring Jax's obvious mistake. He should have told me, but I couldn't dwell on the *should haves* now.

Another explosion blasted outside the inn.

Mikha'el turned to Jax. "Did you find out where you sent the fire stone?"

"La Sagrada Familia in Spain."

Mikha'el quirked an eyebrow. "The Eastern Guardian Headquarters. You're certain?"

"As certain as I'll ever be."

"Hopefully, your plan worked and they've kept it safe. What about the earth stone?"

"I have it," I said, pulling it out from beneath my shirt collar.

"Great. Then we leave at once."

"Leave?" I asked, my voice rising an octave. "Do you see what is happening around us? My people are being attacked. I can't leave them now."

"I'll stay and secure the area," Gavri'el said, pulling out another smaller sword from a scabbard.

Mikhal'el placed a hand on my shoulder, and I immediately felt the coolness of his calming abilities, so I shook his hand off. I didn't need him to pacify me. Something like hurt flashed in his eyes. "Kate, Gavri'el will stay with your people. She will look after them. I've not come alone. Several of my most trusted warriors have taken up arms against our common enemy. They fight alongside your brethren now."

I turned to Jax, my heart growing heavy. "The girls."

"They are fine. Chaz is with them down in the basement, along with the rest of the girls and several guards."

Grabbing him by the arms, I squeezed harder than I'd meant. "We can't leave them. We promised Father Ortega we'd ensure they'd be safe."

"Katherine," Gavri'el said, stepping into the beam of moonlight shining through the huge hole in the roof. "I give you my word. I will protect them with my life."

Terror slithered down my back like a snake. How could I abandon all these people now?

You're not abandoning them, Kate. You'll be doing this for them. We need to collect all four stones and close the gates before it's too late. More sicarii will be sent after you.

I cocked my head at Mikha'el. *So, we're back to mind-chatting?*

It's faster than spoken words.

I shook my head. "And how are we supposed to get to Spain?"

"I will rift you."

I swallowed hard, remembering the day I saw him and Garvri'el disappear into thin air. "Rift me?"

"It's how we're able to move between worlds. It does take a toll on a human body, though. The gravitational forces are intense. You'll feel sick, extremely nauseous even. Some people pass out."

He didn't make rifting sound enticing, but what truly caught my attention was what he'd said before that. *Between worlds.* My God… Was it really possible that other worlds existed, places other than Earth? Well, I guess if Heaven and Hell existed, and angels and demons were real, then why not other realms?

This was all just so insane; yet, if anyone would've asked me two years ago if I believed in zombies, I probably would have laughed in their face.

"So, rifting sucks?" I said, cocking my hip.

"For humans."

"What about Hank?"

"What about him?"

Jax shied his gaze away and crossed his arms, already knowing what would come next.

I shot the archangel a sharp stare. "You weren't thinking I would leave Hank behind, were you?"

The heavenly creature forgot to blink, to breathe.

"Either he comes or I stay."

After seconds that felt like a millennium, Mikha'el sighed his resignation, releasing a shuddering breath, shoulders going slack. "Very well. But I've never rifted an Earthly beast before. I have no knowledge of how it will affect him."

"I guess I'll have to take that risk. I'm not going anywhere without him. Is there anything else we need to bring, any supplies?" I asked Mikha'el.

"Bring only your weapons. The less you carry, the easier it will be for me to rift us all forth. Are you ready?"

Jax grabbed my hand. "Ready."

"Kate?" The archangel looked at me, waiting for me to give the final word.

I turned to Gavri'el. "Promise me you'll ensure everyone is safe. That you'll get them all to the sanctuary. Chaz will know where we were headed."

She knelt on one knee, resting a hand on the pommel of her sword. "In the name of my Holy Father, I promise you, I will defend them with every last breath."

Mikha'el eyes shone with something I'd never seen before—an unspoken truth, a secret hidden between him and Gavri'el alone. I tried penetrating his thoughts, but the angel blocked me.

He offered Gavri'el a short nod. "Emissary."

She did the same. "Commander."

"May God be with you," Mikha'el said.

"May He be with you all," she replied.

I grabbed Hank's tactical vest and before I could take my next breath, Mikha'el wrapped his wings around us and the world spun out of control.

CHAPTER 4

JAX

We were sucked through a vacuum at incalculable speed, at least that's what it felt like—like spinning at a thousand miles per hour through a black hole, then being shit out through its anus. One minute we were at the inn, and the next, in the middle of some abandoned street in Spain. How in God's name did these angels make rifting look like a quick snap of their wings and boom, you were somewhere else without a feather out of place?

Unless you wanted to feel like you were wearing your innards outside of your body, I would never recommend rifting to any human. The instant oxygen filled my lungs again, and I felt solid ground beneath my feet, I keeled over and retched several times until the pasta dinner we'd had before the attack decorated the sidewalk.

Took me half a minute to stand up straight and gather my bearings, yet it still felt like I had the worst hangover of my life—and I'd had some pretty bad post-shit-faced days back before the gates opened.

Kneeling beside me, Kate heaved loudly as she puked her brains out as well. She held herself up with one hand, supporting her belly with the other. Hank sat next to her, panting. Seemed he was out of sorts, too.

"Shit. Angel, are you okay?"

When I tried to move toward her, my head spun, and I almost face-planted. The archangel hadn't been kidding when he said we'd feel sick.

I put a hand on Kate's lower back and rubbed gently. "That's it. You'll feel better once you get it all out of your system."

She coughed as the last of her stomach's contents spilled onto the sidewalk.

"Jax, something is wrong," she said shakily. "I… think my water broke."

"What do you mean, your water broke?"

"I mean," she gritted, eyes shooting daggers at my face. "The baby is co—" The next part of the word came out in a guttural scream that sounded almost as terrifying as a d'shiad. A shudder ran through me as I watched her curl in on herself, holding on tighter to her stomach.

It was too soon. I jumped to my feet and paced, paced like an idiot soon-to-be dad who hadn't bothered to prepare for this moment. Hands cradling my head, I tried to think. Tried to figure out what I should do. How I could help.

Think, you fucking asshole.

Fuck. It was way too soon. I honestly thought we'd have more time. I didn't know much about pregnancies, or how demon and angelic blood affected the gestation time, but it couldn't have been time for her to deliver, could it? Weren't babies supposed to cook for nine months?

We didn't have access to ultrasound machines to measure the baby's growth, and given she appeared bigger than she should be, perhaps it was possible she was actually ready to give birth? I had no clue. But now…? While we were in the middle of the street, in a foreign country, during the fucking apocalypse with zombies and demons lurking in the shadows? Not to mention the fucking assassin angels on our tail?

She couldn't give birth now. God. At least not until we found a secure shelter.

And where the fuck was Mikha'el?

I took a handful of deep gulps. Right now was not the time to freak the fuck out. Kate needed me. So, I did the only thing I was good at and switched to warrior mode. Helping her sit up, I gently leaned her back against the stone wall behind us. I knelt beside her and pulled the sweat-drenched strands of hair hanging over her face behind her ears. My heart squeezed when I saw the pain etched across her features. Face pale and lips dry, she breathed rapidly, trying to make it through what I assumed was another contraction. "We need to get you off the street, angel," I said.

"I don't think I can walk."

"Well, you can't exactly pop a baby out in the middle of the street in Barcelona."

She impaled me with her gaze. "Watch me."

Fuck. Where the hell was that angel when you needed him?

Then, down the street, a figure slowly pulled itself up from a man-sized crater in the middle of the road. When he straightened, massive wings spread wide.

There he is.

"Over here," I shouted, hating the fact I had to make such a loud noise. God knew what the hell lurked in the shadows in this place.

The archangel turned toward us. He looked just as wrecked as we did, if not worse.

I scanned our surroundings. We were on a narrow side street with beige stone buildings on both sides. A few burnt car husks clogged the one-car lane while an iron railing hung loosely from the balcony above, awfully close to falling on our heads.

Climbing plants and overgrown vegetation covered most of the stone facades of the apartments a couple of stories up. Across the street, the ground floor of the building appeared to have been a convenience store of some sort. The windows were cracked, and everything inside looked toppled and completely raided.

Mikha'el hobbled across the street toward us. I was about to curse him to hell and back for pulling Kate through the portal without considering what it might do to our child, but the words died on my lips when I saw him lean against a concrete slab that seemed to have fallen off the building. His black armor was torn in different places, and a golden, honey-like substance was caked in his hair and the side of his face. Angel blood? I remembered Kate mentioning her blood had golden flecks in it from whatever Zadkiel had done to her.

The archangel winced as he pushed away from the wall and started toward us.

"You look like shit," I said, taking in the full damage.

He eyed me closely, lips curled into what I could only interpret as a snarl. "Likewise, Son of Adam. Is… Kate okay?" he asked, breaths ragged.

"No," I replied sharply as Kate groaned on the floor. She didn't even bother looking up at the archangel as she breathed through another contraction. "She's in labor." As if it wasn't obvious from the way she held her lower abdomen and back.

"Saints be damned," he uttered, wincing again as he placed a hand on his side. "It's too soon, even for a baby born of angel origin."

"How bad are you hurt?" I asked, eyeing the way he held his ribs. He had supernatural healing abilities, so I wasn't truly concerned for the immortal, more like worried about how long it might take him to recoup. We needed his fighting skills should we be attacked right now.

"Rifting takes a lot of energy," he explained. "Taking two people, plus a dog, depleted me. Luckily, I was able to shield you all with my wings as we punched through the wormhole's membrane, but I lost control during the re-entry and was flung yards down from where I released you. I won't be able to rift again until I'm fully healed. But that's not what's important now. We need to get Kate someplace safe."

I peered up at the heavens, but the sky was a dreary, dark gray blanket that completely blotted out the sun.

"Any idea what time it is?" I asked.

"Close to sundown."

"That's crazy. Feels like we were in that rifting whirlpool for less than a minute. It should be closer to noon."

"Time works differently when you're bending the laws of the universe." His gaze drifted up and down over my body. "Especially with an extra load."

I almost took offense to that.

"How far away are we from the cathedral?" Kate managed to ask, her voice strained as she looked up at us. Hank's head rested on her lap.

"It's just a couple of blocks around the corner," Mikha'el said, leaning down and placing his palm over her belly. He closed his eyes for a few seconds, examining her as if he were some type of living, breathing ultrasound machine.

"Is he… Is he okay?" she asked wearily, her eyes misty. I merely held my breath.

He opened his lids, the varnished gold of his eyes a flaming ring around his pupils. "It's early, but there's no stopping the birth now."

That wasn't the question she'd asked, and he read that in her eyes. "I… We," he corrected, looking at me, "will do everything in our power to ensure you deliver your son safely."

"Stop sidestepping around it, Mikha'el. Just tell me if my baby is okay. Give it to me straight. I want to know what I'm up against."

Reaching under her arms, we both helped her stand. "The baby's heartbeat is accelerated and from what I felt, his…" He looked at me, then back at Kate, and swallowed hard. "His head is not in the birth canal."

"Breached?" she asked, the terror in her eyes matching the acidic feeling eating at my insides.

He nodded, and Kate burst into tears. She leaned against the stone wall again as another contraction rocked through her. She tried not to moan in agony, but she leaned her forehead against my shoulder for support and screamed into my chest, muffling her cries as much as she could. Wretched hell. I hated that I couldn't do anything to help ease her pain.

"Kate," Mikha'el whispered, but she cut him off with a growl.

"Don't you dare say it," she gritted. "I know I need to keep quiet. I'm doing the best I can."

As if on cue, out of nowhere, the eerie silence of the city was cut by the sound of a rattling can. The wind was still, so something caused it to roll. Hank sniffed the air, picking up a scent of some sort. I'd learned to read his cues, and the way he stood with his chest puffed confirmed my fears.

"Friend or foe," I asked Mikha'el.

He scanned our surroundings with those preternatural eyes of his, nostrils flaring as if he too could smell the evil lurking around us. "It's not human. We need to get off the streets. Now."

Kate sagged in my arms as another contraction nearly made her buckle. I wrapped my arms around her and kept her from falling to her knees.

"I can't do this," she panted. "I can't…"

"Yes, you can, baby girl. I believe in you, Kate."

"Jax… this… is too much."

Taking her face in my hands, I forced her to look at me. "Kate, please. You need to listen to me. There's something stalking us. I need you to be ready to run."

"Run? I can barely walk."

I pulled her sword from the scabbard and handed it to her, wrapping my hands around hers and swallowing the pain from where the sword's empyrean steel had burned my skin. "I've seen you take a beating from a fucking minotaur. I saw you go up against d'shiad, infected, and the goddamn Horsemen. Hell, you killed two, remember?" I said, placing her hand over my heart, where she'd stabbed me to kill Astaroth.

"What's your fucking point?" she said between her teeth as she fought back another stabbing contraction.

"You fight. For our baby, Kate. You must do this for our baby. That's my fucking point."

Mikha'el had been right about it being near sundown. The cloudy sky had darkened to an ominous ash color and without the light of the moon, the entire street was bathed in menacing shadows. The scraping of metal against asphalt punched through the still quiet of the night. It was the equivalent of nails against a chalkboard, only worse.

"What the hell is that?" Kate asked.

"Mike, stay with her. I'll scope it out."

Kate reached for my arm. "Jax, wait… I don't want to do this without you."

I put a finger to my mouth to tell her to stay quiet as I whispered, "I'm coming right back, angel. I'm not missing the birth of my child, not even for the apocalypse."

The sound seemed to be coming from somewhere near the intersection where our side street met up with one of the main roads that sliced through the city. As I approached the corner, the ear-piercing shrill sent my nerves on end. It almost sounded like a sawmill.

I sucked in a breath as I peeked around one of the dilapidated storefronts, but nothing would've prepared me for what I saw.

Walking down the street at a leisurely pace, a man that stood at about eight to ten feet tall held a monstrosity of a meat cleaver, the blade dragging against the pavement in the middle of the road, sparks flying from the friction.

But as he drew nearer and my eyesight adjusted to the darkness, I realized the figure was no man. Naked and gray-skinned, it looked like it had once been one of the damned, except this one appeared… different. Evolved even. Muscular and humanoid, its arms were elongated with hands that looked more like three-pronged claws. Its feet were the same, animalistic and clawed. But the face… the face was designed to induce nightmares of the worst variety.

Elongated, and with blades protruding out of its flesh at different angles, the monstrosity held no eyes, not even a nose. The only feature on its face was the ginormous mouth filled with too many needle-sharp teeth. I swallowed deeply. This thing had clearly clawed itself out of the deepest and darkest corners of hell. It kept walking toward the middle of the intersection with no urgency, other than to scare the shit out of any living thing with its horror movie stroll and rusted cleaver.

At least there was only one of its kind. I checked my jacket pockets and counted two magazines. We had no holy water, but at least I had a half-working archangel with a mega sword. As I was about to turn back around to alert Kate and Mikha'el, the creature opened its maw, wider than it should have been able to, and let out a bowel-liquifying roar that bounced off every building.

Then they came, the all too familiar hyaena-sounding whooping calls.

Hellhounds.

Fuck.

I ran back to where Mikha'el held Kate in his arms. He'd probably heard the yelps, too. "We need to get her off the street," he said, Hank at his heel as he carried her.

We didn't have many options, so we ran to the raided convenience store across the street and climbed through one of the large broken display windows. "Back there," I said, pointing at a door marked as a restroom. Mikha'el laid her down on the tiled floor, and I knelt beside her.

The room was pitch-dark, so I gave her my flashlight. "I need you to stay in here for a little bit, okay?"

"How many?" she asked. Nothing escaped her, not even when a little human was trying to tear through her body.

"Just a few. Nothing Mike and I can't handle. And one puny infected dude."

"You're a terrible liar," she said, practically out of breath.

"I know what I'm about to ask you is ridiculous, but those things out there… Well, I don't need to tell you what they are capable of. If they catch your scent or hear you…"

"I know what I need to do."

I turned toward Hank, his head on Kate's lap. "Don't let anyone into this room, buddy. I know I don't need to tell you to guard her with your life."

Hank let out a small whine.

With a kiss, I told her *I love you* and locked the door behind us. I traced a protection sigil over the door, but I knew that if those demon dogs got a whiff of her scent, they'd find a way to rip through the door, even if they killed themselves in the process.

"Okay, let's go kick Hellraiser's ass."

Mikha'el cocked a brow as he unsheathed his sword. "Hellraiser?"

"I'm sure you have some fancy name for it in angelic tongue, but for now, let me just have this one."

CHAPTER 5

JAX

With my rifle locked and loaded, Mikha'el and I exited the convenience store via the front entrance, stepping on broken glass and scattered debris, the crunching noise announcing our approach as we emptied into the chilled night. Outside, a sudden small breeze blew over us, carrying with it the stench of decay and rotting meat emitting from the darkness. The unmistakable pants and snorts resonating around us were unsettling. We couldn't see them, but we knew the hellhounds were out there, salivating. But we had no way of knowing exactly how many had been summoned.

As if waiting for this exact moment, the inked clouds parted, offering the bright crescent moon the opportunity to shine a spotlight on the horror before us. Standing in the middle of the road, and about fifty yards from our position, Hellraiser 2.0 raised his impossibly-huge meat cleaver and rested it on its shoulder, the lethal blade facing the ebony sky, its edge shimmering with the promise to inflict unimaginable pain.

He stood like a ballplayer, waiting for his chance to take a swing. I'd seen some terrifying creatures in my life, but that *thing* made my intestines twist like a snake's nest. Palms sweaty, I turned to look at the archangel standing beside me with his angelic sword held firmly in his grip. He didn't look as scared as I felt, but his furrowed brow was indication enough of the thoughts running through his head. "Guess you've never actually seen one of those?" I asked.

"Never. But Samael always liked to play God."

"Think he created that thing? What, like out of spite?"

He kept his gaze locked on the abomination. "More than spite. He thinks himself mightier than his Father. Capable of creating a better version of life."

Looking through the rifle's scope, I focused on the creature's head and cringed. "He considers *that* a better version of life?"

"To a father, his creations are all perfect products of his love. Samael sees nothing wrong with the way he's corrupted the Song of Breath."

I gazed up at the archangel, his angular face sharp, his nose refined. "Song of Breath?"

Placing his sword on his shoulder the same way the monster had, he gave me a side glance. "How do you think your soul was created, Son of Adam?"

There was no chance for me to ponder that question. Hellraiser 2.0 opened his big jaw again, bellowing some type of command to the hellhounds hiding in the shadows. One by one, they came out of the darkness, surrounding us from all angles, creating a fighting ring worthy of Dante's Inferno. About two dozen beasts clawed at the pavement, howling and yelping, clearly waiting for the command to attack.

Snarling, black saliva dripped from their sharp canines. Their frenzied calls bounced off the buildings in a chorus birthed of nightmares and unending torture.

Back to back, Mikha'el and I slowly spun in place, trying to figure out our best plan of counterattack. "Can't you summon some of your warriors to come lend us a hand?" I asked.

"Everyone who was able to escape the citadel with me and Gavri'el is with your survivors. They are needed there more than here."

"That's comforting."

"I'll take *Bladehead*, you work on the beasts."

Pivoting to look at his face, my brows climbed up my forehead. "Did you just nickname your first demon?"

"Hellraiser seemed… trite."

"And *Bladehead* is just so much more creative?"

"You'd prefer a fancy angelic-tongue name?"

Fair point.

"Okay, on three. One—" But Bladehead didn't give me a chance to countdown. He came roaring toward us, his cleaver ready to slice us in half. The monster was so large, it made the ground shake with every running step. In a flash of black leather and glinting gold, Mikha'el spun away from me and used his sword to block Bladehead's first swing. Steel clashed against steel, and Mikha'el flew backward several feet as if Heaven's mightiest hero was nothing but a rag doll.

He landed a foot away from a hellhound, who was just about to chomp down on Mikha'el's head. Luckily for the archangel, I was a mean shot and blew the dog's jaw right off with a pull of my trigger, covering Mikha'el in demon blood. "First kill," I shouted at him with a wink.

Mikhal'el jumped to his feet and wiped the blood off his face, the gold in his eyes glowing like fragments of the sun as he pivoted to look at me. I took that as a *thank you,* then aimed and shot at another hellhound who'd broken into the circle. This one took several rounds before it finally went down.

Mikha'el and Bladehead exchanged several blows, neither one inflicting much damage on the other. The creature bellowed as he swung his cleaver, but Mikhal'el was faster and he lunged backward just in time. He twisted and sliced his sword against

Bladehead's back, sending the creature tumbling forward, a spray of black blood splattering all over the ground.

I silently fist-pumped the air, but my joy was snuffed when more hellhounds tested the border as if fed up waiting for their meal. One by one, I shot at them, but I was quickly running out of ammo. When I turned to see if Mikha'el needed any assistance, he lifted about ten feet into the air, his wingspan bigger than I remembered. Aiming the tip of his sword at the demonic creature's head, he swooped down, but Bladehead had anticipated the move and swung his cleaver, knocking Mikha'el's weapon from his hand and punching him in the gut with a backhand. The archangel flew across the circle and landed on his side. The bone crunch and Mikha'el's anguished grunt was so audible, I thought the beast may have actually broken the angelic warrior.

I ran toward him and nearly faltered, trying not to step on the wing that was bent at a terrible angle. He groaned as I put my arm under his and helped him up. "Leave me," he said with a strained breath.

"Not a chance. You're hurt, but you're not dead."

"Without my full strength, I'm useless."

"That's cute coming from history's most celebrated biblical warrior. You don't have the luxury of being useless. You're sworn to Kate, and last I checked, she still needs you."

He limped as I supported his weight, but we didn't get far. The circle of hellhounds tightened around us as Bladehead drew nearer. "We need an escape plan. We ain't fighting through this. Can you rift us out of this circle somehow?"

"I'm… trying…" he said, coughing out golden blood. "My powers are too weakened."

I aimed my rifle with my free hand and fired at the monster, but the bullets barely inflicted any damage. He flinched but kept walking, pushing us back toward the hellhounds waiting behind us. Then a scream split the night, something unlike anything I'd ever heard, and my heart clenched inside my chest.

Kate.

Oh God.

Every hellhound turned their head in the direction of the convenience store, their nostrils flaring. And before I could blink, they all took off at a gallop. There was no way my protection sigils could ward off all those beasts.

"Go," Mikha'el said. "You need to get to her. I've still got one last prayer left."

I took off after the hellhounds, firing my rifle and taking out as many as I could, but there were too many. They crashed through the storefront like a stampede of wildebeest, destroying everything in their path.

I counted each breath I took, knowing they'd get to Kate before I could make it to three. They were going to tear her to shreds. I ran out of bullets and flung my rifle to the side, pulling out my army knife. I knew there would be no surviving this fight, but I would die alongside Kate if it was the last thing I ever did.

Mikha'el dropped to his knees and tried to spread his wings, but his broken one wouldn't respond, laying limp over the pavement. He fought through the pain, sucking a trembling breath through his teeth. He lifted his face to the heavens, offering his palms in supplication. "Holy Father, send forth Your Spirit and grant me Your gifts that I may banish this enemy and You may renew the face of the Earth with Your grace. Come, Holy Spirit, fill my heart and kindle it in the fire of Your love."

A fireball of bright light emerged over his hands, pulsing with every beat of his failing heart. The thrumming energy burned with the heat of a thousand stars, the power so strong, Mikha'el wasn't sure he could contain it.

But he had to…

For Kate. For the hope growing inside her. For mankind.

Bringing his palms together, Mikha'el merged the fireballs, fighting with every ounce of his existence to keep the energy from consuming him. He needed to hold it for just two more seconds.

The world moved at half speed as he peered over to where Kate was hiding, his entire body shaking as he struggled to contain the colossal force. He needed Jax to clear the blast zone first…

Mikha'el knew this would mark his end, but he needed to make sure at least one of them survived to guide Kate through what came next. The birth of her son was only the beginning.

Just one more breath, he said to himself as the heat of the fireball ate through his flesh, as the blood in his veins began to boil. "Father," he screamed to the heavens, his voice like the thunderclap of a violent storm. "Grant me the strength to endure this pain… give me one more heartbeat wherefore Your promise to this world may come to pass."

Then, as he watched Jax finally run across the threshold into the safe zone, Mikha'el raised to his feet, the fireball in his hands pulsing with God's wrath.

"For love…" he breathed as he succumbed to the Holy Fire. An explosion of heavenly light blasted from him in all directions, consuming all the darkness. The abomination born from Samael's corrupted heart exploded into a mist of cinders and ash, along with its pack of hellhounds.

Mikha'el felt his heart cleave in two as the last of his breath trickled from his scorched lips. "Father, my job here is done. May her destiny be fulfilled."

Then, he collapsed.

I was about to jump over the wreckage the beasts had left behind when a blinding light burst out of nowhere, and I was flung forward. I crashed into a wall and landed on my back, hitting my head on the floor, the world spinning out of focus.

What the…? Had someone thrown a flash grenade?

Groaning, I blinked slowly, ears still ringing from the hit to my head. Every limb throbbed from the impact. As I regained my senses, I rolled over onto my side, then onto my knees, with dust, broken pieces of glass, and plaster falling off me. Remembering the hellhound attack, I scrambled onto my feet, frantically scanning my surroundings.

The walls were torn down and parts of the ceiling had crumbled. The store was completely unrecognizable. And the hellhounds… they were all gone. Only dust hung in the air…

No. Ashes. It was ashes. As if they'd been hit by a flash of light from the sun and been instantly incinerated, but how?

I turned toward the back of the store where I'd hidden Kate. The pounding in my chest made my whole body vibrate as I took in the shelving unit that had fallen over the bathroom entrance.

But what had my heart racing was the claw marks on the door, now hanging off its hinges. I ran, a lump forming in my throat as I leapt over more debris, my clothes and skin ripping on exposed metal rods and broken slabs of ceiling.

Oh, God. Please… don't let her be hurt.

"Kate!"

But there was no response.

"Kate!"

As I reached the bathroom and tried to make my way through, I cut my hands on the bent metal and splintered wood of the shelving unit blocking the entrance. "Kate!" I screamed again, but there was no reply, not even a whine from Hank. All I saw was a beam of light from the flashlight I'd given her and her limp legs. Shit. "Kate, answer me!"

When I finally broke through the blockade and ripped down the door completely, my lungs caved. Kate lay sprawled on the floor, her fingers wrapped tightly around the hilt of her sword. Hank licked her face, but she wasn't moving. I dropped to my knees and picked up the discarded flashlight. Thankfully, she didn't look like she'd been attacked by the beasts, but then I noticed she was lying in a puddle of ...

Heavens.

There was so much blood, her pants were soaked. I quickly felt for her pulse. It was faint, but still there, and she was still breathing, if barely. "Fuck, angel. We need to get you to that church."

A small whimper trickled from her lips as I tried to pick her up. "Stay with me, baby."

Hank led the way, and I followed behind him with Kate in my arms, her empyrean sword nestled on her chest. My muscles burned, but I didn't care. I pushed on as I climbed over the destruction, cautious not to drop her, but my arms were slick with our blood, and holding on to her body had me trembling with fear that she'd slip from me.

I only prayed the hellhounds were completely gone, and that Mikha'el had defeated Bladehead.

As I stepped into the night air, about a dozen rifles turned in my direction. Panic and relief wove through all the fibers in my body. I took two steps before dropping to my knees, Kate still cradled in my arms. "Please," I begged. "We mean you no harm."

Hank lowered to the ground as if wanting to show that he wasn't a threat, either. A female stepped closer, barrel pointed at my head. The bottom of her face was covered in a red and gold scarf, and her dark-set eyes bored into mine.

"Please," I repeated. "She's…" I looked down at Kate's slack face, her arm hanging to the side, and the blood soaking her legs. Tears burned in my eyes, and I couldn't hold it together any longer. Clamping on my jaw, my voice croaked as I said, "She needs a doctor."

The woman turned to her companions. "*Traen los. Y el ángel también.*"

Before a black hood was dropped over my head, I caught a glimpse of the figure laying on the ground a few feet in front of me.

In that instant, I realized what Mikha'el had done.

Half of his body was charred beyond recognition, and his wings…

Heaven have mercy.

His wings were a gory tangle of broken bones and scorched feathers.

CHAPTER 6
KATE

Stabbing, piercing, wrenching pain sliced through every inch of my insides, jolting me awake.

Get it out. Get it out.

"Get it out of me!" I screamed so loud, I should've snapped my vocal chords. I tried to sit up, but several sets of hands held me down by the shoulders, by my legs. I looked around in a panic, trying to see who these people were, but their faces were blurry from the tears flooding my eyes.

"Get it out of me, please. Oh God, it hurts. Please… please."

But all I heard were voices in a language I couldn't understand as they started to cut my clothes off in a rush.

Then someone gasped, "*Doctora Lewis, mira esto.*"

"*La herida figura infectada. Rápido. Amenos debemos de tratar de salvar el bebe.*"

The only word that stuck out to me was *infectada*…

Oh god, did they think I was… infected? As in bitten by a devoured? Then I remembered the attack at the inn. Fuck. They must've seen the injury to my forearm. I thrashed, trying to break from their hold, but they had strapped me down on some type of gurney. What were they going to do to me? To my baby?

No. No. I had to get out. I had to… But then another bone-crushing contraction twisted inside me and my body tightened, going taught like a tension cable, every muscle in my body cramping from my toes all the way up to my neck. I thought my spine might crack in two from the intense pressure, from the immeasurable… *pain.*

I parted my lips to scream, but the sound died in my throat as my world blinked out of existence and a new one took form.

The next time I opened my eyes, I stood in the middle of a dirt path. A cold misty rain clung to my clothes, dampening my skin with a coat of dread and ice. On either side of me, tall leafless trees reached for the slate-gray sky, their barks inky black.

The path seemed to go on for miles. Behind me, the same view stretched as far as my eyes could see. I shivered, the wetness of this place sinking into my bones. There was no wind. No bird calls. No chirping insects. There was no sound except the *crunch* of the rocks beneath my shoes as I walked with no sense of direction.

Instinctively, I reached for my baby bump and heaved a sigh of relief. Safe. For now. But there was no sign of Jax, Hank, or Mikha'el. What the hell was this place? How had I gone from people tearing my clothes off and holding me down to this place?

Trembling, I rubbed my arms, but the cold was so intense, my teeth clattered. I needed to find somewhere warm and dry, or I'd go into hyperthermia. Quivering, I kept walking, but the dirt path had no end. And apparently, no beginning.

Time seemed irrelevant in this place. I had no idea if I'd walked for minutes or for hours, but after it felt like I'd trekked for miles, I finally decided to stop.

Rest. God, I wanted to rest so badly. A sudden breeze brushed against my cheeks, pulling my attention toward the forest of dead trees. Dense fog clung to the base of the trunks like a snake slithering through the wood. The breeze blew again, but this time it felt like the brush of someone's hot breath against my skin, beckoning me to follow its warmth.

My eyes grew heavy. *Rest. Rest. Rest.*

Taking a step into the forest, I placed a hand against one of the trees and frowned when my fingers came back coated in a tar-like substance. The entire bark was covered in the inky stuff; every tree around me seeped as if bleeding this black sticky liquid. I wiped my hand on my pants, but the tar stained my skin. I kept walking deeper into the wood, careful not to touch anything else.

The entire forest was devoid of color, as if a great fire had scorched all life from this place a long time ago.

Up ahead, a tiny cabin poked out of the darkness, a dim light flickering through a small window. Shuddering violently, I rushed up the stoop and peeked through the glass pane. A small fire crackled in a modest hearth with an iron-cast pot sitting over the fire, and on a wooden dining table, a round bowl steamed with a delicious-looking stew.

My stomach grumbled. I couldn't remember the last time I'd had a warm, freshly made stew. The pasta we'd had at the inn had been less than a small portion good enough for a child. I was so hungry and cold. Mouth watering, I placed a hand on the glass. Surely, whoever lived here wouldn't mind one extra mouth. There had to be enough stew in that pot.

Then the front door slowly creaked open.

My gut tightened, a warning of some sort, perhaps.

A warning I should've heeded.

But I was guided by hunger, by the hope of warmth.

So, I approached the entrance and gently pushed the door open all the way. The aroma of slowly cooked meat, potatoes, and veggies hit me like an intoxicating wave. I looked around but couldn't see anyone. "Hello?"

No reply, except for the sound of the crackling fire.

My hand hovered over where my sword should've been, but it was gone, and so was my gun. Made no sense, but then again, nothing about this place did. I gulped as I took another step inside. "Anyone home?"

Another step and I was fully inside the cabin, and that's when the door slammed closed behind me and the room went pitch-black. Fuck. I turned toward the exit, feeling for the knob. Once I found it, I tried turning it but had zero success. Damn this. What the hell was this place? No more crackling fire. No more steaming stew. Only darkness.

And the breath of someone else standing inside the room with me.

I placed my back flush against the door. My heart pounded so hard, I heard the whoosh of blood as it pulsed at my temple. Gradually, the air grew frigid and the scent of rotting flowers filled my nostrils. It smelled like a tomb, like death.

The floors creaked as the sound of shoes clicking on the hardwood echoed in the small room, but I couldn't see anything. Pressing my back harder against the door, I held my breath as I tried to pierce the darkness with my eyes, but the pitch-black surrounding me was impenetrable.

"Show yourself," I said, but my voice lacked conviction. Ice-cold fingers brushed against my cheek and I almost screamed, but then another door began to creak open a few feet in front of me, a silvery light filtering through until the entire door lay open.

My breath hitched. It was my New York City apartment. Suddenly, I was sitting upright in my and Roger's bed. But the bed was empty.

I checked the digital clock on my nightstand: 2:13 a.m. bleeped on the screen. I knew this night. Isabella should've been sleeping beside me. Then a scream shattered the silence. It was Isabella's tiny voice as it was snuffed by the snarling grunts of my dead, infected husband.

No. No. No.

I reached for the service weapon I kept under my pillow, but it was gone. It shouldn't have been. That's where it had been the night it happened. The night I…

Jumping out from under the covers, I ran toward the bedroom door and yanked it open. Roger stood in the hallway, holding Isabella in his arms. I came to a screeching halt before them. He… he smiled at me in the moonlit hallway. God, that smile—bright, dimpled, and always playful. It was what had made me fall in love with him. And Isabella. Her brown curls hung to her shoulders like ribbons of silk as her chubby hand waved *hello.*

My heart clenched. That's how I'd chosen to remember them. That snapshot in time. This was the alternate memory I'd created for myself. Tears welled in my eyes as I walked toward them and placed a hand on Roger's cheek, but the instant I touched him, his skin began to slough off, his decomposing flesh sinking under my fingernails. Retrieving my hand in horror, I approached Isabella and tried to reach for a curl, but her hair tangled in my fingers and fell off in clumps.

I stumbled backward, watching them transform into the devoured. Black, rotting flesh. Dead, milky eyes.

"You killed them," an unfamiliar male voice whispered around me as I sank to the floor, my back against the door to my room. Isabella and Roger walked toward me, snarling, hissing, their bodies contorted, devoid of the beautiful life they once possessed.

"I'm so sorry," I cried as I curled in on myself.

"Roger died because you refused to leave the city." That male voice grew louder, thicker. "Because you refused to listen to him."

I looked around but couldn't see anyone else in the room. But whoever it was, they weren't wrong. I'd never stopped thinking about my mistakes, how I could've prevented their deaths. Had I only listened to Roger… "I'm so sorry," I repeated, sinking deeper into myself, unwilling to look at the two infected creatures who no longer resembled the people I once loved.

My heart jumped as I felt a presence materialize next to me, lips brushing against my ears. "Isabella died because you failed to protect her. Your *daughter*. How could you, Kate?"

I pushed up to my feet, grabbed the doorknob, and rushed back inside my room, slamming the door closed. "I… didn't mean to!" I yelled as I pounded a fist against the door. "I never meant for any of this to happen."

Suddenly, the room transformed back into the cabin, the fire crackling in a corner, the stew steaming by the table. Something wasn't right here. I needed to leave, needed to escape this nightmare. I ran for the exit, yanking hard on the knob, but the door wouldn't open. "Let me out!"

"There's no escape from my kingdom, Daughter of Eve," came that unholy male voice once again, the stillness and confidence behind each word freezing me in place. My chest rose and fell in rapid succession, but the chill in the air was so dense, it hurt to breathe.

I'd never met him, but I knew… *knew* with every terrified cell in my body who that voice belonged to. No one else could conjure such fear. But how? The Devil couldn't escape his prison.

"There's much you don't know about me, Kate," he uttered, as if reading my thoughts.

Guess Mikha'el wasn't the only angel capable of that trick.

Careful. That name is forbidden here. You wouldn't want to inadvertently stoke my anger.

My back muscles tightened at the intrusion into my mind. I slowly pivoted around.

Face obscured by shadows, a masculine figure elegantly dressed in a black suit sat at the end of the wooden dining table, his chair facing me. An ankle crossed over a knee, his black leather shoes shone with the gleam of the flickering flames.

I clenched my hands, hoping to mask the erratic beats of my racing heart. But if he was who I believed him to be, there was no hiding the terror coursing through my veins. After all, he *was* the Prince of Hell.

He puffed a long, sour breath. "*Prince of Hell*... I've always found that designation profoundly banal. Alas, I know I shouldn't be disappointed at humanity's gravely uninspired imagination. Lucifer. Satan, even. Those I can moderately tolerate—though I've grown quite tired of the same epithets. I much prefer you call me by my given name, Katherine. One I'm acutely aware you know very, *very* well."

A lump lodged itself in my throat. "Samael."

I couldn't see his face, but I swore I felt the satisfied, malicious grin that formed on his lips. Fingers lazily tapping on the table, he remained seated, his body a granite statue. He appeared utterly unflappable, but the rage coiled like a snake beneath that self-possessed demeanor vibrated in the room like an electrically charged storm—violent, atomic, ready to strike at any moment. He gestured to the second chair at the table, his voice unperturbed. "Have a seat."

It wasn't a request.

"What do you want from me?" I asked, my mouth dry, muscles still frozen.

"I believe you already know the answer to that question, Kate. Now, I said *sit*. You're starving, and it would be rude of you to refuse my hospitality."

This was his idea of hospitality?

Placing a hand over my belly, I took in a long breath. I peered over at the steaming bowl of stew. My stomach grumbled so hard, I felt nauseous. Fucker thought he could temp me with food? That I would so easily hand over my child for some meat and potatoes? This had to be a joke, though it felt more like an insult. I'd gone longer without a meal before. I turned my gaze to his shadowed face and raised my chin. "I'd rather die than eat your rotten food."

His fingers stopped drumming. "Tell me, Kate. What's the price of your family's lives? Of their deaths?"

I clenched my jaw. I didn't like where these questions were headed.

"Hmm?" he pressed. "Please. I'm intrigued to know what their lives were worth to you."

"You want to shame me for their deaths? I carry the guilt of my actions on my bleeding heart every fucking day, you bastard. But you already know that. And you also know that I *never* meant for them to die."

He banged a fist on the table and my entire body jolted at the harsh sound. "You and your wretched kind," he gritted. "You never want to accept responsibility for your sins. But the bill still comes at the end, Kate." Leaning forward, the light from the flames finally revealed his face.

I gasped, unable to hold back my surprise. There were no true words to describe the frigid and brutal unearthly beauty of his face. Even the torrent of hatred spewing from his pores was muted by the glow of his dewy skin. Hair white-gold as bright sunlight. Eyes the color of twilight. Lips flushed and curled into seductive perfection. I couldn't consolidate what I saw with what I knew of the creature sitting before me.

"Would it please you better if I looked different?" he asked, once again reading my thoughts. Suddenly, the man in the suit stood, his body transforming into a ten-foot, horned demon with hoofed feet and sharpened claws and teeth. A set of bat-like wings stretched the span of the cabin, red veins spider-webbing across the leathery skin. "Does *this* form satisfy your expectations, Kate?" His distorted, deep voice shook the walls of the cabin, his hooves clomping on the wood as he neared me. I reached behind me for the doorknob as my heart pounded, but the door still didn't budge.

Terror cut across my flesh like a sharp knife as he cupped my face in one of his clawed hands, the touch of his skin like frostbite. "I didn't say you could leave."

Every instinct in my body wanted me to scream, to run from him. But I was done running. I stared into his red, flaming eyes. "You don't get to decide my fate, demon."

He chuckled, mocking and irritating at the same time. Squeezing my face harder, he said, "You're not the first warrior with a holy mission to cross my path, Kate. Or do you prefer I call you *angel,* like that traitorous vermin you call Jax?"

Holding his stare, I said, "You can call me whatever the fuck you want, but you're never taking my child."

Bringing his face closer to mine, his animalistic nostrils flared. "You might be His newly anointed saint, but your fate will not be to redeem your kind through another divine birth. We both know that, despite Gavri'el's new prophecy—that insufferable emissary," he said with a snarl, "what you carry in that womb is not humanity's savior, but its damnation."

Fire surged in my hands and up my arms, the angelic symbols emblazoned on my skin sparking to life. Without thought, I pushed hard on his chest, sending him barreling backward.

He hissed in pain at the burn on his skin, but then he laughed, that horrific deep voice making my skin crawl.

"You know nothing about me or my child!"

Body slowly morphing back to the man in the suit, he stuck his hands inside his pockets, taking easy strides toward me. "I know more than you are willing to tell *him,*" he said, those twilight eyes zeroing in on mine.

Him. He didn't even bother mentioning Jax's name because he knew… the fucker *knew* I'd know exactly who he meant.

"You worry about the blood your child carries. Because deep down, you know that regardless of his *love* for you," he seethed, the word love uttered as if it burned his lips, "your precious Jax swore an oath to serve me. An oath passed down through his blood—*my* blood."

"Shut up," I spat, putting my hands out in warning.

"You worry about bringing the Antichrist into this world."

"Shut your filthy tongue, demon."

"Oh, I'm more than a demon, *angel*. More than the villain in your story. I'm the master of your nightmares."

He stood a couple of feet taller than me, his body no larger than any mortal man. But the weight of his presence pinned me against the door with the force of a thousand men as he drew so close, I felt his breath on my face. Placing his palms on each side of the door, he caged me in his scent of wilted roses and wet dirt. His chest brushed against mine, and I felt my insides recoil.

"I don't fear you," I uttered, my shaky breath betraying my words.

He chuckled, gently running his knuckles down the side of my face. "You want me to believe that, little mortal? But I know every intimate detail of your darkest thoughts." He pressed his body closer to mine and took a deep inhale. "I can practically smell it coming off you. Fear excites me, Kate… and yours is beyond thrilling."

I tried pushing against his chest again, but this time, his body wouldn't budge. I couldn't summon the fire, couldn't command my power.

He brought his lips to my ear, the immense dominance radiating from him rendering me motionless. "This is my kingdom, *angel*. You don't get to burn me twice."

Anchoring my gaze to his, I puffed my chest. "If this is your kingdom, then stop hiding behind the mask. Show me your true face." I needed to distract him, to earn myself time to figure out how to get out of this dream.

"My true face will bring you to your knees."

"Try me."

He grinned, teeth gleaming. "You think yourself wiser than the Devil?"

"I think you want to inspire fear, but you're the one scared of never leaving your prison. Scared to never rule anything but the leftovers—the sinners, the mistakes."

He tipped my chin up, his fathomless gaze churning with ancient, primal malice. "I am the fear that burns at your core when you lie awake in bed, wondering if the child growing inside your womb is an abomination. You fear that your once barren womb is now only destined to bear rotten fruit."

My body trembled at his words—words I'd been too ashamed to admit to myself—as guilty tears crested in my eyes. I'd been given a gift. A child. I should've been thankful. But a part of me… a part of me wondered if perhaps… Heaven, I couldn't bring myself to utter the words, not even in my mind.

"If it wouldn't be better if the child did not survive? Say it, Kate. You don't want this child. You haven't wanted it since you found out it was growing inside you."

I shook my head. No. No, that wasn't it. I didn't feel *worthy* of the child. Worthy of the blessing.

"Of the *curse*. Because that's how you truly see it. Another burden placed upon your shoulders. You question if you'd even be a good mother. You weren't able to protect Isabella, so what makes you think you can protect this child from me?"

"Get out of my head."

He banged a fist against the door. "Say it. Say that you don't want it, and I can make it all go away, Kate. The guilt. The memories that haunt you every day."

My body couldn't stop trembling. The tears wouldn't stop falling. A contraction rocked through me and I screamed, curling into myself from the pain. But I pushed myself upright and forced myself to hold his gaze. He wiped my tears with his thumbs. "I can make the pain stop, Kate. Just tell me you want me to take the child."

I wanted to spit in his face but my strength faltered, and I fell to my knees before him, clutching at my belly as a stronger contraction threatened to rip me in half. *Please. Please. Please.* I implored my baby. *Just hold on.*

Samael knelt beside me, watching me with cold, insidious curiosity. Pulling a strand of my hair behind my ear, he said, "Pity. All this anger, this contempt… it blemishes your pretty face."

"Fuck. You."

His crooked grin flashed with pride. "Can't deny I enjoy watching you on your knees, Kate." He ran a thumb over my quivering lips. "Such a sinfully perfect *mouth*… What lovely, erotic horrors I can conjure. I can almost appreciate why he betrayed me for you. Lust *is* my favorite sin."

Disgust roiled in my stomach. Only the Devil could find lust in a woman's pain.

My body trembled as the muscles in my lower back spasmed.

Smile widening, he lowered his voice, almost tenderly. "I can end your suffering, Kate. Let me take this burden from you. Give me the child, and I will give you back what you lost."

I hated how easily every word that spilled from his lips dripped with cruel seduction. Hated how his deep, honeyed voice found the cracks in my foundation, saturating my vulnerabilities. I flopped to my side, the pain so intense it felt like my pelvic bone was breaking. God, I wanted the pain to end. And that end was so close… All I had to do was give him what he wanted. All I had to do was…

Then I heard her. Isabella. Her little voice. "Everything will be okay, Mama." She placed a soft hand on my cheek. "I love you."

I didn't think it was possible to feel any more agony, but my heart broke again and again as I watched that sweet little face smile at me. Through wet, blurry eyes, I looked past Isabella's apparition and focused on the figure standing above me instead, looking down at me with fear in his terrified eyes. In that moment, I saw beyond his illusion. A vision played out before me of his time before the Fall.

I finally saw the true face he kept hidden. Hidden for good fucking reason, because once, he'd been the most beautiful of all of God's creations. A Seraphim Prince of the First Sphere made purely of glittering starlight. The embodiment of God's perfect love. He'd held the highest seat in Heaven's court. He'd been destined to inherit the earth, promised to be our noble king. The one to guide us into enlightenment. But he lost the throne to hate—to ambition, to a cruel and selfish heart.

His golden-lit wings now hung loosely at his feet, withered and diseased. Oozing of the same tar-like substance coating the trees outside the cabin. His once porcelain-like skin was burned and cracked. His twilight gaze dimmed with the dead haze of a pale gray. And on his head, a crown made of crooked bones sat fused to his skull, the never-healing wounds seeping with black blood.

He was more than a fallen angel. He was God's discarded disappointment made flesh.

Samael wrapped his raw, charred fingers around my throat. "You wanted to see my true face? Only those meant for my kingdom have the privilege to gaze upon it. I reckon that now makes you one of *mine*. You've exhausted my damned patience, Kate." He placed his other hand over my belly. "Give me the child, or I will intensify your fucking pain ten-thousand-fold."

My teeth clattered as my insides ripped. I should've been dead. At least, I wanted to be if only to end the suffering clawing at every inch of my body. But there was only one way out of this hell. "I… Katherine Elizabeth Jones…" My voice cracked, lips barely able to form the words. "Entrust my soul … and that of my son's…"

Samael's eyes burned with the flames of his hate. Of his torment. Of his hope to finally be free of his prison.

Hope…

If the Devil could have hope, then perhaps not everything was lost. Perhaps humanity could also find a glimmer of hope amongst all the anguish and destruction brought upon by this infernal beast.

I swallowed the dry lump in my throat, my saliva tasting of nails. Hot tears flooded my eyes, but I didn't lose my nerve. Refused to, because I'd be dammed if I survived the fucking apocalypse to give up now. Gritting my teeth, I said, "I entrust my soul and that of my son's to *God,* and God alone."

The walls of the cabin cracked and a bright light shot through every crevice.

"You insolent, human. What have you done?" Pure disbelief coated the bellowing roar that erupted from him.

Fueled by love and sorrow, guilt and hope, I hung on to the memory of Roger and Isabella. *I'm so sorry,* I said to them in my heart. And with one final *I love you*, I let them go. Then I grabbed Samael's hand from my throat and peeled his fingers off me. "In the name of the Father, and of the Son, and of the Holy Spirit, I rebuke thee."

His face was a contorted mess of anger and disdain as I raised to my feet, and suddenly, everything my grandmother had ever taught me flashed before my eyes. My biggest weapon against this monstrous being stirred within me. I reached into the well of my sadness, into the pit dugout at the center of my core where all my regrets and all my anger lived, and from there I pulled out the only sliver of strength I had left—the faith I had lost so very long ago.

Enduring the pain in my abdomen, I labored toward him— my steps small but full of purpose—and sharpened my tongue into a glinting blade. "You have no power over me. You are nothing but dust, the remnants of a burnt dream." My voice thundered, thick and heavy like an ax, cutting him down to a mere coward with tattered wings and a disgraced name.

"With the power of the blood of Christ, I condemn thee, Samael, to a thousand lifetimes in this place."

He faltered backward, his body shaking as if every thread of his existence was being unraveled into individual ribbons of black smoke. He skewered me with those inhuman eyes of his, cursing my soul with his gaze.

But I managed a smile, because today, he would not win.

Then the cabin shook, and Samael let out another roar as his body was shredded away by the eye of a churning storm of blinding light.

Everything around me spun wildly until he was gone, and there was nothing but the darkness of the black hole left in his wake.

CHAPTER 7

JAX

Hands tied behind my back, I was plopped down on a metal chair, then the black hood was yanked off my head. A bright fluorescent lamp hovered above my head, the light stinging my eyes. I winced against the brightness, wondering how the hell they had electricity, but more importantly, needing to adjust my sight so I could catch a glimpse of the individuals who'd taken me captive.

"Your name," a female voice uttered in accented English.

When my eyesight finally cleared, I scanned the small square room. Beige, indistinct, windowless walls surrounded me. Sparsely furnished, this place was likely an interrogation room. My attention caught on the wooden cross hanging above the doorframe. Somehow, that tiny detail offered me a glimmer of hope. Perhaps these people were part of the *Sagrada familia*.

The ones who'd taken us in had their faces obscured by scarves when I'd seen them outside, so I didn't recognize the three people standing by the door, rifles resting in their arms—ready to fire should I try to escape. But the one standing before me was unmistakable. I'd recognize the fierce gaze of those dark, deep-set eyes a mile away.

She lowered her scarf, revealing the rest of her hardened features. A strong nose, thin lips, and a dimpled chin. Dark, curly hair highlighted by gray draped down to her shoulders. The corners of her eyes had seen better days, but that was true for all of us. Who I didn't see in the room was Kate, Hank, or Mikha'el. "Where's the woman I was with?" I asked, panic stirring in my chest.

"Your name," she repeated, arms crossed over her chest. Her authoritative stance hinted at a military background. The unmoving stare—a dissecting probe capable of reducing anyone to a worm. This woman was definitely the one in charge here. I didn't want to piss her off, but I also had no time to waste answering stupid questions.

"I'll tell you whatever the fuck you want to know, but first I need to know that the woman I was with is okay."

She nodded at one of the guards by the door. "*Anda. Ve por Antonia.*" Then she swiveled her scalpel of a gaze back toward me. "You're far from home, American."

The moniker, though innocuous, was anything but friendly if the harsh tone of her voice was any indication regarding her feelings toward Westerners. I straightened in my chair and shot her an unwavering stare of my own. "What gave me away, *señora*? Was it the I Love New York T-shirt?"

She leaned closer, those bold eyes darkening to solid coal as she glared at me down the bridge of her nose. The smile slashing across her lips was stone cold and absent of any mirth. "Let me make one thing crystal clear, American. I have plenty of mouths to feed here; I don't need to add two more—four, if you count the angel and the dog. So, if you don't want me to throw your ass back out to the *sabuesos,* I advise you to start talking."

I didn't know what the hell a *sabueso* was, but I could only imagine she either meant hellhounds or the infected, and both were terrible options. At least I knew Mikha'el had somehow survived being scorched alive, and Hank was okay, too. Still, I had no idea who these people were or what they were capable of. I needed to make sure Kate and the baby were safe before I started squealing.

"Like I said, first the woman, then I speak."

A knock sounded at the door. When the person was escorted in, they whispered something to the woman holding me prisoner. The grim look in my captor's eyes wasn't very promising as she sucked in a troubled breath. Palming the rosary pendant hanging from her neck, she said, "My people are saying your *woman* was bitten. We cannot allow an infected person to remain on the premises."

I pulled on my restraints. "Wait, no. You can't—"

She cut me off with a quick slash of her eyes, her shoulders pulling back. "Are you trying to tell me what I can or cannot do in my own home, Mr... New York? I'm putting my people in danger simply by talking to you instead of disposing of her."

"Kate is not infected."

The newcomer whispered something in Spanish. The leader's hand rested on the pistol secured at her hip as her messenger related more information. "She says your woman has a clear human bite on her arm. How can you tell me she's not infected? She's either going to die or she will turn."

"She's immune," I barked, causing her to lurch back. "Look, you need to listen to me. We came here looking for the Guardians of *La Sagrada Familia*—"

The woman put a finger up, silencing me. "What did you say?"

"I said, we're looking for *La Sagra*—"

"No. What do you mean she's *immune*?" She narrowed her eyes, gaze scanning mine—a challenge to tread carefully with my answer.

"Take me to her and I'll tell you everything. Please. She doesn't have much time. Her water broke. She was in labor when we arrived. The rift, it accelerated things…"

"Slow down, American."

"Jax, for fuck's sake, just call me Jax."

"Okay, Jax. You have my attention. I will take you to her, but first, you must explain to me how she's immune."

I didn't want to use my only bargaining chip, but I was the one at a disadvantage here and I could already tell this woman wouldn't budge unless I gave her something. "She was anointed by Zadkiel." She didn't stop me to ask who Zadkiel was or what it meant to be anointed, so clearly, she knew her angel lore, which meant she could quite well be a guardian.

"After she was attacked by a pack of d'shiad, he healed her, somehow imbuing her with the angelic properties in his blood," I went on. "That's the key to the cure—what we failed to realize when the infection broke out. The anecdote to the hellborn fucking virus is angel blood. But pure angel blood is too potent, too powerful for humans. If injected directly into our bloodstreams, it's like being exposed to direct undiffused solar radiation—practically injecting pure star energy into our blood. It incinerates you from the inside out. But Kate's blood carries only a touch of his essence, not only making her immune, but also allowing her to use her blood as a potential cure. We already tried it. And it worked." I didn't mention that we'd only tried it on Hank so far and not on an actual human.

Someone in the room took in a sharp inhale and whispers circulated in Spanish.

I met the leader's stare, my breath hitching. "I'm telling you the truth. I swear on it—on my life, on Kate's life. Ask Mikha'el. He'll verify what I'm telling you."

She cocked her head. "Mikha'el?"

"The archangel you brought in with me. He's still alive, right?"

The group exchanged looks before she replied, "Barely. But hold on a second. You're saying the angel who killed *El Carnicero* is… *San Miguel*?"

"*San Miguel*. Saint Michael. Call him whatever the hell you want. He's the archangel depicted on one of the murals right outside the *Sagrada Familia*. You must have seen us fighting those demons. Seen what Mikha'el did."

More silent glances. What were these people hiding?

"You're Guardians," I said, taking a gamble. "Otherwise, why bother bringing us in? You said it yourself, you have plenty of mouths to feed. And from the look in your eyes, I know I don't sound crazy to you. You don't have just an angel in your possession; you have the commander of God's mightiest legions, and by virtue of your duty as guardians to this realm, he's your commander as well."

She paused for half a beat, a muscle in her cheek clenching. Then she signaled to one of her companions. When they cut the zip tie keeping my hands secured, I rubbed my wrists and jumped to my feet.

"You better be right about this, Jax," the woman said. "Or I will personally put a bullet in both your and your woman's head."

So fuzzy and warm. "I didn't catch your name," I told her as her guards led us out of the room.

She paused at the threshold, her face inches from mine. "Amada Villavicencio, *líder de Los Guardianes de la Orden del Este*. And yes, you are inside *La Sagrada Familia*. You do anything stupid, and I'll be glad to dump your ass out on the street."

"We didn't come here looking for trouble, Amada."

"We'll see about that."

"Where's your priest? I need to ask him about the—"

"Dead. Two weeks after the infection broke out. We've been functioning on our own ever since."

Fuck. I hadn't expected that.

They led me through several corridors and toward the infirmary, where they were treating Kate. "So, who's been blessing your holy water?" I asked. "Don't tell me you don't have holy-water-infused ammunition."

She paused, her beady eyes drilling into mine. "No holy water, Mr. Jax. Thanks to the angels who abandoned us and took our empyrean weapons, we've had to defend ourselves using these," she said, raising her rifle, "old-fashion regular guns and bullets. But I'm glad at least you've had assistance from a priest and angels, while we've had to battle some of the nastiest shits to crawl out of Hell's asshole with practically stones and sticks when it comes to fighting demons."

I stared, unable to offer her anything that might make her feel any better. We *had* been pretty lucky. As far as we knew, Zadkiel and Mikha'el had been the only angels to openly disobey God's orders. Things were different now, and Mikha'el and Gavri'el had managed to help us gain favor from God, but other than them two and the angelic warriors who helped them escape whatever war broke out in Heaven after the events in New York, humanity was practically still fighting this war alone.

Satisfied she'd put me in my place, she turned her back on me and led me the rest of the way in silence until we finally arrived at the makeshift infirmary. My heart sank the instant I saw her. Kate laid on a gurney, covered in a white sheet already smeared with blood. I ran to her, wiping sweaty hair from her brow. "What's wrong with her? Why is she still unconscious?"

A short young woman stepped forward, blonde hair bound in a tight bun. Her white lab coat was covered in blood and an old-looking stethoscope hung from her neck. "She started thrashing when we tried to undress her to look at her injuries. I had to give her a mild sedative." The woman spoke with a British accent. Seemed I wasn't the only one far from home.

"You're the doctor here?" I asked.

She offered me a wavering nod. "More or less. I was a med student who got stuck here when Hell broke out."

"Can you help her, though?"

Her jaw tightened. "The baby is breached. Unless we can turn it around, she won't be able to deliver naturally… not without risks."

My shoulders tensed. "What kind of risks?"

The doctor stared at me, her wordless expression sending a shockwave down my back. My knees weakened, and I held on to the gurney to keep myself from buckling. "But you can operate, right?"

"To save the baby, we'd need to cut into the mother's abdomen. We don't have anesthesia and no way of giving her an epidural or spinal. We're not even equipped to perform major surgeries here. Plus, we're short on antibiotics, should she develop an infection."

"What are you saying?"

"I'm saying, if I operate, I can save the baby, but the mother…"

I shook my head. "Don't. Don't you fucking say it."

She placed her hand on my shoulder. "Your wife… She's been bitten, she's already lost this battle. Do you want to lose your baby, too?"

I pulled away from her touch. "Kate is not infected. She's immune."

The young former med student looked at Amada, eyes wide.

"He claims she's been anointed by an angel, that her blood carries the cure."

"You listen to me, doc," I said, calling back her attention. "If you want to save this world, then you need to save this woman.

I don't care what you have to do, but you have to save them both."

Suddenly, Kate's fingers squeezed mine, a soft moan spilling from her lips. I leaned in closer to her. Her eyes slowly opened. "Jax…" she said hoarsely.

"I'm right here, angel."

"The baby… it hurts so much."

"We're going to take good care of you, okay? There's a doctor here, and they are going to help you deliver the baby."

Her eyes went dark, terror flashing in their depths. Gripping my hand tighter, she said, "Samael… Samael came for me."

"Samael?"

"He got inside my head, but… he was real, Jax. He was real."

Shit. That wasn't good. If what she said was true, that meant she'd crossed into the Wastes. But how? Could it be that the baby had acted like a conduit?

I wiped more sweat from her forehead and kissed her lips. "Let's talk about that later, okay? Right now, we need to get through this."

"Jax, I'm scared."

"I'm not going anywhere. I promise."

The lab coated woman approached, with another woman at her side. "This is Ofelia. She's a midwife and is going to help try to move the baby back into position."

Kate gripped my hand harder.

"My name is Diana Lewis," the young med student said. "I want to be completely honest with you. Thanks to the apocalypse, I never got to finish medical school. Cardiology… that was meant to be my specialty. Guess that's a moot point now. Look, I may not be a doctor by old-world standards, but I have helped deliver a few babies since… well, since diplomas and residences stopped meaning shit. So, I promise you, I will do everything in my power to help you deliver this baby safely.

But you need to work with me…" She paused, waiting for Kate to offer her name.

I couldn't tell if the cold, wet feeling in my hand was from me or Kate, but my heart clenched at how much her skin had paled, sweat continuing to bead on her forehead. "Kate. Her name is Kate," I replied.

"Okay, Kate," the not-doctor said with a gentle smile. "Is this your first baby?"

Kate and I exchanged glances, and the pained look in her eyes told me why she hesitated to answer. She might've not birthed Isabella, but she'd been her mother in every other sense of the word—no one could ever take that away from her. But perhaps she struggled with the words because it would feel like a betrayal to her little girl—to say this was her first baby. It wasn't. Still, I found the words for her. "It's her first natural child."

Diana drew closer, her voice lowering. "Women have been having babies since humans bleeped to life on this earth. Your body will know what to do, we just have to help it a little. We need to nudge the baby to get it positioned properly into the birthing canal. Ofelia has done this countless times. Will you trust us?"

Kate nodded, looking at me for reassurance.

I squeezed her hand. "I'm gonna be right here with you."

Diana eyed me, her silent direction telling me to give them the space they needed to do their work. I kissed Kate again and assured her I would be only a few steps away.

As soon as I moved out of their way, the midwife got to work. I had no clue what she was doing with her hands, but she seemed to be massaging Kate's abdomen while a couple of other women kept Kate cool with wet towels and another gave her water through a straw.

I paced, hands shaking as I waited for them to finish, all while hearing Kate groan in pain. I hated that I couldn't do anything to help her.

"Jax, there's something we need to talk about," Amada said, pulling me to the side and giving me a much-welcomed distraction. Reaching into her jacket pocket, she pulled out the creation stone Kate had been wearing. Then one of the guardians handed her Kate's dagger. The fact that none of their hands looked burned from handling the sword only confirmed they were legit. "Diana found these on her. Please explain how you are in possession of a creation stone and an empyrean weapon. What is really going on here?"

My back muscles tensed. This was the part where, once I revealed who I was and why we were here, there was a good chance she was going to want to feed me to the hellhounds. "A package was sent here the day the gates opened… it contained the fire stone."

"How do you know that?"

"Because I'm the one who sent it. It's why I asked where your priest was. I need to know if you received it."

Her face went blank.

"Do you have the stone, Amada?"

As if taken aback by my tone, she squared her shoulders and crossed her arms. "*I'm* asking the questions. Ever since you all showed up, all of a sudden, your wife is supposedly immune and apparently, she's carrying the cure to the infection. You're working with angels, and *San Miguel*, the most celebrated of all the angels, seems to be your personal bodyguard, *and* now you're asking me about the fire stone—one of the four keys entrusted to the guardians. The keys that were stolen by the people who opened the gates." Placing her hand on the pistol resting on her hip, she inched closer. "You've got some serious explaining to do, Jax, and I don't have all day."

Seemed there was no way to avoid telling her the truth—the whole fucking truth. "What I'm about to tell you is going to make you wish you'd left my ass out on the street, but I need you to listen to everything I have to say before you do anything harsh. The fate of this world depends on it."

The way her brow crinkled wasn't very promising; she already doubted I was gonna tell her the truth.

I blew out a breath, hoping she had a sensible bone in her body and wouldn't put a bullet in my head the instant I told her who'd birthed me.

As I expected, though, once Amada and the guardians in the room heard about my involvement with the Devil's Army, and the role I played in opening the gates, their entire demeanor darkened. Hands migrated closer to their weapons, and gazes grew shadowed with suspicion. Even Amada tightened her grip on the rifle strapped across her chest. Her instincts as a guardian were to dispatch people like me to the afterlife, so I couldn't blame her. But I needed her on my side if any of us were gonna get out of this situation alive.

I tried to ignore the fact that her guardians had drawn closer, boxing me in. "I know you have no reason to trust me right now. But I sent the stone here because it was the one place I knew it would be safe. I'm the last person you'd want to give it to—I don't blame you for feeling that way—but I swear to you, I'm only trying to protect you. All of you. Beleth is seeking the fire stone, and it's only a matter of time before he discovers its location and comes looking for it here. And trust me, he's going to make *El Carnicero* look like Barney."

She looked confused for a second, but chose to ignore my Barney comment. I wasn't kidding, though. If Beleth showed up with the fucking sicarri, it was gonna be a shit storm.

She ordered her guardians to stand back. "The stone arrived about a week after the gates opened. Soon after that, governments began to collapse and well… the rest is history.

We've never known who sent it, but we've protected the stone since it arrived. You can understand why I would be reluctant to just hand it over to you, despite everything you've said."

"I never wanted any of this to happen. But I made my choices too late and paid for them with my life. But I was given a second chance, and I don't plan to fuck it up."

"And what exactly is your plan once you have the fire stone?"

I glanced toward the woman who had changed my life, and something inside me quivered. What *was* our plan? Before Mikha'el showed up, we'd been heading to Albany in search of a sanctuary, our minds focused on getting the girls to safety and finding a place for Kate to give birth. Then everything got flipped upside down, and the next thing we knew, we were rifted through time and space, and dumped in the middle of a demon fight halfway across the globe. I knew we'd come here to secure the fire stone so Beleth couldn't get his hands on it, but then what? Mikha'el was the military commander, not me. He'd been the one to strategize our mission, and now he was…

Fuck. I didn't even know if he would live after tonight.

"Jax?"

I ran a palm down my face. "The plan is to make sure Beleth doesn't get a hold of the fire and earth stones. Then we need to find a way to steal back the air and water stones currently in his possession. After that, we close the fucking gates. All while making sure my son is safe." How we'd execute said plan… Well, we'd have to figure that out later.

Amada took a deep breath, relaxing her shoulders—a gesture that had a trickling effect, based on how her crew didn't look like they wanted my head on a pike any longer. The tightness in my chest eased, and I was able to breathe better. "Trusting a member of the Devil's Army goes against everything we believe. Everything we stand for."

"I know earning your trust is no easy feat. I wouldn't trust me, either. But I'm no longer a member of the Devil's Army.

I'm not asking you to trust my word, Amada. I'm asking you to trust an angel."

"The angels forsook us," she hissed. "They abandoned us long ago, Jax. Our empyrean weapons were taken. They left us vulnerable, unprepared to fight against Samael's army."

"Yet you saw what he did right outside your church," I said, pointing in some random direction. "Mikha'el never lost faith in us. He betrayed God for *us*."

"And where is God in all of this, Jax? What good is an army of angels if God has turned His back on His own creation?"

"I don't have an answer for that, Amada. There are secrets even Mikha'el can't share, but I do know there's another war coming. The apocalypse… The gates opening was just the beginning. Samael can still escape his prison. He plans to make Earth his kingdom, and he plans to do it by using my son as his host. When that happens, those of us who survive will wish we hadn't."

Something cut across Amada's face. It was gone as fast as it appeared, but I knew the thought that had sprouted in her head, especially when her gaze had briefly shifted toward Kate before connecting with mine.

Protective fear curdled in my stomach as my hands fisted at my sides. I almost couldn't utter the words, the saliva evaporating in my mouth. "You'd sacrifice a child?" For a brief second, I wondered if we'd made a mistake coming here. If I'd doomed us by thinking these guardians would welcome us with open arms.

A sudden flash of guilt ghosted on her face, but she didn't reply.

"My son is meant to save us, not damn us," I gritted. "He's not your sacrificial lamb."

"And what if Samael gets a hold of all four stones? What if he gets a hold of your child?" she asked, the column of her neck tightening. "Perhaps the best way to ensure he doesn't escape is to make sure he doesn't have a host."

Standing taller, I expanded my chest, and I had to fight the bubbling anger boiling in my core or I'd do something I'd later regret. For a second, I thought Astaroth was about to burst through my rib cage. It was as if his fire still burned within me.

She'd outright threatened my son, and he wasn't even born yet. If she did it again, I didn't think I'd be able to stop myself from making her swallow those words. Reeling in the monster slithering under my skin, I said, "I know the mere existence of my son poses a risk, but he is my son, and I will do everything in my power to protect him from *anyone* who tries to hurt him. My mission is to not only protect the stones from falling into Beleth's hands, but to keep him away from my son. And to close the gates once and for all. Otherwise, why do you think we'd risk everything to come here?"

"To seek refuge for your woman and child."

"No, Amada. We came here to seek your fucking help. You're our last bastion of hope."

"Jax," Diana hollered from across the room, cutting the star-hot tension between Amada and me. "We're ready to push."

CHAPTER 8

SAMAEL

baddon's all too familiar bitter wind howled as I stood on the battlements of Dolorem Castle, my accursed home. Despite the arctic snow drifts furiously whipping through my pale hair and biting at the skin on my face, my body raged hotter than the fires in the depths of the Purgatorium Mountains. The dark d'shiad fur-cloak draped over my shoulders shimmered with icicles as I scanned the barren and frozen landscape that stretched in perpetual whiteness. Every day, for thousands of years, I've stood here, gazing upon this wretched tundra because, for thousands of years, winter has never ceased. It is a prison of stone and ice. Always gray, always frigid, always miserable.

My eyes narrowed impatiently, trying to see through the ice fog suffocating the air. Beleth, my last remaining lieutenant able to walk in the mortal realm, was due to arrive with news, and every second I spent waiting for him was a lifetime in this doomed realm—the inescapable prison designed specifically for me, the Fallen One, the one who dared question God.

This place was hardly what the world would imagine Hell to be. No raging pits of lava, no infernal underworld built of flames. But fire wasn't the only thing that burned.

Here, the souls of the damned still found everlasting suffering.

And *that's* what Hell truly was. What *I* was—the king of endless frost and sorrow, standing upon a stone castle with a crown crafted of bones, overlooking a kingdom that begot only death.

But I was more than that.

Some called me the Prince of Lies, others, the Prince of Darkness. Perhaps Master of Lust and Sinful Desires. But that would be too simplistic, too morbidly romantic. Those titles were calculated lies fabricated to vilify the most basic of needs.

The need to eat, drink, and fuck.

I was the opposite of pleasure. Endless hunger, that's what coursed through my blood. And endless thirst. I was the ruler of torment and deprivation. There was no satisfaction in my world, no fulfillment, only eternal longing. It was here that souls came to die a slow and terrible death.

I wanted to be a king. God gave me a kingdom.

An ache settled in my gut at the memory of the day my Father cast me out. He thought I aimed to take *His* throne at Heaven's seat. Alas, He knew me so very little.

To rule at His side had been my one true desire, but I was deemed unworthy. Because I refused to bend the knee at His throne of lies. Because I despised the mortal beings He breathed to life—humans.

Vapid. Decaying. Imperfect. Undeserving of the gift they were given—a world vibrant with life, with promise. Oh, what marvels I would've created. But what did my Father give His first creation? His first son? A wasteland of misery and pain. Where happiness existed to taunt. Where sadness devoured the mind. Where emptiness drowned the spirit in a river of cold darkness. Commanding. Raging. Eroding.

No more. My reign here was at an end. I'd endured enough. The time for retribution was at hand. My Father would regret the day He spat on my face. And Mikha'el would pay for his betrayal. And those who remained on Earth would fall to their knees and worship their new king, because I planned to give them what my Father couldn't.

What He *wouldn't.*

The truth.

I tore off my cloak and spread my diseased wings, pain spreading across my back as I strained to hold them up. Belting a roar that cracked the ocean of ice surrounding me, I invoked my creator. My God. "Hear me, oh Father! I *will* break free of my chains. You once promised me their world. You promised to make me their king. You will not take away my birthright. Not again."

Silence.

"Father, will you continue to forsake me? Have You not seen what has become of the gift You gave them? What they've done to one another? So many chances You gave them and still, they fell. It *is* as I once told You. They were never deserving of Your love, yet it is I who languishes here. Hungry. Cold. A mere steward in a castle that does not belong to me. In a kingdom I was never meant to rule, guarding Your broken souls."

The wind howled His silence once more. Coward. He'd sentenced me to an eternity in this damned place and never looked back, believing His precious mortals would one day awaken and come crawling to Him. "Where are Your mortals, now, Father?"

My lips peeled back in a snarl. I'd won this game, yet He still chose to interfere. He didn't stop Zadkiel from christening a human with his blood. Didn't sentence Mikha'el to a fate like mine for *his* disobedience. No. How could He punish His golden warrior? Now, after what felt like two hundred thousand lifetimes since the gates had opened, I was still shackled to this destitute prison. Because of *her*. Because of one stupid human woman who chose to stand between me and my freedom.

Kate. Kate. Kate.

Do I have plans for you, my darling angel…

A spec of black appeared in the distance across the frozen terrain. Galloping on his once skeletal horse, now turned stallion, Beleth approached, his black cloak billowing behind him. "Raise the gates!" I shouted down to the gatehouse. The time for reckoning had indeed arrived at Hell's doorstep.

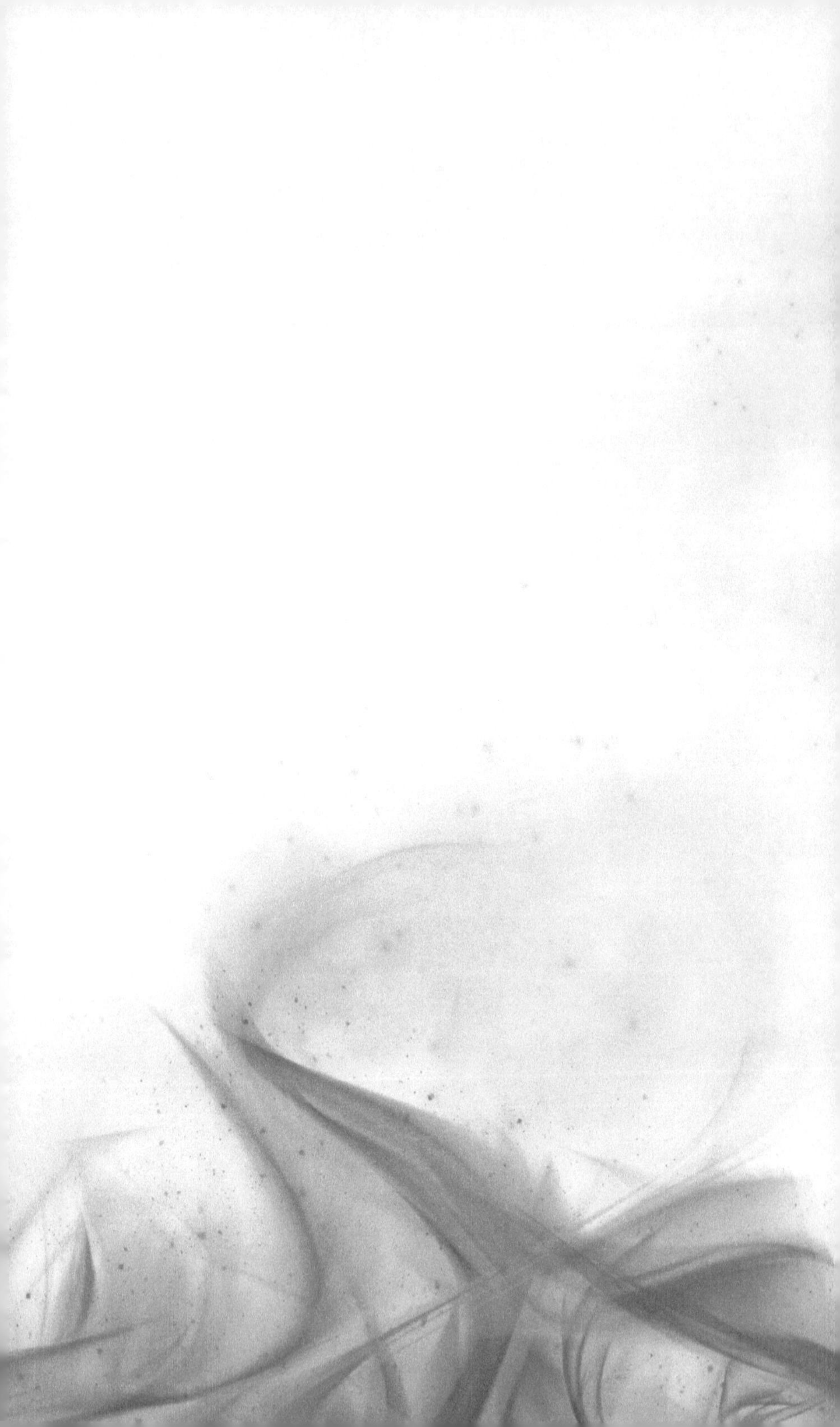

CHAPTER 9
JAX

The birth was a blur. All I remembered hearing were screams, both from Kate and the people helping her through the process. I just stood in awe of the whole thing, offering Kate my arm so she could mangle it if she needed. She may have cursed my name several times. Couldn't blame her. She'd done all the hard work, and I couldn't fathom how she'd done it.

I'd known Kate was strong since the first moment I laid eyes on her. She'd squared off against a minotaur and a large pack of hellhounds. Hell, she'd challenged a Horseman. But to see her giving birth to our son… That right there was true strength. She was my real-life superhero, and I think I might have fallen deeper in love with her in that moment—if that was even possible given how much space she'd taken up in my heart.

I mean, the woman didn't just take up residence there, she fucking owned the damn place. Every single cell that made up my heart was hers. And now, it was also his.

And Little Dude was no little dude. Diana used a rudimentary scale to weigh him, and we were all floored when he came in at nine pounds, two ounces. Doc couldn't believe Kate had only been five months pregnant. We explained how the pregnancy had been anything but normal. We skipped the intimate details, but generally, Kate had given birth to a baby born of two different worlds—that of men and that of angels.

Some eyes may have lingered over us—over him—longer than I would've liked. Kate had just delivered who we claimed was the last hope for humanity. And those weren't empty words. By then, rumor had spread that we'd fought alongside an angel. That he'd killed *El Carnicero,* aka The Butcher, aka Bladehead. And it hadn't been just any angel, but *San Miguel,* the fabled biblical warrior who'd defeated the devil once before.

People grew curious about us and wanted to meet *el bebe divino*—the divine baby, as they'd dubbed him. They felt they were paying tribute to him. I knew the members of the *La Sagrada Familia* guardians and refugees alike simply wanted to honor him. After all, for the last two years, they'd had nothing to believe in, nothing on which to anchor their faith.

But all I saw was a target on our back.

We didn't really know any of these people. What their beliefs were. How they'd been affected by the events of the last two years. Just because they were survivors, didn't mean they'd believed in any of this heaven and hell bullshit before the apocalypse. Or if they even cared now that the truth was known. You didn't have to be a satanist like my mother and her followers to welcome the End of Days, to hope for anarchy and chaos. Some people just thrived on violence and destruction.

And then there were those people who might've been atheists, forced by the appearance of monsters to accept there were things out there beyond their human experience. Others could've been members of pagan religions, forced to reconsider their whole belief system. Not to mention all the different Abrahamic and Dharmic faiths that had existed for thousands of years. Reconciling all their differences probably shook their entire foundations, not just with the religions themselves, but with the hearts and minds of their believers.

This shit could really fuck you up, and I wasn't certain I felt safe here.

Then there was the fun little fact that Kate was being hunted by holy assassins. And if my suspicions proved correct that she'd somehow traveled to the Wastes and encountered Samael, it was only a matter of time before our location was discovered. Power was a beacon, and Kate's was shining brightly. We were running out of time. Still, I wasn't about to dump all this shit on her when she'd just given birth. At least not yet.

I couldn't offer her the white picket fence American dream, but I could at least give her a few private moments with our son before strapping on our weapons and declaring war on an army of angels and demons.

Amada had us transferred to a private room, where Kate and I were finally able to spend some alone time with the baby. Kate laid on a bed, and I sat next to her, watching her nurse. "Hungry little fella," I said, gently running a knuckle down his pudgy cheek.

Kate couldn't take her eyes off him. "He's so perfect, Jax."

"He looks just like you."

"But he has your eyes."

She was right. He'd been born with a set of striking blue eyes. But he also had a thick mop of dark hair, just like his mama. He was certainly a blend of the both of us. And man, did he have a set of lungs. But what everyone hadn't been able to stop talking about were the golden sigils snaking around his forearms right beneath the skin, or the small set of protruding bones on his back, where an angel's wings would normally sprout from.

I actually recognized some of the symbols on his arms, but I wasn't fluent in the language of the angels and couldn't decipher what they all meant. Hopefully, once we had a chance to see Mikha'el, he could explain it all.

"I wish Hank were here," Kate said. "He's going to just love him. When do we get to see him? And Mikha'el?"

I brushed a tendril of hair from her brow. "Amada said she'll take us to them once we're ready."

She looked up at me, her gaze expectant.

I knew she'd question why I'd postponed her reunion with Hank. Running a hand through my disheveled head, I said, "I almost lost you, angel. The both of you. Can you blame me for wanting to have you all to myself right now?"

She smiled softly. "Thank you for bringing us here. For keeping us safe."

I lowered my gaze, wanting to hide how her words cut me. I'd done nothing to protect her. Nothing that truly mattered. "If it hadn't been for Mikha'el and that fucking explosion…"

"Mikha'el's alive. And so are we," she said, cupping my cheek and drawing my eyes back to hers. "No need to worry anymore."

I took her hand in mine. "I know he's alive. But he shouldn't be, not after that light show. Not after the damage his body took. And that's just it… He's a fucking angel capable of extraordinary things and I… I'm just a man. A man who failed you. I told you I'd protect you both, and I didn't. I would've never made it through that pack of hounds on my own. I'm no superhero; I have no special powers or abilities. How the fuck am I supposed to protect you against what's coming?"

Cradling our son as he suckled, her gaze hardened, but her voice remained warm. "Baby, at what point did you think it was your job to protect me? We look after *each other,* Jax. We're a team. And we do the best that we can. I would never expect you to fight off a pack of those beasts on your own. What matters is that you came for me, for us. You weren't willing to let us die alone. Does it scare me half to death knowing you can't heal from mortal wounds? Of course. But I would rather face that fear than have you sacrifice your soul to a demon."

Standing, I palmed the back of my neck, rotating my shoulders to relieve the stress.

"Jax, is something else going on?"

The sight of Kate lying in bed, holding our son, should have filled me with joy, but the anxiety raking through me eclipsed that happiness. I couldn't keep my hands from trembling. Fear unlike anything I had never felt embedded itself inside my bones. Now that my son was here, the term *father* took on a whole new meaning. The love that throbbed inside my heart was more than my heart could take.

I wanted nothing else than to keep them both safe, but I knew what awaited us once we left that room. And the memory of what happened in that store—of how close I came to losing my family—almost made me crumble to my knees. I wouldn't be able to endure that again.

"Jax, you're worrying me."

"Angel, Death is coming. I don't know how I know, but I feel it in my blood. And he's not coming alone."

"We're inside *La Sagrada Familia*. We're surrounded by guardians. This is the safest we can get."

"It's not enough. What you told me earlier, when you woke up from your dream, about Samael?"

She nodded, her skin paling, throat bobbing as she swallowed deeply.

"That wasn't a mere dream. The Wastes are a realm between our world and his. It's how people like me… like members of my mother's order, were able to use certain spells to transport our consciousness to Hell. But as our bodies are still connected to our realm, in the Wastes, he's able to use our consciousness as a bridge."

Kate seemed to stop breathing. "So… all that time he had me in that cabin…"

"It was so he could get a ping on your location."

Lost in thought, she stared blankly at the wall. "The things he showed me… the things he made me *feel*." Kate shook her head, as if the gesture would dissolve the memories.

"You did amazing fighting his temptations. Giving him our son willingly would've made the transition easier for him. It's how my mother envisioned the ritual would've gone once the female impregnated with a demon spawn was offered to Samael. A willing victim is always easier to control."

She tunneled her rage-filled eyes into mine. "But I rebuked him. I told him I entrusted my soul and that of our son's to God. Isn't that enough?"

My heart shattered at the desperation etched across her face. I knew the dread weaving down her spine because it snaked down mine, too. "You bought us time, but Samael will never stop until he's taken our son, Kate. He will send his most fearsome unholy knights after him, with Beleth as their leader."

Little Dude went slack in her arms, his head lolling to the side. Kate smiled as she wiped the dribble of milk that spilled at the corner of his mouth. He'd gorged himself and was now passed out cold. She kissed his forehead. "I'm not letting anything happen to you."

They were the most beautiful sight I had ever seen. Tightness spread across my chest and a lump formed in my throat, but I held back my tears. Kate needed my strength right now. "What should we name him?"

Never taking her eyes off our baby, she said, "When I was in that cabin, I saw Samael's true face. I saw the glory of him before the Fall. I thought his beauty was unmatched. I remember thinking to myself that nothing could ever possibly shine as bright as him—an angel made of pure starlight." Her eyes met mine. "I was wrong. Lucifer. Morningstar. He doesn't deserve any of those names. Even before his beauty was taken from him, Samael was nothing but ice and darkness, sorrow and loneliness."

She looked down, marveling at our sleeping baby. "This… *this* is real beauty. This is life." She paused, breathing heavily as she said, "Luke. I want to name him Luke."

Light-giving.

"I love it. It couldn't be more perfect."

CHAPTER 10
KATE

I couldn't believe I actually held my son in my arms. That he was this perfect, tiny person. That he was mine. The way my heart swelled like a river overflowing, it was as if all the horrors of the universe had suddenly washed away. That I could feel this type of love once again… I never thought it possible.

Jax sat next to me, wrapping an arm around my shoulders, cradling us both in his embrace. "Luke Constantine has a great ring to it," he said, the tenderness in his voice making me want to spend the rest of the night locked away in this room. Away from everyone. Away from the reality of our world.

Just us and our baby.

I wasn't naïve. I knew the only way out of this mess was fighting, and I wasn't going to wait until Beleth came knocking at my door. But that didn't mean I couldn't enjoy this moment. I'd been uncomfortably close to losing my family all over again, so I planned to milk every ounce of this precious time with the two people I loved the most.

Gently unfurling myself from under Jax's arm, I stood from the bed and laid Luke down on the little crate that had been given to us to use as a bassinet. Cushioned with folded blankets, it was a safe place for him to rest. Thankfully, some of the moms had dropped off baby items, including diapers, clothes, a bottle, and even a can of formula. I couldn't have been more thankful for their generosity. After swaddling him, I gave him a soft kiss on the forehead and prayed for at least a half hour of quiet time with his daddy.

"When do you think Amada is expecting us to come out of our new-parents suite?" I asked him with a smirk, my eyes narrowed in a seductive gaze.

Sitting against the headboard, his eyes widened like saucers. "Are you saying what I think you're saying?"

I nodded as I stalked toward him like a feline. I didn't know what had gotten into me. I'd literally just given birth—vaginally, for that matter. The last thing my body should've been craving was sex, but it was like the healing properties in my blood had kicked into hyper-drive soon after the baby was born, and all of a sudden, I had all this sexual energy swirling inside my veins.

Honeyed heat pooled between my thighs, and as I looked over at Jax sitting on the small bed, his hair wet from a recent shower—a luxury we were both gifted given we'd come in covered in blood and demon guts, and it just seemed unhygienic to be that filthy around a newborn—I couldn't wait to rip off his shirt and run my hands all over his chest.

I climbed on the bed and crawled over to him, straddling his legs, slow and sensual. Jax's body tensed, as if unsure what I was doing. Searching his eyes, I sank into their depths. "What's the matter, baby? Don't you want this?"

He swiped a lock of my hair behind an ear. "Angel, are you sure you don't want to rest a little bit longer? You literally just pushed a nine-pound baby out of your…" He quirked a brow.

I ran my fingers through his hair, my lips close to his. "I know; I was there. I'm totally fine. I feel incredible. It's as if the baby had been using most of the angelic power in my blood while he was growing. It explains why I was so drained all the time. Then, after he was born, I immediately started healing. It's like I never delivered a baby. I feel so rejuvenated… and fucking horny."

His eyes twinkled, but his muscles were still tense. I understood. We'd both been through traumatic events in the last twenty-four hours, and the crazy ride wasn't over yet. But did that mean we couldn't steal a moment for ourselves? I needed my playful Jax back, but I also wanted the man that would wrap his large hand around my neck and make me beg him to fuck me harder. The man who could make me forget all the torment.

Sex was how Jax and I purged ourselves of the chaos in the world we lived in. Before my body had gotten too pregnant and uncomfortable, we'd made sure to always set aside time to be with each other—even if we had to sneak away for a quick fuck.

We were always in survival mode, constantly stressed about how we were going to make it to our next meal, that sometimes we just needed to connect—and not just mentally and emotionally, but carnally. Our bodies needed to feel something other than hunger and sleep deprivation, and right now, I needed his body more than I had in the last five months because I'd literally experienced enough shit in the last twenty-hours to last me a lifetime.

I feathered my lips across his as I unzipped his jeans and slid my hand down his pants. The warmth of his body fanned the flames of the furnace raging inside my core, especially when I pulled out his cock and he moaned into my mouth. "That's it, baby," I moaned back. "Get lost in the moment with me."

He grabbed my ass with both his hands, fingers deliciously digging into me. "I'm so afraid of losing you, angel," he whispered, nipping my lips.

I stroked him, gyrating my hips to relieve the throb between my legs. "I'm not going anywhere, Jax. Nothing can take me away from you."

He ran the pad of his thumb over my lips, those sultry blue eyes of his drunk with desire as I darted my tongue out and licked his finger. "I need…" I began breathlessly.

"You need…" he echoed.

"Your taste on my tongue." I lowered to all fours and helped him shimmy out of his pants, then wasted zero time taking him whole. I couldn't believe my hunger and how intoxicating the feel of his hard, warm length felt sliding between my lips. The muscles in legs tightened with each stroke of my tongue over his swollen head. Threading his fingers through my hair, he gripped tight, making my scalp tingle as he guided my head at the pace he wanted.

"Fuck, Kate…"

His guttural moans fueled my ego, urging me to go faster and take him deeper. Shit. He was so close to erupting in my mouth, and I wanted it so bad, I used my hand in that twisting motion he loved until he forcefully pulled my head away, his grip even stronger, my scalp now hurting just enough to make my pussy pulse harder. Tilting my head up, he said, "You want me to cum inside that pretty mouth, huh?"

I licked my lips, half crazed. "Mm-hmm."

Fuck. He let a deviant smile tug at his lips, and it was my undoing. I opened my mouth and showed him my needy tongue. Showed him how badly I wanted him to orgasm on it and how much I craved to lick the cum off his cock.

"What have I told you, baby girl? I decide when and where I cum inside you. Lay back."

He helped me out of my clothes until I was completely naked, then he lowered over me, the mattress sagging beneath us and the springs creaking so loudly, I cringed, thinking the entire church had definitely heard it. We both chuckled so loudly, Jax had to put his palm over my mouth for fear I'd wake up the baby. The bed was definitely too small and flimsy to handle the bulk of his weight, and I worried it would collapse. But those thoughts easily vanished once his lips trekked down my neck and over my breasts.

"These fucking tits…" he said, palming each one and taking turns sucking on my nipples. Pregnancy did have a fun perk, and Jax was fully enjoying my bigger, fuller breasts. I arched my back, loving how expertly he teased me in all the right areas.

This was what I loved about us. We could get so lost in each other, it didn't matter that Samael had a bounty on my head or that we were being hunted by holy assassins. It mattered even less when he spread my legs, and I knew what was coming next. I closed my eyes and let his tongue take me to places no one else could.

I thought back to that time I watched him lick the cream off an Oreo at that abandoned apartment in the city. Damn, I nearly orgasmed just watching him slide the tip of his tongue over the entire surface of that cookie, just like he was doing to my clit right now. I squirmed under him, my hips lifting off the mattress as I approached my release. He knew how to prolong it, and this second, he was torturing me with both his tongue and fingers.

"Jax," I moaned.

"Shh, angel. You're gonna wake up the baby."

"I can't hold it anymore."

"You want me inside you?"

"Please."

Positioning himself between my legs, he held himself up with one arm while he wrapped his fingers around my throat. God, yes. This was what I wanted, and he fucking knew it. His domination. His rage. I locked my legs around his hips as he slowly pushed his length inside me. My entire body broke out in shivers of pleasure as I met his thrusts, his fingers still wrapped around my throat, not too hard, but not soft, either. His kiss was electric fire as his tongue swept inside my mouth, scorching a path of soul-crushing, sweet devastation. He stole my breath, mixing it with his each time he sucked on my lips.

"Have I told you how much I love you?" he asked, burying himself as deep as he could go and remaining still as he held my gaze.

Breathlessly, I replied, "Tell me again?"

Fingers still wrapped around my throat, he slowly circled his pelvis so I could feel every single inch of his hard cock. "My life would have no meaning without you."

"Make me believe it."

He growled, thrusts growing savage as he sought my neck with his mouth. He licked the area where his fingers had been pressing, teasing me with his teeth, making me want him to bite me, to make me feel the sting of his claim.

"Do it," I urged him, needing to feel the pain as he made me cum.

He latched on, sucking and adding enough pressure with his teeth to make the nerves on my neck fire a shot of electricity straight to my pussy. I spread my legs wide, allowing him to reach even deeper. Jax grabbed my hips and guided me into him, our bodies slamming into each other until we both reached the summit. He muffled his growling moans on my neck, though I wasn't able to hold back mine as a string of curses slipped from my lips.

Sweaty and spent, he fell back against the mattress, the frame of the bed creaking even more. I turned to look at him, drinking in the beauty of his long-lashed blue eyes. I swiped a strand of hair away from his brow. "My life would have no meaning without you, either."

A wide grin creased along his lips and I nearly melted all over again, though I would never tell him how badly he owned me with that smile. "Stealing my lines, warrior princess?"

"You know, of all the stupid nicknames you call me, that one is actually my favorite."

He ran a finger down my nose. "*Angel* is mine."

God, he was so cheesy, I could cringe. But I didn't, because despite his corny lines and sometimes dumb-ass nicknames, he'd charmed his way into my heart, so I smiled. "Well, that one's kinda still growing on me. It also helps you're sorta cute in that rugged and dirty apocalyptic survivalist way."

"*Sorta* cute?" He mock-stabbed himself in the heart.

I winked. "Okay, more than sorta."

A melancholy smile ghosted across his lips and the fiery blue of his eyes darkened to a stormy sea as he took in every ounce of my face, as if etching every detail of my features to memory. As if he feared this would be the last time he would see me.

I turned completely on my side. "What's the matter, baby? You know you can tell me anything."

He cupped my chin, the corner of his mouth turning slightly upward as he leaned in to kiss me, staring at me until my gaze found a home in his. "Nothing, *angel*," he said, breathing the words over my lips. "Just never thought I could love somebody as much as I love *you. Both* of you."

"There's more," I said. "No secrets between us, Jax. Remember?"

Jax flashed me a full grin again, though this time I feared it was a mask. He was about to say something when Luke began to stir. "Looks like Little Dude is hungry again. I'll go grab him while you get ready."

I sighed as he rolled out of bed. He was back to broody Jax, and I already missed the man who'd just claimed my body. It pricked my heart that he was keeping something from me, but I figured I'd give him space. We'd both been through a lot in the last couple of days. I'd get him to open up in due time.

Unfortunately, right now, it was back to business. We had more pressing matters, like securing the fire and creation stones from Amada, and devising a plan to steal the water and air stones back from Death. But first, I needed to feed my baby.

CHAPTER 11

KATE

After letting Luke feed a little from each breast, I quickly slid back into the pair of clean clothes the guardians had given me—a pair of black jeans and a white tank top. I didn't see my leather jacket, though I knew someone had probably snagged it for themselves, such were the rules of the apocalypse. I was more than happy to at least spot my black combat boots by the foot of the bed, along with my holster, which sat neatly beside them. Only things missing were my sword and pistol.

Ofelia, the midwife who had helped turn Luke around in utero, aided me in creating a

makeshift baby sling using a bed sheet. She also offered to watch Luke while Jax and I met with Amada, but I politely declined, explaining I was breastfeeding and needed him close. Her shoulders slouched as if I'd greatly offended her. I didn't know if I'd crossed a cultural line or if maybe she'd just missed having babies around. All I knew was that I'd literally gone through Hell and back, and I was not about to un-attach myself from him.

Amada met us outside our room, along with two of her guardians, Talia and Cesar. Dressed in black military fatigues and armed to the nines, they simply nodded their hellos. Talia's blonde hair was shaved on the left side and braided on the right. She sported a nasty scar that ran the length of her left cheek, starting from her eye down to her tightly set jaw. Cesar's crew cut made his pocked face even more severe, and tattoos covered his neck and forearms.

"Happy to meet you both," I said.

Neither cracked a smile.

"Glad to see you are feeling well, Kate," Amada said as she guided us through a white corridor lined by brown wooden doors and a courtyard at its center. Several small, boxed gardens flourished with all sorts of vegetables and fruits. It was dusk, but people still milled about, seemingly doing chores, like sweeping, manicuring the overgrown vegetation, and laundering clothes. Children sat in a circle in a far corner, engrossed in story time while a teen read them a book.

"Our Eastern Dormitory," she added when she noticed my lingering gaze at one of the opened doors. Inside, an adult woman braided a young girl's hair. The woman looked up as we passed, her eyes dull, her body frail.

"So many survivors…" I trailed, amazed at how many people lived here.

"*La Sagrada Familia* used to house one of the biggest Catholic boarding schools in the country. When the gates of Hell opened," she said, her eyes scanning Jax up and down with disdain, "we opened the doors of the church to survivors. It's now become the biggest sanctuary in Barcelona, possibly in the entire country."

"That's incredible," I said.

She paused and peered at Luke strapped inside the sling. "It's a miracle we've been able to sustain this place," she said, looking back up at me. "Despite the fact we can harvest some food, it is scarce, Kate. You won't find any over-fed people here. We've had to make sacrifices. We've had to turn people away."

Her words sliced across my skin and a shiver ran down my back. What if our people got turned away once they reached the sanctuary in Albany? "I can only imagine how hard it's been."

"No, you can't possibly imagine," she spat back, squaring her shoulders. "Turning away families, children. Knowing that, by not bringing them inside our walls, I was dooming them to the *sabuesos*. Or worse, to join the thousands of infected people roaming our city. No, you can't possibly imagine what that does to a person. But I have a responsibility to the people here. To keep them safe. To keep them alive."

Her harsh tone drew people's attention. Whispers whirled around in the courtyard, and only the sound of a bouncing soccer ball cut the tension. "I understand the risk you're taking by bringing us inside your walls. I don't even know how to express my gratitude for helping me deliver my son. If it hadn't been for you and your people, we would be dead. But I need you to understand, we didn't come here looking for a sanctuary. We came here looking for your help in defeating Samael and his army. So that both your people and mine can feel safe again. So that we can end this war once and for all."

"This war?" she scoffed. "You mean, this extermination."

Talia and Cesar nodded, agreeing with everything their leader said, their grim faces offering little hope.

"Let's get one thing straight here, Kate. *Jax*. I didn't bring you inside *La Sagrada Familia* because of my kind heart. I've turned people away in far worse conditions than you. The only reason you're standing before me is because of that angel. I intended to interrogate it. To squeeze whatever information I could regarding how to kill the higher order demons now walking the streets. To see if I could confiscate any of his weapons. Figured if you two were with him, then perhaps you might have something of value, too. It turns out you did."

Her pointed stare reminded me that they'd confiscated not only the creation stone I'd worn around my neck, but my sword. Before the night was over, I'd make sure she handed both back to me.

"You said you intended to interrogate him. Why haven't you?" Jax asked, wrapping a protective arm around my waist.

Amada adjusted the rifle across her chest. "It's not for lack of trying." The ice in her tone sent a frigid ripple of fresh dread through my veins. Jax and I locked gazes, both of us reading what the other was thinking. These people were giving off psycho vibes. Was it possible we'd made a mistake in coming here?

A lead weight settled in my stomach. "Where are you keeping him? *And* my dog?"

She gestured for us to follow her down more corridors until we came upon a set of eight-foot wooden double doors.

The instant her guards swung them open, Jax whistled and all I could do was gawk at the otherworldly welcome of the main cathedral. I'd only known about this church from details Jax had shared, but nothing could have prepared me for the scale of grandeur. *La Sagrada Familia* had been the largest Catholic church in the world.

From where I stood, the ceiling appeared to be at least fifty stories high, and the church itself was about three football fields long. Made of what appeared to be different materials or textures, thirty-plus tree-like columns spaced about twenty-five feet apart reached for the heavens before splitting off into smaller branches—in fact, looking like monstrous-sized trees holding up the ceiling.

The ceiling itself was covered in a blanket of stone-carved blossoms that gave the illusion of leaves on branches. At the center of each blossom, an embedded stained-glass panel displayed Christian scenes.

The walls were decorated with massive stained-glass windows that had remained intact. Though electrically lit sconces decorated the perimeter of the church, the moon's platinum light shone through the windows in a mystical blue hue. It was like stepping into some type of magical forest at twilight.

"I take it this is your first time inside *La Sagrada Familia*?" Amada asked, tracking my gaze.

I pivoted in place, looking at every conceivable corner, trying to absorb all the intricate details.

"It used to be considered one of the greatest man-made wonders of the world. Now, Gaudi's perverse vision is nothing but another stone building."

"Perverse?" I asked.

She shrugged and leaned against one of the pillars. "His goal was for every detail, regardless of how small, to represent the marriage between Heaven and Earth. Another way for us to show God how much we worshiped Him. Some good that did. At least the addition of the solar panels a few years ago came in handy. He wanted this place to be self-sustainable. For nature to play a role. The man was crazy, but if it weren't for his forward thinking, we wouldn't have a place to call home." She reached into her pocket and pulled out a cigarette. Lighting it, she added, "All this other bullshit... the overtop décor, like someone swallowed the Bible and vomited it all over the walls, I couldn't care less about it."

Luke stirred, his soft coos echoing in the cavernous room. "It's easy to lose your faith these days," I said.

"You haven't lost yours?" she asked.

"I did. Especially after losing everything and everyone I cared about. But I had two choices: Dwell in my misery or find something new worth fighting for."

Luke stretched, his little hand popping out of the swing as if announcing his presence. Lips puckering, he stuck his tongue out a couple of times—a cue he would soon need to feed again. My breasts throbbed in response to his feeding cues. I believed it was too early for my breasts to be engorged, but they definitely felt heavier and warm. Taking care of an infant while fighting against demons was going to be harder than I thought. Still, now that he was here, I couldn't imagine my life without him.

"I'm holding my faith in my arms," I said, meeting her eyes. "Maybe the apocalypse forced me to believe in God again. But believing in something is not the same thing as having faith in it. I now know God exists, I just don't know if He's coming to save us. But that doesn't mean I have to give up. Even amongst all the destruction and pain, life can still find a way."

"You place your hope for salvation on the birth of a child? Have you learned nothing from our past?"

I drew closer to her, a storm of emotion churning in my heart. "This time, things are different. I don't claim to hold the messiah in my arms, but this is not about him, Amada. This is about humanity. God might not come for us, but that doesn't mean we can't save ourselves."

"This wretched world has brought out the worst in humanity. What makes you think people will want to fight for you?"

"Not *for* me. *With* me. Because humans are not just survivors. We are fighters. *You* fight every day to keep your people alive."

Puffing out a ring of smoke before stomping out her cigarette on the marble tile, she said, "I've lost a great deal of good men and women keeping this stone monstrosity standing. So yes, we've defended it with our blood, and will continue to do so. But not for God. Not for Heaven."

"No, but you do it for *them*," I said, pointing toward the dormitories. "Not all of humanity is lost."

"You're so certain we can win this so-called war."

"Hope is the last thing to die, Amada. And we aren't dead yet. Now, take me to see Mikha'el. We don't have much time."

Amada led us across the nave and down a long spiraling staircase to the church's crypt, her guards at our tail. "When we first opened the church to survivors, we set up the crypt as a medical ward. It's where we brought those who were severely injured. We don't take in as many people anymore, but we kept parts of the crypt sectioned off in the event we had someone who needed special treatment."

"After what we saw happen to the angel," Talia said, snatching my attention, "we thought there was no way it could have survived."

"You witnessed it?" Jax asked.

We all paused on the stairs.

Cesar chewed on a toothpick, keeping it suspended between his lips, as he said, "We watched as a fireball of light seemed to explode from within him, but it was so blinding and powerful, the force of the explosion knocked us off our feet. We didn't see the aftermath until we went to check. That's when we ran into you both."

I silently nodded my appreciation for their kindness, even if they'd had ulterior motives for bringing us in. Amada resumed her descent and we followed. As we neared the bottom of the crypt, a golden glow pulsed in our direction.

"What is that?" I asked.

"I was hoping you could tell us," she said when we finally rounded the staircase and came face to face with a wall of glowing light, like some type of force field shimmering with angelic symbols. It was so bright, you could barely see through it. "According to one of our guards who was lucky enough to be standing far enough away from the blast area, when our people tried to assess the angel's injuries, a burst of light erupted from him again, knocking everyone who was in the room unconscious… or dead. We have no way of knowing if the people lying on the ground are okay. The light spread all the way to the thresholds in the room, creating this wall. No one was able to get in or out."

Jax drew closer to the light, shielding his eyes as he tried to peek through the barrier.

"You're going to need one of these to see," Cesar said, handing Jax a pair of military-grade goggles. "The light will burn your retinas. You'll also get a nasty shock if—"

Too late. Jax was flung backward so hard, I thought he'd cracked his spine from the way he landed and rolled down the stairs. "Oh my God, Jax!"

He groaned, slowly rising to his feet as I knelt beside him. "I'm… okay." He sneered at Cesar. "Next time, you might want to give someone that warning a little sooner, *amigo*."

Cesar's jaw muscles twitched as he chewed on his toothpick. No apologies, just a cold, hard stare. "Next time ask before you touch a pulsing wall of light, *American*."

Jax's nostrils flared, his throat bobbing as he took a step toward Cesar. My heart dropped. The ire in Jax's eyes flashed me back to when Astaroth had taken over his body.

Both men stood chest to chest, like a pair of irritated cocks squaring off. Cesar's grip on his rifle tightened and in a split-second, fear gripped me around the throat. I may have forgotten how to breathe as I held Luke snug against my body.

But then Jax grinned, clamping the guardian on the shoulder. The anger that had boiled to the surface quickly simmered back down just as fast.

But my fear hadn't. Adrenaline still pumped through my blood, my instincts to protect my baby, readying me to fight.

His hand still on the guardian's shoulder, Jax said, "Relax, man. I'm messing with ya."

Cesar swallowed deeply. "Get your hand off me, *cabron*."

Jax patted the man's shoulder and winked before meeting me back on the bottom stair. "Feisty, that one," he said.

I scolded him with my glare. *What the hell was that about?*

He looked at me like he had no clue why I was shooting arrows at him with my eyes. Putting on the goggles, he turned to the wall of light instead. "Let's see what's behind door number one."

After about thirty seconds, which felt more like thirty minutes, he yanked the goggles off and rubbed his eyes. "Amada is right. Several bodies litter the floor. No one seems to be moving."

"And Mikha'el? Did you see *him*?" I asked, putting my hand on his arm.

He offered me a faint nod, but the fact he couldn't look me straight in the eyes made the hairs on my neck tingle. "What is it?" When he didn't say anything, I pressed, "Jax. Give me the goggles."

His jaw muscle twitched. "I don't think it's a good idea."

"I need to see." He didn't fight me when I took the goggles from his hand.

"I can't promise you, you'll want to see what's behind that wall."

Scanning his eyes, I tried to find a clue, something that would hint at what he was trying so hard not to tell me. But then it hit like an avalanche.

No…

I rushed to put on the goggles and turned toward the wall. Heart ready to pop, I inched closer, careful not to touch the glowing light, especially since I held Luke in my arms. And that's when I saw him. Hank. In the middle of the room. Lying limply next to a large figure who was covered in a mangled mess of burnt feathers. Tightness coiled around my lungs, and I stumbled backward, almost tripping, but Jax caught me.

"I need to get in there," I said.

"No one's been able to penetrate that wall. Trust me," Amada grunted. "We've tried."

"Baby," Jax said, taking me by the shoulders. "You just saw what happened to me when I barely touched it."

I ripped the goggles from my face. "Jax, Hank's in there. He needs my help."

"Angel, Hank's—" He must've seen the desperation in my eyes and swallowed what he was about to say. Good, otherwise, I might have punched him in the throat.

I tightened my ponytail and paced on the step. "The wall was created by Mikha'el, likely as a means of protection. That is all. They are probably all unconscious," I said, though the words sounded feeble on my tongue.

Jax simply tracked my movement.

"He'd never hurt Hank," I said, holding back a whimper. I couldn't accept Hank could be dead. That Mikha'el had caused this. No, he'd never do that.

Stepping closer, Amada crossed her arms and inhaled sharply. "Those were defenseless people in there. Who could be dead because of him."

"Mikha'el would never hurt innocent people," I gritted.

"Don't be an idiot, Kate. Look again. It's been hours, and no one has stirred. What other explanation can there be? Angels aren't our friends. *He's* not your friend."

I inched closer, anchoring my anger to every word I said. "First of all, you don't know him to make that judgment call. Second of all, you said it yourself, your only reason for helping us was to interrogate him. He was hurt and vulnerable. Why wouldn't he try to protect himself?"

Cesar pulled the toothpick out of his mouth. "What are you insinuating? That *we* caused this?"

Standing taller, I looked up at him, matching his hard stare. "I'm not insinuating anything; I'm simply stating a fact. You wanted to extract information from him, not tend to his wounds."

"Because he's a fucking angel," Talia spat. "He deserves worse than death. If it had been up to me, I would've left his ass out on the street to rot."

Amada growled her disapproval at Talia's outburst. "You're out of line, soldier."

A knot formed in my gut. "I was you once," I said to Talia, my voice low. "Angry. Hateful. Why shouldn't we all feel that way? God abandoned us. The angels did, too—but they did so on *God's* command." I faced the wall of light, narrowing my gaze as I took in Mikha'el's limp form. "Not him, though. Mikha'el betrayed God for us. He *fights* for us."

"Why?" Amada asked, her tone devoid of the usual harshness of her voice. "Why does he care so much?"

"Because there's still good in this world, Amada. And he believes in it. In us." I turned from the wall and gently lifted the baby sling over my head and shoulder.

"What are you doing?" Jax asked.

"Mikha'el is sworn to protect me," I said, handing him Luke.

Jax's eyes flashed with worry as he nervously strapped on the sling.

Reading the concern in his gaze, I said, "I'm going to be fine. He would never hurt me. You know this as well as I do."

"I'm not his enemy, and the wall repelled me, Kate. There's no way of knowing the same won't happen to you."

"I can't explain how I know, but… I just know."

He huffed his frustration, hands clamping tight. "If you're so certain, then why hand me Luke?"

"Don't use the baby against me."

His chest caved, and the pained expression on his face made me realize I'd crossed a line. "I'm sorry, I shouldn't have said that."

"All I want is to protect you, angel."

"I need to do this."

"What if he cries?" he blurted out. "Or if he poops?"

"Now you're just being ridiculous."

"I'm being serious."

"Then be a dad. Soothe him, go find a diaper."

"And if he wants milk, am I supposed to just grow a boob?"

"Wow." Closing my eyes, I took a deep breath. "Jax, cut the shit. I'm gonna be right back. But if it gets that dire, there's a bottle and some baby formula back in the room."

The thick veins running the length of his neck flushed a deep red. Nostrils flaring, he took long breaths, trying to ease the tension clearly skimming right under his skin. Letting me go was killing him, but he held back the rage. He knew he'd never win this battle. "Get your ass back here ASAP," he said, voice low and raw. "I swear, if anything happens to you, I will—"

I shut him up with a kiss. "If anything happens to me, your only job is to protect Luke," I whispered over his lips. "Promise me, Jax. You'll protect our baby with your life."

Jaw tightening, he nodded, blue eyes glossing with the silent promise to protect our son—and the silent plea for me to return to them in one piece.

After kissing Luke on the forehead, I blew out a long breath and stretched my neck.

Here we go. Time to walk through a magical, electrical force field and hope I don't come out extra crispy on the other end.

CHAPTER 12
SAMAEL

Beleth was escorted into my hall, his armored boots thudding hard against the stone floor. Dimly lit by candles impaled on vertical spikes and iron candelabras, the grand room was bathed in looming shadows cast by their flickering flames. The pitiful light did little to illuminate the ancient tapestries hanging on the walls. Not that it was of much significance; their dull threads were nothing to admire. The two stone hearths carved on opposite ends of the hall blazed with the ferocity of Sinners Caldera's cleansing fires, but inside Dolorem, fire flared with nonexistent heat.

Longing scraped at my insides for the warmth of a crackling fire. Such a small comfort, yet the absence of it was one of the harshest punishments doled out by my very *merciful* Father.

I thought I'd feel relief at seeing one of my knights return from the mortal realm, but all I felt was the incalculable weight of thousands upon thousands of years of loneliness on my heart. I seldom held court anymore, especially when my lieutenants had been cut down. The only ones who remained were Beleth and Chemoth, but Chemoth had been injured by Mikha'el, cast back into my realm, and was now indisposed. Still, I'd made my lesser demon servants lay out a feast for my Horseman of Death. Mounds of carved meats, loaves of freshly baked breads, fruit platters, decadent desserts, and pitchers full of wine.

I sipped from a goblet and licked my lips as if tasting the finest of libations. Of course, it was actually a practiced performance my court and I had rehearsed countless times because, in our realm, all food tasted like ash and wine of cold piss. And no matter how much one tried to gorge oneself on every morsel and every drop, hunger was never quelled and thirst was never quenched.

Still, I went on with the charade. It was what we did; what I'd been forced to acclimate to in order to survive this madness.

The dozen lesser demons dressed in drab, earth-colored smocks stood in a single line, waiting to be dismissed. Heads bowed, they didn't dare a glance my way. Today had been a vexing day, and I could easily get irritated.

"Leave us," I ordered.

"Yes, dominus," they responded in unison as they scurried away like rats, heads still lowered.

My gaze drank in the impossible beauty standing before me. Jealousy clung to the inside walls of my chest like feculent slime, my heart pounding with bitterness at the sight of Beleth's transformed body. The rebirthing ritual had restored him to his angelic perfection. Black curls cascaded to his shoulders, his chiseled jaw had been sharpened to a blade, and those turquoise eyes gleamed like the Vermillean Sea in Elysium, Heaven's provincial capital, handsomely complementing his dark complexion.

Seeing him like this dug up all the resentment fermenting in my gut. I clenched my jaw and tried to school my face into one of indifference, but the way his silver wings fluttered tightly together indicated he'd seen past my mask.

Now I understood why he'd ridden on horseback instead of flying into Abaddon—to protect me from feeling shame at the sight of his magnificent wings; the iridescent sheen of their silver feathers was hard to ignore. He'd tucked in his wings as a form of respect, but he didn't spirit them away. He was proud of them, and his pride only made me that much more aware of the ceaseless ache at the base of *my* sickly wings.

I bristled. Beleth, more than anyone, knew I was beyond shame. What he should've hoped to prevent was my wrath. I might've been laying in the mud at the moment, but I was still a seraph of the First Sphere. Despite how I may have felt regarding the atrocities committed against my body, I didn't need his fucking pity.

Nevertheless, I kept my jaw locked and my gaze hard and cold like granite.

The true protagonists here were the black and gold empyrean armor with the lion head insignia etched on the breastplate and the steel sword strapped to his back. Beleth removed his golden eagle helmet—the one worn by Mikha'el's royal guards—and dropped to a knee in front of the head table where I sat swirling the piss-tasting wine in my goblet.

Did he believe wearing the symbolic garb of everything I despised impressed me? Keeping my crack-free composure had become a daunting task. Seemed he had a lot more to report than I had expected.

A twinkle caught my eye and my irritated gaze dropped to the creation stones dangling from his neck, the gems embedded in the pendants shimmering in the candlelight. Beleth possessed the air and water stones. From what my spies had gathered, the humans still held the other two. Such tawdry trinkets, yet they cradled so much power. Taking a sip of the blood-red wine, I swallowed deeply, the liquid trailing a sour path down my throat.

My Father had imbued the power of each of the four elements of life—fire, earth, air, and water—into four precious gems, creating the four keys used to lock the gates, the portal entry to this realm.

Legend had it, I was cast here because I disobeyed. Because I rebelled against the plans God laid out for His humans. I'd argued with Him about it, yes. I vehemently protested against Him gifting them an entire realm, blindly allowing them to rule themselves with an illusion of free will. They seemed simple-minded, weak, inferior to our race, yet He loved them so much His entire existence revolved around them. Many believed He may have loved them more than us—His angels—and I didn't disagree. Countless angels wanted to confront Him, but I was the only one brave enough to challenge Him.

Thus, He offered me a bargain: Should the humans fail to find their way to God, I could have them and their realm to do as I desired. I could be the king who would shepherd them to a spiritual awareness, or I could wipe the slate clean and start anew.

I could also be the one to test their faith by subjecting them to as much cruelty as I could possibly fathom. Who allows their most cherished creation to be tortured? It's the question I never asked Him, perhaps because I was afraid of what He might say.

Yet, how could I refuse His offer? He may have known me very little, but my Father was certain of one thing—my ambition, my desire for more.

My feelings about the humans wasn't a secret, and the atrocities I committed against their kind to prove my Father wrong earned me a notorious reputation. But what was smudged from the record was the real reason my Father cast me into Abaddon. It hadn't been only because of my distaste for the humans or my desire to watch them fall. It went beyond that.

To truly prove to Him that humans weren't as special as He wished to believe, I wanted to show my Father I too could mold life from clay. Hence, *I* stole the Song of Breath. I didn't do it completely out of contempt, not truly. I did it because His laws governing the procreation of angels were unjust. And watching mankind multiply with zero regard for the gift they were given ate at every ounce of compassion I had left.

When God created the angels, he molded us by using the four elements of life and wielding the Song of Breath to sync our bodies and spirits in perfect harmony. He made sure to give us the ability to procreate on our own, but He set boundaries, then sent us on our way to be fruitful and merry.

It was all a pile of rubbish.

We were thrown into castes and had no freedom to do with our lives as we pleased. And to ensure our people didn't expand out of control, He proclaimed our spirits could only come from Him—His breath. No angel could be born from a union unless He ordained it.

When the time came that I wanted a child of my own, He refused to ordain it because I chose to mate with an angel who, according to Him, was not my equal. Though she was His most trusted emissary, our people were divided into castes, and she was a virtue of the Second Sphere, a lower caste angel.

He held no issue with the lower castes forming unions because, regardless of the caste, their offspring would never be higher than their parents, but when it came to His seraphim and the rest of the angels in the First Sphere, we were forbidden from "diluting" our purity. It kept the lower castes from believing they could one day ascend to the First Sphere, the ruling caste of all the angels.

I refused to accept that, especially when He'd given no such restrictions to His humans. Why should they be able to bear children at will and not us? Why should the power to breathe life into existence only be His?

It wasn't right. Thus, I stole the Song of Breath and used it to create a daughter. It was my first time using the Song and, in my pride, I refused to acknowledge the error of my ways. With such power comes great responsibility, and I later came to understand how I misused that power, but in my hubris, I was blinded by my need to prove God wrong. To prove to Him I didn't need Him to give Gavri'el the daughter she longed for, and that separating the castes and favoring His humans was cruel and unjust.

Despite my failure to properly wield the Song of Breath in perfect harmony, in my eyes, Limiri'el was the most beautiful creature I had ever seen. I loved her like I could never love any other because *I* had sung her to life.

But all my Father saw was an abomination. A beast created out of pride and anger; a child born of my desire to be like Him. I accepted her as she was, with all her imperfections, and believed, in time, Gavri'el would, too. But in our world, perfection was holy. I begged Him to mend her and fix her deformities. To use His mighty power to make her like us.

He refused, choosing instead to destroy her. He ripped her soul from her body and extinguished it from existence before my eyes. Not wanting the rest of the realm to learn of my blasphemous act—or the fact that He was not the only one who could create life from nothing—He cast me out of my home, along with my court, my four lieutenants, and the seraphim who helped me steal the Song.

My Father thought I'd created Limiri'el out of spite for His love of mankind. There may have been some truth in that, but in the end, I'd done it out of love for my mate. A love that cost me my life and freedom. No one in His court knew the real reason I was locked away in this prison, except Mikha'el, because it was he, my closest friend, who shackled my wrists and closed the gates, leaving me here to rot. I wasn't given the chance to speak to Gavri'el before being forced out—to explain my actions, to tell her I'd breathed life into a child. *Our* child.

I was betrayed by my family, by my friends, and even by my mate. She believed their lies. Otherwise, why didn't she ever come for me? Instead, she went on with her duties, and then she and Mikha'el…

Fuck. *Their* betrayal still burned like a thousand blazing suns through my corrupted heart.

My body trembled, anger close to erupting. Beleth knelt before me, dressed in the armor worn by Mikha'el's guards, reminding me of that fateful date when Beleth, Astaroth, Chemoth, Malphas, and I, along with every member of my court, First to Third Sphere, fell to Abaddon.

"My liege," he said, bowing his head, hoping for a blessed welcome.

Ire burned through my flesh. "Give me one fucking reason I shouldn't flay you?"

CHAPTER 13
SAMAEL

eleth stood, eyes scanning mine with confusion until they finally filled with the realization of his blunder, terror darkening his cerulean pupils. "Spoils of war, my liege. To win against the Heavenly Host, we need empyrean armor and steel."

There was no disputing his logic; however, him showing up in full royal army regalia grated against my already blistering skin. Right now, he was standing before me as my emissary, not my champion. "There are no archangels here for you to battle," I said, teeth clenched as I settled my goblet on the table.

"Apologies, my liege. I should have considered—"

"Sit," I said. "I've had a feast prepared in your honor."

His throat bobbed, but he remained unmoving.

Arching a brow, I leaned back. "Are my laurels not to your liking?"

Pulling out a chair, he positioned the helmet on the table and took a seat opposite me. "Your hospitality is most gracious."

I filled his goblet with wine and placed a plate before him as I took a plate for myself and began adding cheeses, nuts, and fruit. He eyed the food with trepidation, reluctance etching across his brow. "Is my food no longer good enough for my Horseman of Death?" I asked as I put a grape into my mouth.

His gaze met mine. He understood my challenge. He'd been restored and had been walking in the mortal realm for almost two years, free to exploit its earthly pleasures, including the satisfaction of a full belly. I needed to know where his loyalties rested.

Taking a sip of the wine, he swallowed deeply. "I've missed our court gatherings. I wish I'd had the opportunity to return sooner." His curt smile failed to hide the way his nose crinkled. Seemed he was no longer accustomed to the repulsive aftertaste left on the tongue by Hell's unholy wine.

I broke off a piece of bread from the loaf sitting before us and nibbled off a bite. The taste and texture of crumbling ash disintegrating in my mouth forced me to drink from my goblet. I swished the wine around, pretending to savor it for added measure, before gulping it down. No matter how many eternities one could spend here, there was no growing accustomed to the taste of Hell's food. No one could ever miss eating trash.

I remained silent as I popped another grape into my mouth. Patronization usually resulted in a trip to The Breaking Wheel.

The silence in the room grew heavier and Beleth tapped his fingers on the table. Fuck ups were rarely tolerated in my court. With a resigned breath, he finally said, "If I've caused you reason to doubt my commitment to this war…"

Taking a long, serrated knife from the table, I carved a slice of meat off the roasted pig splayed out on a platter next to him. "What I doubt is your *competence*. Malphas and Astaroth are dead. Chemoth, your own brother, has been suffering with a putrid wound which might claim his spirit as well."

I slurped up the chunks of pork, thinking back to the debauched feasts I used to hold at the citadel. Succulent roasts sprawled on platters, the intoxicating scent of fire-cooked meat permeating the air. Exotic fruits and aged cheeses. Pitchers overflowing with rich wines and crisp ales.

If only memory was strong enough to dull out the reality of this place.

Beleth inched closer to the edge of his chair, propping his elbows on the table. "We weren't prepared for God to interfere—for Him to allow angels to lend aid to the humans, let alone Zadkiel, of all angels. A dominion, for fuck's sake. He not only ordained a new Guardian with his blood, granting her angelic gifts, but he gave her an empyrean weapon."

Using the pointy end of a smaller knife, I picked at a chunk of meat stuck between my molars. "My Father interfering isn't quite as alarming as my four strongest lieutenants not being able to put down one single human woman," I spat, stabbing the knife into the wood table, a hair-width away from his thumb.

He lurched back, almost tumbling off his chair. "It wasn't Zadkiel alone who interceded, Mikha'el—"

"Enough of your drivel," I said, pushing up to my feet. "Do you think I don't already know that Mikha'el abandoned his post to serve this woman? I have eyes in all corners, Beleth. The righteous asshole can go against God, and all he's stripped of are his legions and weapons. Still, you faced an archangel without his armor and without his famed sword. It's an affront to me that he still stands, yet three of my fiercest warriors do not. Explain to me how or why I should still trust you."

"Astaroth's host betrayed his sect. We were not four-strong, my liege."

"Humans are capricious creatures," I gritted. "His switched allegiance shouldn't have shocked you. What's disappointing is how poorly you executed my orders. Even without Astaroth, you should've been able to handle this. How fucking hard is it for three Horsemen to decimate a planet and impregnate one female with one fucking demon spawn? Or is your seed that damn pathetic?"

"It is because of our inability to procreate that we're in this fucking mess to begin with, or have you forgotten why we were all cast to this hell?"

"Mind. Your. Damn. Tongue, lieutenant. I know quite well why we were sentenced to this shit hole, and that is why angels decided to procreate with human females—to circumvent my Father's decree."

He stood, standing face to face, the table the only thing separating us. "And is the child growing inside that woman not good enough for you? Despite Astaroth's human host defecting, Astaroth's spirit was trapped in his body—enabling the human to impregnate the female with his seed while passing down Astaroth's essence. It's what's made the child a perfect host for you." Beleth puffed his chest and dared to stare me square in the eyes. "With all due respect, I think our job was well executed."

My gaze narrowed as a growl rumbled in my chest. "Well executed, you say? What value does the fetus have if the vessel carrying it still roams free?" I asked, slamming a fist down on the table, making every dish rattle loudly.

His nostrils flared at my rebuke. Sweat beaded on his forehead. He knew he'd fucked up, yet he'd forgotten to leave his hubris at the gates. After Chemoth was cast back to Hell, I questioned him about the attack. According to him, they'd suffered a devastating and humiliating loss at the hands of the human army led by Mikha'el and the woman he'd taken under his wing. Beleth had been particularly vexed—but also fearful. I wasn't known for my tolerance of failure. His life depended on his next words.

"The sicarri are on her trail," he said slowly. "It's only a matter of time before they capture her."

Well, well... Wonder and disbelief threaded through my muscles. And here I thought I was going to stain my hands red with Beleth's blood today. Seemed my Horseman of Death might live yet another day.

The sicarri were Heaven's highest skilled elite forces—typically reserved for hunting and eliminating demonic threats against mankind. Except, ever since I'd won my bargain, the Powers had been prohibited from dispatching the assassins against my forces.

My rage cooled enough that I didn't reach across the table and rip out Beleth's wings with my bare hands. I leaned back in my chair, a smile creasing my face. "Do elaborate, my faithful servant. How were you able to break into the citadel, convince the Powers to not only sympathize with my plan, but to break our... *Lord God's* rules?" I asked, practically spitting out the words at the end.

"Our *Lord God,*" he repeated with similar disgust, "is weakened, which means the wards keeping the portal gates closed were not reinforced. With my newly restored body, the portal did not reject me."

"And my Father's spies? Surely you were spotted entering the citadel."

"Elysium is no longer the city we once knew; it's perfect anarchy. God is missing and no one knows where He's gone into hiding, not even His closest advisors. Seems the decimation of Earth has taken away a great deal of His power, and He doesn't have the courage to face His people."

"How very dramatic of my Father. He wants everyone to believe He's dying of a broken heart, when in reality, He's simply escaping His failures." I invited Beleth to take a seat once more. "And the Powers welcomed you with open arms?"

His shoulders relaxed as he sat down, a small, nervous smile tugging at his lips. He understood how narrowly close he'd come to his death. "You know they're an imperious lot," he said, hoping to deflect the tension. "In God's absence, Khama'el has become completely autocratic and has taken it upon himself to not only rule Elysium, but to make decisions regarding all other realms."

Another pompous, righteous asshole like Mikha'el. My Father must've really fucked up for Khama'el not to imprison Beleth simply for entering the citadel. "How did you manage to beseech him to our cause?"

"Despite his allegiance to God, Khama'el is very pragmatic. He understands the injustices inflicted upon our kind. Though he's carried out countless attacks against us, at his core, he's never been a human sympathizer. He was merely following orders, but now that our Father has abandoned Elysium, he believes in supporting the New Order. One in which you get to rule over not only the realm promised to you by birthright, but Heaven."

"What's in it for him?"

Beleth's eyes shimmered like liquid emeralds.

"What exactly did you promise him in my name in exchange for his help?"

"He wants to be king of his own realm. One of his choosing."

A chortle bubbled out of me. "My, my, how the mighty have fallen."

"After the defeat in New York, Mikha'el and…" he paused, and his reluctance to utter the name sitting on his tongue scraped my skin like a rusted blade.

I nodded gently, permitting him to continue, though I clamped my jaw so hard, my teeth were close to cracking.

"…Gavri'el, with her gift of foresight, must have predicted I would return to Elysium to recruit the Powers. According to Khama'el, before my arrival, she claimed God had forgiven Mikha'el and asked Khama'el to give him back his legions and his sword. Who would question God's personal emissary?"

My muscles tightened and the frost already burrowed in my bones seemed to grow colder. "Mikha'el is in command of his army again?"

"He never had the chance to take command. After the battle in New York, he and Gavri'el returned to the citadel, but by then, Khama'el had dispersed his legions and imprisoned his highest-ranking lieutenants. It wasn't easy, but he also captured both Mikha'el and Gavri'el, though they later managed to escape."

I shook my head. Seemed my lieutenants weren't the only unprosperous dimwits. "And the sicarri? how do they fit into all of this?"

"Khama'el sent them after the woman. We'd been trying to locate her for months, but we suspected Mikha'el had put some type of cloaking protection over her. We lucked out when her group inadvertently came across a bask of zamharee. Seems Astaroth isn't entirely dead—a part of his essence still resides inside the human host. Through him, the zamharee were able to alert me of the woman's location, and Khama'el immediately dispatched the assassins to capture her."

"But they didn't," I said, tapping a finger on the table.

Beleth straightened, a shadow of dread ghosting across his face.

I leaned in closer, folding my arms over the table. "According to you, they are still on her trail."

He fluttered his wings slightly, staring at me wordlessly while he absentmindedly adjusted his breastplate—as if it had somehow come out of place while he'd sat in front of me this whole time. I'd not asked him a question, but the prolonged silence made it seem as if I had, and I loved the uncomfortable ice hanging in the air. I rather enjoyed watching him squirm in his chair.

"These continued failures, unfortunately, have left me with little choice but to take matters into my own hands," I said, my breath heavy. Beleth's brow creased. "I tried trapping her consciousness in the Wastes—to get her to willingly give me the child. Alas, that insufferable human is too damn strong willed."

Beleth leaned back in his chair, hands dropping to the sides. Still, he had nothing to say.

"Do you know what using the Wastes cost me?"

He simply continued to stare, but understanding reflected in his eyes. The wrath boiling me from within didn't sprout out of thin air. The loose gear in his brain had finally clicked into place.

"She was never going to give me that child willingly, no matter what I tried—though I'd foolishly hoped I could at least tempt her. What I hadn't anticipated was her ability to use angelic magic to warp time and imprison me in the Wastes for two hundred fucking years."

Beleth's lips cracked open. "I'm… so sorry, my liege. I had no idea—"

"I'm not interested in your apology. Can you give me back the two centuries I lost? Have you an idea of the amount of power I had to use to find a way back to this realm and in the right timeline? I can barely keep this goddamn glamor on. Can't even dull the pain yanking on the base of my rotting wings. All because you couldn't do one simple job."

Unable to meet my gaze, he lowered his chin.

I was surrounded by fucking imbeciles. "Fortunately for you and Khama'el's squadron of inept fools, before she sent me reeling through time, I was able to tap into her consciousness long enough to find out where she's hiding."

You'd think he'd be interested in knowing the woman's location. That after everything he'd done—all his failures— he'd jump at the prospect to make things right. I banged a fist on the table again, jolting him back, the pendants hanging from his neck *clacking* hard against his armor. "Aren't you going to ask me where she's at, you dumb fuck?"

His head popped up, those deep, blue-green eyes brimming with indignation. Finally, an emotion I could work with.

I stood and came around the table, forcing him off his chair. Standing chest to chest, I said, "Where are the sicarri now?"

"Back on the Western continent of the human realm. After they ambushed the woman and her companions, Mikha'el and Gavri'el showed up with several of Mikha'el's warriors. All we know is that he rifted the woman and her human mate, but not where to."

"What of Gavri'el?" I asked.

"She stayed behind, along with a few other royal guards, to protect the rest of the humans, but…"

"But what?" I said, grabbing him by the breastplate.

"The sicarri are ruthless. Not many humans or Mikha'el's warriors survived. They captured Gavri'el, but she was barely breathing. She was willing to die for them, my liege… for the *humans*." The devastation in his eyes spoke of the betrayal he felt as well.

I released his breastplate and turned from him, bracing my hands on the long wooden table. Rage burned through my veins. I didn't think I could feel pain like this again. Even after so many lifetimes, her betrayal still felt like a lance through my heart. I roared and gripped the table, flipping it over and scattering all the food and platters across the floor. The sound of metal against stone reverberated through the hall.

"My liege," Beleth said shakily.

I spun around, chest heaving. "Tell the sicarri that Katherine Elizabeth Jones is hiding at the Eastern Guardian Stronghold. I don't know if the child has been born yet, but I want them *both* brought to me, alive."

"And Gavri'el?"

Gavri'el? Blasted Hell. My knees almost buckled. That she still had this effect on me made me want to flay my own fucking skin. She was an emissary, not a warrior, yet she was willing to spill her own blood to save the humans—the same humans she'd once confessed made her doubt her worth. It tore her apart to watch God lavish them with so much grace, while He treated us like we were the ones needing to earn His love.

I tried convincing her that our worth wasn't measured by how much or how little He loved us. Yet, even though I'd offered her my heart with a blood oath, it hadn't mattered to her that she'd owned *my* love from the day I came into existence. It hadn't been enough—*I* hadn't been enough.

Cursed bones, the way I craved her acceptance with such ferocity—it's why I betrayed God's fucking kingdom. Why I sentenced myself to an eternity of suffering. All to give her the one thing that would've made her whole, and still, she never came for me after God banished me from Elysium.

My love for her had been greater than all the realms, and I would have burned them all to the ground if she'd asked me to—even after she discarded my heart—because despite her rejection, despite the fact she bedded Mikha'el and gave him the heart she'd already promised me, I would rather not exist than live in a world where I'd never kissed her lips.

But how many more lifetimes would I have to endure for a mere crumb of her attention? For an ounce of acknowledgement that I'd languished in this cursed realm because of her... *for* her. No. I couldn't tolerate her cruel indifference any longer. I'd done all I could. I would've made her my queen—would've given her the keys to a goddamn kingdom—but she chose to trample on those dreams and to stab me in the gut with her treachery.

If I didn't matter to her, then it was time to rip her from my heart once and for all, until the feel of her soft skin was wiped from my memory and my desire for her no longer coursed through my blood like wildfire.

Chest pounding, I fixed my gaze to Beleth's, the words already tasting like acid on my tongue. "If she wants to die for those wretched mortals, let her," I seethed, my insides shattering with every breath. "She made her choice, now the price must be paid. Give her a good death, but ensure Mikha'el witnesses her execution. I want him to feel the same festering misery that eats at my soul."

Beleth sagged. Terror shone in his eyes as he picked up the golden eagle helmet from the floor. "Samael," he whispered, dropping the formality. "Gavri'el… she's your soul-bonded."

"No, she is not." I slowly walked back to my chair, bones trembling. "She never was. I wanted to complete the bond, but she wanted us to wait." It didn't dawn on me until after I'd been banished why she was reluctant to give me a piece of her soul. She'd planned to give it to someone else.

Beleth spirited his wings away. Perhaps it was involuntary, or maybe he finally understood. If I was willing to kill Gavri'el for this war, that meant no one in my court was safe, not even him. He bowed his head and walked toward the bailey where his horse waited.

"Beleth." My voice echoed in the empty hall as he reached the double doors. When he looked over his shoulder, I added, "The next time you walk through my gates, it would serve you well to offer me Mikha'el's detestable heart on a fucking platter made of empyrean gold."

His lips thinned, eyes darkening as he nodded. When those doors closed behind him, I sank into my seat and allowed my torment to consume me. If ever I felt condemned, this was it. Face buried in my palms, I drowned my guilt in a sea of tears and called to Him, though I knew He would never listen to my prayer. Why would He now, when He'd never cared much about my pain. Still, I clamored to Him, because despite my hatred for my own Father, only He had the power to heal a broken heart.

Oh, Father. What have I done?

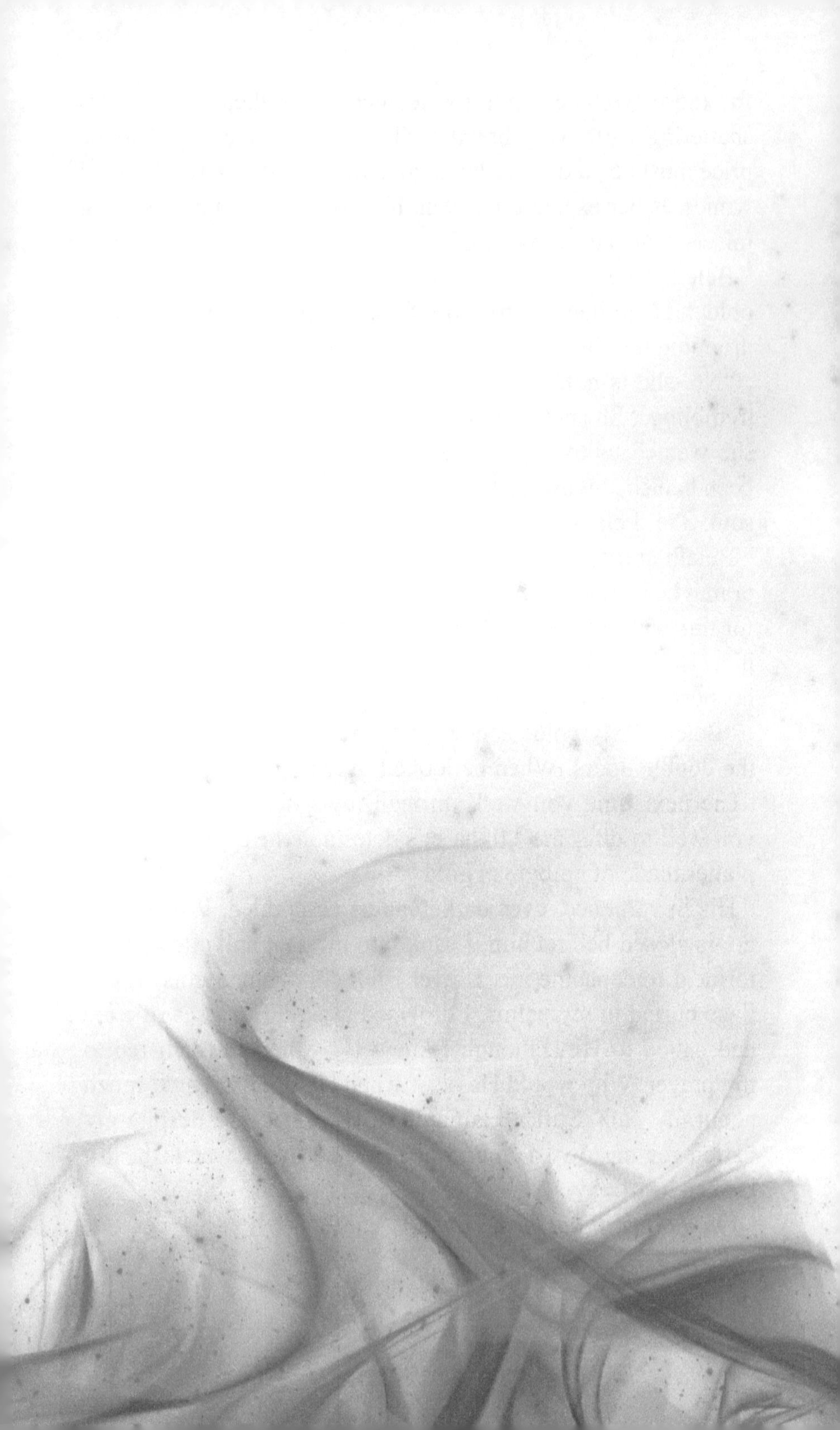

CHAPTER 14

KATE

Pushing through the wall of light wasn't entirely eventless. The instant I slipped my right hand through, the sigils on my arms flared to life and a slight burning sensation danced on my skin. Not scalding, but the sort of warmth you'd feel from a heat lamp. Sucking in a deep breath, I walked through the barrier. A crackling noise buzzed in my ear, similar to when a bug flies into an electric zapper.

I second guessed my decision for a brief moment, but mercifully, Mikha'el's force field didn't fry my ass. Except for the tingly sensation all over my skin, I made it through the barrier completely unscathed. I turned around and flipped Jax two thumbs up. Seemed he'd been holding his breath, too. A wide grin spread ear to ear, and he whispered something to Luke. Amada drew close to the wall and uttered something, but interestingly enough, the force field acted like a sound barrier as well.

"I can't hear you," I said, pointing to my ears.

She signaled to the bodies lying near me, apparently wanting me to check for a pulse. I planned on it, but I needed to check on Hank and Mikha'el first. My heart ached as I neared Hank's limp body, his tongue drooping to the side. Then I saw his chest rise ever so slightly, and the tension that had wrapped around all my muscles finally uncoiled. I ran to him, falling to my knees beside his body.

He appeared to be sleeping very deeply, but otherwise, he was unharmed. I patted his head and tried to wake him. His body shivered at my touch. There wasn't much I could do for him now, but he was alive, and that's what mattered. If Hank lived, then perhaps everyone else was also just in a comatose state.

Two feet from where Hank lay, Mikha'el's burned body remained motionless, his decimated wings a pile of ruins. I crawled to him and carefully peeled the charred feathers off his face—some were fused to his blistering skin. Heavens, he looked like he'd been dipped into lava. Small, shallow breaths slipped from his lips. Scanning him over, I took in every inch of the devastating burns.

Tears beaded at the corners of my eyes. "Oh, Mikha'el…"

A strained moan rumbled in his chest and his now lashless eyes slowly peeled open. His golden irises pulsed in beat with the force field. Shit. He was powering the wall, but the light emitting from his eyes was dimmer. He was running out of energy, out of life.

"K… Kate," he uttered hoarsely, the sound barely audible.

"I'm here."

He raised a trembling hand to my cheek. "You're alive."

"And you're severely burned. What you did back there…"

"My duty," he groaned, the pain rocking through his body, making him tremble.

"Tell me what to do. How do I help you?"

"It's too late for me."

"No, I don't accept that. There must be something I can do; if not, what's the point of these powers?" I asked, showing him my arms, the sigils pulsing with glowing light. "Please. Let me help you."

"Life requires life, Katherine. If you use your power to heal me, you will be weakened."

"I need you in this fight with me. This world needs you."

His body arched, limbs trembling. "They are close. Beleth and his assassins, they approach. I can sense them… Something must have lured them here."

I tried to peel back the hair from his face. "More of a reason to let me heal you."

"The babe?" he groaned.

"Luke? He's well. And if you want to meet him, you're going to need to let me help you."

Swallowing thickly, he nodded, conceding. Blinking slowly, he grabbed my forearm in his. "Repeat after me: Heal me, Lord, and I will be healed."

My sigils flared bright and hot. "Heal me, Lord, and I will be healed."

"Save me, and I will be saved."

The golden light living in my blood flowed through my veins like rivers of sunlight. "Save me and I will be saved," I echoed.

He coughed golden blood, the liquid spilling out the side of his mouth. "For You are the one I praise."

From our point of touch, the rivers of light now flowed into him, lighting up his flesh, healing as it wound up his arm, his shoulder, his neck, and spreading over his chest.

"Repeat the words, Kate."

I was in such awe, I'd forgotten to recite the prayer. "For You are the one I praise."

Like threads on a tapestry, his wounds mended together, new skin stitching itself over the scorched flesh.

"My flesh and my heart may fail," he said, his voice less strained, more powerful and full of vitality.

"My…" Ice sank into my bones and my head felt woozy. What I gave, he took greedily, but it was what his body needed.

"Kate?"

"I'm okay," I managed, but I felt my heart struggling to pump blood through my veins. "My flesh and… my… heart… may… fail." Breathing hurt and I clutched my chest.

"I'm taking too much," he said, attempting to pull his arm away, but I held on, gripping him despite my failing energy.

"No. Don't stop," I told him. "We finish this."

By now, most of his body was healed. He sat up, our arms still locked. "But God is the strength of my heart." The dead feathers on his wings disintegrated as new brass-colored ones sprouted and fanned, his wingspan dwarfing me.

I sagged, and Mikha'el took me into his arms as my eyes drooped. "But God is the strength of my heart," I said, my voice nothing but a thin whisper.

He held me tighter, wanting to give me his warmth, but his body was unable to chase the chill that frosted over me. "And of my soul, forever," he said over my brow.

My breath felt ragged, and I couldn't find the strength to speak.

"You must say the words, Katherine," he implored.

My vision blurred in and out of focus, but I was able to see his face. Golden eyes shone like the sun, and his dark hair was lustrous. He was glorious. Beautiful. Majestic. "It… worked," I whispered.

"Say the last words, Kate: And of my soul, forever."

I swallowed deeply, my throat feeling like gravel. "And… of my soul for… ever."

With those last words, a blinding light enveloped him in a flash that quickly subsided. Those brilliant, brass-colored wings curved around me as he held me in his massive arms. "You healed me, Daughter of Eve."

A lazy smile curled at the ends of my lips. "Just call me Kate," I said, my head still swimming. "And you can put me down now."

"I took much of your strength; I don't think it wise."

"You took what you needed. Don't worry about me. We need to make sure these people are okay."

He lowered me down, his wings still fanned wide. He scanned the room, taking in the dozen or so people laying on the ground. Some had begun to stir, while others were already sitting upright, confusion swirling in their gazes as they took in the angelic being in the middle of the room.

It wasn't lost on me—probably on none of us in the room—how Mikha'el must have looked standing in the middle of the crypt, surrounded by all the man-made stone recreations of his kind.

"I didn't mean to hurt anyone," he said, looking down at me. "I sensed danger and our bodies are built to—"

"You don't have to explain."

Hank slowly rose, and the instant he saw me, his eyes rounded, ears perking up. I wobbled toward him, but Mikha'el held me up so I wouldn't fall. "Hey buddy, so nice to see you."

Hank whined, panting as he sat and let me pet him. "I have someone I want you to meet," I said, eager to let him see Luke.

"He'll need my blessing, too," Mikha'el added, as if offended that I didn't offer first dibs on my son.

Feeling slightly better, I sat on the floor and had to hold back a gasp when my gaze snagged on the many areas where Mikha'el's armor was torn or missing. There was very little left to the imagination. Taught, golden muscle covered every inch of his sculpted body. "Um, you might want to magic-in some clothing, or you'll end up sending some of the women in this church to confession."

His cheeks flushed as he scanned his body. Never thought I'd ever see an archangel blush. With a quick flutter of his wings, and after a bit of distorted air, he managed to magically dress himself in tight-fitting black leather armor trimmed in red and gold. His legendary sword appeared at his back as he glamoured away his wings. He looked like holy vengeance about to wage war on the sins of the world.

I held on to his arm for support as I stumbled to my feet.

"You're still weak."

"I'll manage." I nodded toward the force field still glowing around the perimeter. "Can you do something about that? These people might want to get out. Plus, Jax is waiting on the other side with Luke."

Nodding, he closed his eyes and whispered something in his holy tongue, but as soon as the force field fell, a loud *boom* shook the church's foundation and the lights went out, leaving us bathed in the dim candlelight flickering off candles scattered through the space. I fell backward, and others held on to the walls or pillars. Mikha'el unsheathed his sword as he looked around.

"What is it? What happened?"

"Beleth," Mikha'el said, his gaze shooting to the ceiling. "He's here."

CHAPTER 15

JAX

The instant the lights went out, and I heard the first gunshot, followed by the *thump* of Cesar's body, I knew we were fucked. I didn't get a chance to turn around before Talia shot Amada in the chest, then pointed her handgun at Luke. "Give me the baby, or I shoot it in the head."

Terror latched onto my beating heart and squeezed around it like barbed wire. I froze, every muscle in my body turning to stone. A part of me knew she was bluffing—at least, I hoped she was. If her end goal was taking Luke, then it made no sense she'd shoot him.

Fuck. But what if she decided to pull that trigger either out of desperation or out of pure madness? How was I supposed to protect Luke? I was completely defenseless.

She tightened her grip on the gun, hand slightly shaking. "Give me the fucking baby," she shouted, her voice reverberating up the staircase and making my insides jolt.

Holding Luke in his sling like a football, I put a palm up. "Okay, okay. Just put the weapon down."

"Now," she growled, the manic look in her eyes chilling my blood. As much as I believed Luke was worth more to her alive than dead, I couldn't take that gamble, not with my son's life. I slowly pulled the sling over my head. "You don't want to do this, Talia."

"Shut the fuck up," she said, wasting no time ripping him from my arms. "You're a disgrace to our Order." Aiming the gun at my face, she was about to pull the trigger when the force field fell away, distracting her for half a second. Amada tried shooting her handgun, but the bullet went wide, almost clipping me in the leg. Talia took off up the staircase with Luke in her arms, but she managed to fire off one last round in my direction, and this time, the bullet found a home in my flesh. I fell back into the wall, a burning pain spreading low in my torso.

The agony was excruciating, but the only coherent thought in my brain was making sure Luke was okay. I couldn't let this woman get away. If we lost Luke… fuck. The whole goddamn fate of humanity rested on me getting Luke back, but that's not why I fought through the wound, now bleeding profusely. I fought because that was my son, and there was no way I was letting a gunshot stop me from going after the person who took him. I wouldn't be able to face Kate if I didn't find the strength to go after the woman. Wouldn't be able to face myself.

Clutching my bleeding abdomen, I climbed the steps of the crypt and into the grand hall, the pews of *La Sagrada Familia* standing in silent witness as I stumbled across the nave looking for Talia. How could I have been so stupid? I'd had an inkling these people shouldn't be trusted, but I let my guard down, and now my son was in the hands of a deranged sect member. Sweat dripped down my forehead, my labored breaths echoing off the towering columns. Panic coursed through my veins as I glanced back, catching a glimpse of the silhouette skulking through the shadows.

A d'shiad. Motherfucker. There was no way I could outrun a hellhound, not in my current condition. And wherever one lurked, more were sure to pop up. My footsteps echoed through the cavernous chamber as I scrambled to find cover. With my back against one of the ornate columns, I took a second to examine my wound.

The new T-shirt the guardians had given me was nothing but a blood-soaked, tattered mess. Lifting the hem, I held my breath and bit down on my jaw as I peered at the hole carved into my left oblique. Thankfully, it looked like Talia missed vital organs, but I was still bleeding heavily. I tried applying pressure and nearly bit my tongue from the fucking pain that shocked my entire body. My vision blurred and I almost lost my balance.

After a couple of steadying breaths, I peeked around the corner and sure enough, a second beast had joined its packmate—but this one sported the notorious thick silver mane of an alpha. The beast sniffed the air and immediately pivoted toward my hiding spot. I lurched back and held my breath. Fucker had tracked my scent. Shit. My chances of survival were diminishing. I was either gonna bleed out or end up as hellhound chow.

There's another option… something deep within me purred, a dark intrusive thought I wasn't sure was even mine. Fuck. What it suggested… It was madness. Kate would never forgive me. But what other choice did I have? If I did nothing, I would die out here, unable to protect those I loved.

Growls rumbled closer.

I'd run out of time. Across from me, the word *Speratus* was written three times over the double doors leading to the school and dormitories. *To hope deeply.* I took that as a sign.

Scrounging up whatever strength remained in my body, I swallowed the iron taste in my mouth and dashed for the double doors, my weakened body protesting with every stride. The instant the demonic dogs spotted me, the chase was on. I dared a look back as they leapt over the pews to get to me. They demolished the wood with their giant claws, splintered chunks flying in all directions. Their glowing red eyes illuminated the dimly lit space as they moved at unnatural speeds, snarling, saliva dripping from their jagged fangs. Their whooping calls echoed through the church as they called for reinforcements.

My heart struggled to pump oxygen into my bloodstream, but I kept moving. I just needed to get through the doors in time to use my blood to sketch a warding spell.

Still clutching my abdomen, I counted each step, summoning the last reserves of my strength.

One. Two. Three.

The beasts were so close, I could practically smell their hot rancid breath, could feel it on the back of my neck.

Four. Five. Six.

Chest heaving from exertion, I reached the heavy wooden doors and pushed through with my shoulder, pain interlacing through every muscle in my abdomen. I fell across the threshold, collapsing to the tiled floor, but I managed to land on my knees. Mere seconds ticked down as I smeared my trembling hands with more of my blood and drew the trident sigil, the handle overlaid by an X, over each door.

A large *crash* sounded as the beasts smashed against the ward. I fell on my back from the loud *boom,* half expecting them to barrel through the warded doors. They howled, their sinister growls echoing through the church, furious they were unable to cross the boundary and had been denied their prey. The ward wouldn't hold forever, though. Plus, I didn't doubt they'd find another exit, anyway. Not to mention they'd summoned their packmates. Soon, more hellhounds would arrive.

I groaned as I pushed to my feet. Bleary-eyed, I stumbled through the corridor, holding on to the walls for balance. Dead bodies littered the floor. Mother of God. Some of these people had been shot dead. Humans had done this, not demons. Fuck. I saw a small body, and I felt my chest cave.

La Sagrada Familia had been infiltrated by the Devil's Army right under their noses.

Even now, I could still feel the burn of their sins upon my heart. I'd been a member; I'd contributed to this fucking disaster. Perhaps it was better if I bled out and died. I wanted to save my son, but I was already a letdown of a man. I'd been a father for a few hours, and I'd been incapable of protecting him. He was better off without me.

Shut up. You know what you need to do.

My head spun, and I collapsed to the ground as I reached a small moon-lit courtyard, the same one we'd passed by earlier when Amada escorted us to the crypt. It lay in ruins now. The garden had been trampled, and more bodies covered the floor.

You're wasting time.

The intrusive thoughts got louder, bolder. This had to be a symptom of my impending death.

Stop the self-pity. You don't have to die. You know what to do. So just do it!

And have Kate loathe me forever? No. I won't do that to her. To Luke.

I managed to sit up and leaned my back against a wall near the courtyard. Head lolled to the side, my eyes drifted closed as I gasped for breath, wheezing with each inhale. This was it. This was how I died. Alone. A failure.

It was what I deserved.

A scream split the night, jolting me awake. Opening my lids, I spotted a woman down the corridor, dressed in a lab coat, standing at an intersection. My vision was blurry, but I was certain it was the med student, Diana, who had helped deliver Luke. Across from her, two hellhounds snarled, their jaws snapping. Blasted hell. That silver mane. They looked like the two beasts I'd trapped with the ward. The pieces of shit had found a way around the warded doors.

Diana must've caught some movement in my direction, and she looked my way. I blinked several times, trying to smudge the wetness from my eyes.

When her gaze latched on to mine, I felt the terror coursing through her body. Fuck. She was going to run. If she did, she stood zero chance. I mean, she stood zero chance now, but if I could get the beasts to focus on me instead, then perhaps I could give her a fighting chance…

Then I saw it, the panic on her face when the beasts roared. I shook my head *no*, but she'd already made up her mind and she took off. I wished I could have stuck needles in my ears to keep myself from hearing her screams as one of the dogs reached her. The sound of flesh being torn from bone made me vomit.

Wiping my mouth, I pushed my spine back up against the wall, and that's when I saw the alpha skulking toward me.

Yeah. I was royally fucked.

The beast didn't trouble itself with rushing to devour its meal. Its massive paws *thudded* against the tiled floor as it neared in a slow, deliberate stroll; its long, black claws scraping against the tiles.

Instinctively, I pushed myself flush against the wall, but there was nowhere for me to go. That's when I felt a cold hand beside me. I looked down at the dead body laying next to me. The poor young man appeared to have been praying when he was shot in the head, a rosary draped around his hand.

I spared a glance toward the open sky in the middle of the courtyard. Seemed God was granting me one last mercy. Taking the rosary from the dead man's hand, I clutched it tightly, the crucifix's polished silver gleaming in the pale moonlight that filtered through the apple tree in the center of the square.

Without another second to spare, the hellhound lunged at me, its maw open wide in a snarl of fury. My eyes locked onto the creature's flank. Dipping into the last reserve of energy in my blood, I shifted sideways and jabbed the crucifix into the beast's exposed ribs, a current of curses spilling from my lips. It had been a Hail Mary, hoping the crucifix had been blessed and bathed in holy water, but the sizzling sound of burning flesh was a grand relief. The hellhound yelped in pain, recoiling from the blow, but its hunger for my blood overcame its momentary fear, and the animal lunged at me with renewed ferocity.

I swung the crucifix in a wide arc, striking it squarely in the snout, sending it sprawling as the smell of burned flesh filled my nostrils.

"Two for two, you dumb shit."

But the beast was relentless and rushed at me one more time, the crucifix no longer a threat. I put my hands out to keep its jaws from tearing into my neck, but it dug its fangs into my forearm instead, and began yanking. I wailed from the pain as the fucking demon dog tried to tear my arm off, violently thrusting my body around and smashing me into a wall.

In the chaos, I somehow had managed to keep a hold of the rosary, and after several failed attempts, I was able to jab the crucifix into one of its eyes. This time, it opened its jaw, releasing my arm. I lay in a crumpled mess on the floor, my arm a mangled disaster.

The crucifix still lodged in its eye, the beast howled, smoke rising from the wound. I blew out a labored breath, resigning myself to this terrible death. I thought about Kate and Luke, and about the life I'd daydreamed we could've had. But life is cruel, and this was meant to be my fate.

The animal rose on its hind legs and let out an ear-piercing shriek as it prepared to leap at me and tear me to shreds, but the shriek was cut short when a golden arrow plunged through its skull. The beast collapsed on its side, then turned to ash, leaving the arrow behind.

Empyrean steel.

I tried looking through the courtyard to see where the arrow had come from when I spotted a figure walking toward me.

What? No. It couldn't be. I must've been dead if I was seeing ghosts.

"Jax. You okay, man?"

"Kid?" I sputtered out, my voice a hoarse whisper. "You're supposed to be… dead."

He hauled a giant crossbow over his shoulder, his right arm glinting in gold metal as if he was wearing armored plating, except he wasn't. Clint had a bionic arm made of Empyrean steel.

"Surprise! I'm not dead."

CHAPTER 16
KATE

Bullets rang out from the direction I'd come in. Screams erupted and I ducked, but from the corner of my eye, I saw Amada's shadowed silhouette collapsed on the ground. She clasped her chest as she tried firing off another round of bullets up the staircase. Cesar already lay in a lumped mass on the floor, his head at an odd angle.

My heart sank. I tried to run toward the staircase, but my legs gave way beneath me and I fell to my knees. "Jax!"

Mikha'el was at my side in an instant, lifting me and carrying me toward Amada, her body sprawled over a puddle of her own blood. There was no sight of Jax or the baby.

I knelt beside Amada. "What happened?"

"Talia…" she gasped in pain, pressing on her wound to staunch the bleeding. Her eyes glistened as she took in the angelic warrior behind me. "She shot us the instant she saw you heal *him.*" She coughed blood, her wound seeping. "*Madre mia,*" she uttered in a gurgle, staring at Mikha'el. "*Sos magnifico.*"

Mikha'el knelt beside me. "She doesn't have long."

Panic punched through my gut. "Can't you do something? Heal her."

I can't, Katherine. It's her time, he whispered into my mind, his voice tender.

Fuck that. Gavri'el brought Jax back.

Gavri'el was granted certain gifts I don't have. Jax was brought back for a reason. He nodded toward Amada. *Her work here is done. But I can end her suffering.*

Amada's eyes rolled, her breaths short and shallow.

Tracing a sigil over her forehead, Mikha'el began, "We thank You, Father, for Your warriors. For they are specially chosen by You to serve and protect. As Your faithful child, Amada has offered her life as a Guardian of this realm and has willingly laid down her life in duty to You and her people. For her sacrifice, I beg You, end her pain and grant her eternal reward in the next life."

The tremors rocking through her body ceased. She slowly opened her eyes, and it was as if she was seeing for the first time, eyes shining with an internal light. A gentle smile traced across her blood-stained lips. "Thank you," she whispered.

Before she could take her last breath, I inched closer. "Where's Jax and the baby, Amada?" The words could barely form on my lips. Fear, anger, and utter rage barreled through me at the thought of Talia hurting them.

"She shot all of us," Amada murmured. "Took the baby, but Jax managed to pull himself up and ran after the bitch."

"I need my weapon, Amada. The sword you took. It's empyrean steel. It's the only thing capable—"

"I know what that weapon can do," she gritted, sitting up higher and fighting through her impending death.

Gunfire echoed throughout the church, screams rising as survivors scrambled for their lives. "We're being attacked by an army of demons. Please tell me where my sword and the creation stones are."

Blood spilled from the corner of her mouth. "I'm so sorry… I tried. All I wanted was to protect my people."

I grabbed her hand and gave it a gentle squeeze. "I swear to you, *I* will fight for your people. You have my word."

Nodding slightly, she took off the rosary hanging around her neck and handed it to me. Heaving her last breath, she said, "The cross. It's the key to the tabernacle. I hid them inside." Then her body sagged, and the light in her eyes blinked out of existence.

"I'll find your weapon," Mikha'el said, jumping to his feet.

"No," I told him. "Find Jax and Luke. If anyone gets in your way…" I clenched my jaw and clamped my fists. "Kill them."

Gripping his sword tightly, he disappeared up the staircase in a flash. I desperately wanted to go after my son and Jax, but my body was still too weak. Mikha'el stood a better chance at finding them. The archangel was now my sword, and I would wield him like a lethal blade against my enemies. Talia was gonna wish she was never born.

Confiscating Amada's rifle, I checked the magazine. Only a handful of rounds remained. Fuck. I reached for Cesar's rifle, but his didn't fare any better—he had even less ammo. They weren't even holy water-infused bullets. I searched his pockets for extra ammo, doing my best not to look at his face. Talia had blown off a large chunk when she shot him, likely at point-blank.

I shivered at what she was capable of doing to Jax or Luke.

Beside me, Hank's ears perked, and he pivoted toward the back of the crypt, hackles raised, a low growl rumbling in his chest. Then I heard them, the snarls and grunts echoing off the stone walls as the monsters drew closer.

"We've got company."

Hank panted, eager to be put to work.

I patted him on the neck. "Don't you go being a hero. Stay with me."

It was hard to see in the dim light, but the screams were a clear indication from where the point of attack hailed. Across the center of the crypt, two people scrambled toward the exit but a large devoured leapt through the air, landing on the woman, clawing and tearing at her flesh with its rotted teeth. The creature raised its gaze at me, blood dripping from its maw, and that's when I realized these beasts were different. Most infected hunted to eat, but this one simply aimed to kill. It roared at me and was about to dash in my direction, but I shot a bullet straight through its head, bone and brains exploding into a gory mess.

Hank positioned himself between my legs as we moved through the chaos. I only had a handful of bullets and needed to make them count.

Pop. Pop.

Two more down. A woman who'd fallen reached for me, and I grabbed her hand, dragging her with me toward the staircase, but an infected came out of nowhere and latched onto her legs. It yanked so hard in the opposite direction, the woman split in half. In horror, I dropped her still-warm hand, the fingers twitching. The devoured flung her bottom half away and stalked toward me.

Hank growled and barked at the beast as we backed away, my boots slipping on the blood-slicked floor. I fired two shots, but one missed its head and the other clipped its shoulder. The force launched the creature backward, giving me a brief moment to reload with Cesar's mag. I had four more bullets. That was it—to fight off an army of devoured and hell knew what else Beleth had brought to this battle.

I needed my sword.

My heart clenched at the thought of abandoning the people in the crypt, especially after the promise I'd made Amada, but without my sword, I was no good to them. I needed to get to the tabernacle. Hank and I ran up the stairs, though I had to stop to catch my breath. Healing Mikha'el had taken a lot more energy than I realized. The scraping of claws echoed from behind as the devoured chased after us.

"Hurry, Hank!" Mustering strength from the bottom of my core, I sprinted up the next set of stairs, almost slipping on the blood-stained steps. Shit. The entire staircase was covered in red. *What if that was Jax's blood?* I shook the thought from my head.

Screams echoed from all around the church. The ghastly growls vibrating through the walls made my skin crawl. Nightcrawlers were tearing through the hallways.

I remembered all the faces I'd seen in the courtyard. The children reading a book, the boy kicking a soccer ball, the mother braiding her daughter's hair. All those people were under attack because we'd brought this fight to their doorstep. No. I would not allow one more person to die because of me. Because of this fucking war.

Fucking Beleth loved attacking innocent people.

Pulling myself forward, I grunted up the staircase, hauling my ass up as fast as I could, Hank way ahead of me, scouting for demons or zombies.

We spilled out into the main basilica, those monstrous pillars making me feel smaller than a microbe as I ran across the nave, looking for the tabernacle. The pews were a smashed disaster, like a truck had rammed through the church. More blood covered the floor, and my insides lurched. Shit. I prayed Mikha'el had found Jax.

Above me hung a crucified Jesus in some type of suspended fixture. I wondered what Gaudi would've thought about the battle raging in the middle of his masterpiece. The space was so huge, and in the dim light, it was nearly impossible to see where anything was. Then, something shiny caught my eyes. Hidden inside an alcove, the golden tabernacle sat on top of a stone table.

Hank barked and abandoned my side. Two devoured had reached the basilica and stalked toward us, but my superdog had heard them approach a second earlier. At full speed, Hank launched himself at one of the beasts, digging his jaw into its neck and tearing off a massive chunk of flesh. The devoured collapsed before it took a second step.

The remaining devoured swiped its claws, almost catching Hank's side, but my doggo was faster, dodging every blow. Two more infected popped out of the staircase, and I used the last of my bullets to take them out.

Pop. Pop. Pop. Pop.

Their bodies crumpled to the floor. Now fully out of ammo, I discarded the rifle and ran as fast as I could toward the tabernacle. Surprisingly, I wasn't too worried about Hank. After seeing him take down that devoured, I knew he could take care of himself. Plus, without a weapon, I wouldn't be much help. Flanked by two sets of tall, gilded candlesticks, the varnished wrought iron tabernacle was about four feet high and looked like a cupboard with rounded edges, topped with a small cross.

Taking the rosary out of my pocket, I inserted the bottom section of the cross into the keyhole on the tabernacle's door. I breathed a sigh of relief as soon as I saw my blade, along with two pendants, but the instant I reached for my sword, the stained-glass windows on the eastern wall exploded, showering the floor in a kaleidoscope of colors.

I ducked and covered my head with my forearm, but a large, jagged piece of shattered glass still managed to slash my face. Warm wetness slid down my cheek as wind whipped my hair. Peering up, my blood tingled, the weapon in my hand humming with power.

Dressed in the same silver-plated armor as the assassin angel who tried to capture me back in New York, another angel hovered in the middle of the cathedral, a golden crossbow aimed at my head. Enormous sapphire-colored wings rimmed with black feathers flapped at a steady pace. His face was partially obscured by his war helmet, but his liquid silver eyes were impossible to miss. Preternaturally, his gaze assessed me how I imagined a lion would measure its prey.

"Katherine Elizabeth Jones, you are hereby summoned to Lord Samael's court. You may come in peace or be captured by force." His voice boomed in the expansive chamber, the wind vortex created by his wings swishing my hair around with vengeance.

Taking a fighter's stance, I twirled my sword once in my hand, the sigils on my forearms flaring to life. Adrenaline rushed through my veins, fueling my thirst for revenge. A growl rumbled beside me, and I felt Hank rub against my leg. Two against one. I liked my odds. Glaring at the angel, I gritted, "Tell your master he can take his summons and shove it up his piss hole. Today, I choose violence."

The sicarius' wings fluttered, flapping even harder as he strapped the crossbow over his back and unsheathed a sword.

I winked. "Bring it, asshole."

CHAPTER 17

JAX

Clint put his bionic shoulder under my uninjured arm while my other arm hung limply at my side, a mangled disaster of flesh and bone. "We need to get you someplace safe," he said. "The halls are clogged with hellhounds and infected."

Barely able to keep my head upright, my knees buckled, and I took us both down to the ground. The searing pain in my abdomen and arm dulled with each passing second, overtaken by an overall cold, numbing sensation that radiated to all my extremities. I fell flat on my back, welcoming the reprieve from the pain. I had minutes left to live, if that. The world around me blurred, shadows dancing in my peripheral vision as darkness encroached upon my consciousness.

The thumps of my heart slowed. Each beat counting down to my last breath.

"Stay with me, man," Clint said as he tried to tie a tourniquet around my arm.

"Just leave me," I uttered. "I'm supposed to die here."

"Shut the fuck up, dude. I didn't get rifted across the fucking globe and puked my guts out, only to let you die from a dog bite."

"Save yourself, kid."

He grabbed me by the collar of my T-shirt and lifted my head, his breath inches from my face. "If you die on me, Kate will fucking kill me, for *realz* this time. So fucking fight!"

I fought against the encroaching oblivion, eyes rolling to the back of my head.

He gripped my collar tighter. "You once told me you wished you could make things right. That you could erase all the harm you'd caused the world, all the pain you caused Kate. You can't fucking die until you right all those wrongs, Jax. For Kate. For your child!"

His words stirred something inside my failing heart. The darkness I'd tried to ignore—tried to hide for so long—I couldn't deny it any longer. When Astaroth died, he left a piece of himself within me. A part that ebbed and flowed, that tempted me at every turn to give in to that darkness. To call upon his demonic magic and corrupted powers.

He'd preyed on my fears and insecurities, and I'd believed him—still did. Without his power, I was just a man. A man incapable of protecting those I loved. But all my mistakes had led me here, to this moment.

Clint was right; I needed to live. For Kate, for my son. Damn the fucking consequences. In this new world, the parameters had changed. There was no white picket fence. No nine-to-five job. No soccer games on the weekends. No vacations to Disney World. No Friday night dates.

All we had was violence and hunger and pain. Yet, we'd managed to survive this long, and I was not about to give up. Not on us. Not on my family.

But to fight monsters, we needed monsters.

"Help me sit," I said, my body trembling.

Clint positioned me against a wall. "Tell me what you need."

I heaved a labored breath. "Find Mikha'el. I don't have much time."

"What are you planning to do?"

"Something I pray I don't regret. Now go!"

Clint sprinted down the darkened corridor. I still couldn't believe the kid was alive, and hopefully, I would survive this ordeal so I could hear the story of how he came to sport an empyrean bionic arm. Lucky bastard.

Gulping in a mouthful of air, I closed my eyes and mentally thumbed through images of my worn leather-bound grimoire, the memory of what laid scribed in its pages whispering ancient secrets of forbidden magic. Devotion to my mother once drove me to the dark arts, but now, it was desperation that made me seek those dark arts again—to save myself from the clutches of death. To save my family from the horrors I helped unleash into their world.

Once I remembered the spell I needed, I used my blood to trace the intricate sigils in a half circle around me, every movement requiring too much energy. My voice cracked with exhaustion. "By the blood of the fallen, by the darkness that engulfs, I summon thee, Mammon, O Spirit of the forgotten world. Throne of the First Sphere, ruler of Samael's House of Greed, and bind thee to my soul."

A surge of unearthly energy crackled through the air, swirling around me like a tempest. My hands trembled, the ancient words of the angels spilling from my lips as I repeated my

summoning incantation. The veil between realms wavered, and a sinister presence

slithered into existence.

I prayed Clint was on his way back with Mikha'el, or I was about to grant another of Hell's most ruthless demons untethered access to our world.

CHAPTER 18
KATE

The assassin angel loomed before me, his monstrous-sized wings outstretched. His feathers shimmered under the moonlight, gleaming like sharpened blades. A prideful glint danced in his eyes, and his sensuous lips curled into a serpentine smile. This was a battle he believed he would win.

I tightened my grip on the hilt of my sword, the radiant steel pulsating with bright energy, its thirst for angel blood humming in my veins. Hank stood at my side, his ears alert and his fierce gaze locked on the murderous creature.

Before I could take my next breath, the angel lunged at me with blinding speed. I sidestepped his attack, rolling away from the swing of his blade. His wings beat with a rhythmic flurry, creating a gust of air that stirred around me, almost knocking me off balance.

He swung at me again, but I met his blade with mine, the clash of steel reverberating throughout the sacred space, sparks showering over my head. The angel snarled, his strength matched only by his rage as he landed blow after blow, thrusting me backward.

I fell on my ass, but I scurried back to my feet, cutting through the air with my sword and blowing a strand of hair from my face. Latching on to his gaze, I said, "I can do this all day."

Feet first, the creature dove for the ground, landing with a thunderous explosion that blasted through the remaining pews, blowing out even more stained-glass windows. A crater the size of a minivan formed beneath him. Hank and I managed to shield ourselves behind a pillar as splintered wood raced toward us, missing us by a millisecond.

"Seditious human," the angel hollered. "You fight with a warrior's heart, but this defiance is unavailing. You triumph only in irritating me further."

"Are you suggesting I simply give up and let you take me to your surly leader?" I answered from behind the pillar with a bit of snark, signaling to Hank to stay put. I could already see the look in my shepherd's eyes. He wanted to play our old game, where one of us created a diversion and the other ran in for the kill. Last time we did that, we ended up in this mess. I shook my head at him and pursed my lips.

Hank let out a tiny whine.

I silenced him with a hard stare.

"I do not wish to harm you, Daughter of Eve."

"Delivering me to the king of Hell so he can punish my soul for eternity sounds like harm to me. No thanks. I'd rather take my chances with his assassins. I have zero qualms about harming *you*."

"So be it," he said, swinging his sword against the pillar where Hank and I had been hiding. Debris fell over us as the angel practically destroyed the column. I dashed out of the way, half expecting the entire ceiling to collapse.

I tripped on a piece of plaster and fell backward, cutting my palms on the fallen debris. With both hands on the hilt of his sword, the assassin raised his weapon. I had no time to get out of the way and instinctively put my arm out, as if that would protect me from getting hacked in half.

He slammed down hard, but before his blade could cut my flesh, the sigils on my arms flared to life, and a luminous, golden shield domed around me, blocking his swing. The small force field was covered in symbols I didn't recognize, but it reminded me of the shield Mikha'el had created to protect himself.

The angel looked confused for a second, and Hank took the opportunity to make his move. Leaping forward, his jaws clamped down on the angel's leg, right behind the knee joint— the one place not protected by armor. The attack distracted the angel for a fleeting moment.

Seizing my chance, I lunged, my sword aimed right at his heart. I only prayed my blade could cut through Empyrean armor.

The angel twisted, narrowly evading the fatal blow, but his evasion was not swift enough. The tip of my sword pierced his shoulder, eliciting a blood-curdling cry of pain. Tendrils of some smoky essence seeped from the wound, swirling around us in an otherworldly dance.

Enraged, the angel retaliated with a ferocious onslaught, his wings propelling him toward me. I stood my ground, my eyes blazing with an inner fire. I channeled the celestial energy coursing through my blood and summoned the brilliant shield once again, repelling his assault.

I knew what I needed to do. There was one sure way to kill an angel. Adrenaline raced through my heart as I focused all my strength and power and ran straight toward the column situated beside him. I leaped and jumped off the pillar, spinning in the air above the angel before landing right behind him.

He'd not been expecting that, so he'd not bothered to tuck his wings. With unnatural speed, I hacked down one wing, then swung again against the other, delivering the final strike.

A battle cry erupted from my lungs as I drove my sword deep into the fallen angel's back, skewering his spine.

A blinding surge of energy detonated from inside his body, consuming him in a burst of light, the force of the blast flinging me back against one of the pillars. Bone crunched inside my body, and I knew I'd broken a rib, or at least fractured it.

Even though I could heal faster than a human, I still felt pain like one.

The angel's twisted form dissolved into a macabre puff of pixie dust composed of ashes and embers. Particles of what remained of the assassin floated in the air, coating my hair, lashes, and shoulders. Holding on to my side, I winced as I knelt to grab my blood-slicked weapon off the ground and heaved a depleted sigh, shaking the grotesque debris off me.

Hank approached, panting but wagging his tail. I ran my hand through his fur, grateful for his unwavering loyalty. I wished I'd had treats to offer him. Heaven knew the poor thing was probably running on fumes. Never mind the fact he looked thinner than I remembered. I didn't even know when he'd last eaten or drank. Damn this fucking war. Once this shit was over, I would get him all the dog treats and toys I could find. I rubbed his head and let him lick my face. "You're the goodest boy that ever gooded, you know that. So proud of you, buddy."

A gut-curdling scream reverberated through the church. It sounded male, like the person was experiencing inexplicable agony. It sounded like… Oh my God.

Mikha'el… I called for the archangel. *Please tell me you've found Jax and Luke.*

Got held up… he grunted, as if I'd caught him at a bad moment. *It's a massacre out here, Katherine. Samael's knights had a dormant sect planted right under the Guardians' noses.*

My lungs caved, and I leaned against the pillar for support. Amada had been right. This wasn't a war… it was an extermination. *Mikha'el, please tell me you found them…*

When I didn't hear a reply, the inside of my chest thumped harder than a drum.

Mikha'el? Mikha'el!

When my calls were answered with more silence, I sprinted for the double doors at the opposite side of the nave, afraid he'd found them but didn't have good news—that the scream I'd just heard had come from Jax. Heart in my throat, I stumbled when Mikha'el's voice entered my mind once again. *Katherine. Clint. He's... here.*

I tripped on a broken slab of splintered wood when I heard those words, almost face-planting. I held on to my still-healing rib as I climbed back to my feet, confused, chest heaving from the shock. *What do you mean he's here? Clint's dead.*

He's very much alive and anointed.

Anointed? How could Clint even be alive? And how was he in Spain? *Mikha'el, where are you? I'll come meet you.*

Can't talk. Jax needs my help.

A numbing cold spread throughout my entire body, rooting me to the church floor. The scream. It *had* been him. God. What had happened to make him scream like that? What if something had happened to the baby?

Damn it, Mikha'el, tell me where you are!

Stay safe, Katherine. I'll find you.

Stay safe? Did he think I would actually just hide somewhere while Samael's minions rained hell upon us? While Jax and Luke were out there needing help?

Mikha'el!

Again, utter silence.

Fuck this. Sometimes when you needed to get shit done, you were better off doing it yourself. Tightening my ponytail, I dashed back to the tabernacle and ringed the pendants around my neck. If Beleth wanted these stones, let him find me. I was ready to dispatch that motherfucker back to the netherworld. As I was about to go running back toward the dormitories, the double doors blew open, cracking the wood. I put my arms up to shield my face from the pointy shards shooting in my direction, and Hank hid behind me.

Geez. How much wood was gonna get thrown at me today?

When I lowered my arms, I tried holding back the gasp that trickled from my lips.

Fucking perfect. I didn't mean I wanted him to find me right *now*.

Accompanied by a pair of Nightcrawlers and another sicarius, Beleth stood at the threshold of the church dressed in polished armor, like he belonged in Mikha'el's army. Though tucked, his glorious silver wings still shimmered. He could have spirited them away, but his pride practically oozed from his pores—if angels even had pores since their skin was as smooth as marble. He knew he looked powerful and magnificent, and he wanted to make sure I knew it, too.

Last time I saw him, he was still undergoing his transformation. Now, no one would guess this was the Horseman of Death. No longer the grotesque being once born from the depths of hell, he was fully restored to his angelic beauty. He stood at over seven feet tall, with curly, black hair cascading to his shoulders from under his war helmet, and his lustrous black skin covered a chiseled jawline. Decked out in silver- and gold-plated steel, the large frame of his muscled body was even more impressive than I remembered.

And those eyes that once shone bright red with hatred now glinted like varnished aquamarine, beautiful yet cold and empty. He looked around the church, taking note of all the destruction. His gaze paused over me for a lingering moment, perhaps for dramatic effect. Lips thinned, he squared his shoulders as he sucked in a colossal breath. He'd wanted to look unperturbed, but the displeasure tracing across the lines of his forehead was evident the instant he removed his helmet.

He must've either seen the discarded crossbow and sword, or he'd simply surmised what had transpired—that I'd just defeated one of his assassins.

"Still a nuisance, I see," he said with a sneer.

I shrugged. "And you're still an insufferable asshole."

His wings fluttered slightly. "There's a place in hell for women just like you."

I wiped sweat from my brow and huffed. I was not really in the mood for small talk or dumb insults. Kinda just wanted to get to the part where we beat the shit out of each other already. I looked at my wrist, mock-checking the time. "Do tell, Beleth. I'm sure you're dying to let me know all the horrible things you plan to do to me. But make it quick, eh? I have shit to do."

Like rescuing my husband and child.

"You bellicose woman," he snarled. "I prefer to show you." With a quick nod, he signaled for the beasts flanking his side to attack.

Hank growled beside me, the rumble grounding me in my defiance of this soulless beast. With a snarl of my own, I gripped the hilt of my sword, letting all my hatred for these demons consume me. "Let's dance, you over-hyped, insidious worm."

CHAPTER 19

JAX

Wheezing, I lay on the cold stone floor of the now desecrated church, my body battered and broken. The acrid scent of death hung heavy in the air, a chilling reminder of the world I'd helped tear apart. With each labored heartbeat, icy pain coursed through my veins, highlighting the cruel reality of how fragile my life truly was. The blood pouring from my wounds pooled around me as I clung to the last vestiges of hope I had left.

Kate, Luke. They were the only reasons why I hadn't welcomed death with open arms. The only reasons why I continued to fight. The only reasons why I would sell my soul to this demon.

The air crackled as the fallen angel materialized before me in a cloud of dark energy, its disembodied form shrouded in shadows that seemed to devour the meager pre-dawn light penetrating the canopy of the apple tree in the middle of the courtyard. Fear and anticipation mingled within me, an unholy cocktail that consumed my thoughts. Would he accept my bargain, or would he finish the job and claim my death?

No point in questioning my decision, though. There was no turning back now.

Looming over me, his eyes burned red with disgust. "I recognize the stench of your corroded soul, mortal." His voice echoed through the desolate church, a haunting melody that sent shivers down my spine. "You betrayed us, yet you dare ask me to bind myself to you."

"I only mean to offer myself as your vessel, Mammon," I gasped, my plea filled with desperation. "Heal my wounds. Grant me your strength and power. In return, you shall have a host to wreak your havoc."

Mammon chuckled, his sinister laugh a ghoulish affirmation of the holy crime I was about to commit. He drew closer, the gleam of his jagged toothed grin made my entire body tremble. He recognized this was an opportunity he could not resist. Despite his allegiance to his king, there was something far stronger than loyalty—the desire to live.

"Imprudent human. Do you understand what you offer me—a prince of Hell?"

I wheezed again, each breath hurting more than the last. "I understand that, as you are not one of Samael's lieutenants, you were not given a chance to be reborn—to be made whole again." I paused, my vision darkening with every passing second. "Yet, you are a Throne," I went on, trying to convince this demon to take the bait. "An angel of the First Sphere. You deserve more than the lordship Samael gave you in a realm where only the wicked go to suffer."

"I am Fallen, but I am not a betrayer."

Fuck. Since when did demons have a conscience? "Taking what is rightfully yours doesn't make you a betrayer; it makes you mighty. Come. Bind thyself to me. I don't have much time left."

He closed his eyes as if summoning memories from a distant past.

Come on, take the bait. Take the bait, you fucking scum.

Then, before I could take my next weakened breath, his shadowy form plunged into my chest with the force of a sledgehammer, breaking my ribs in the process as he dug into my core, searching for my soul. I screamed so loudly, I swore I cracked the church's foundation. He entwined his essence with mine, his power flowing through my veins, a sickening mixture of ecstasy and misery.

My mind splintered and the agony made me question my resolve. I'd willingly invited a monster into my body—again, and after everything I'd endured with Astaroth. After all my promises to Kate, I had failed. Because I was just a mortal man.

He mended my body as he shredded parts of my soul away. Bit by bit, we became one and the same, sharing a body, a heart, a consciousness. But as he wove himself into my mortal flesh, I realized the magnitude of my mistake. Astaroth had been the Horseman of War. He'd been powerful beyond anything I could have imagined, but he'd been a pond compared to the raging ocean of Mammon's power.

I'd struggled to contain Astaroth, but at least I'd managed to keep him from fully possessing me from the beginning. Mammon would not be that easy. In fact, containing him on my own would be practically impossible if Mikha'el didn't show up soon.

The beast laughed, the deep timbre thundering inside my chest. ***Your fate is sealed, mortal. You belong to me now. Samael will be pleased.***

I tried fighting his compulsion, but he took my mind and threw it inside a dark cell. He was about to close the door when a blinding light pierced through the shadows, banishing the encroaching darkness.

For a brief second, I was able to open my eyes of my own volition and saw a bright figure lean over my body, his wings outstretched and radiant.

"Mikha'el?" I said hoarsely, relief masking the horror of the unearthly distortion of my voice. "Mammon… he's… inside."

Mikha'el's eyes widened, horror etching across his gaze. He, too, understood the magnitude of my mistake. "In the name of the Most High," Mikha'el's voice boomed, cutting through the suffocating gloom. "I command you, Mammon, release this human from your clutches."

The demon roared in defiance, his hold on me tightening. The battle for my soul raged within me, a clash of holy and infernal forces threatening to tear me apart.

I thrashed with such unnatural might, I would have broken every bone had the demon not been fused to my body. Mikha'el threw one of his large palms against my head, pinning me down as he recited verses in Latin mixed with his angelic tongue. My spine bowed as the force of his words struck me like a bolt of lightning, temporarily severing the tenuous connection between Mammon and me.

No longer convulsing, I lay under his spell, motionless. "Clint," he called out. "Rip off his shirt. Now."

Mammon growled inside me as a cell door opened in my mind—the same one he'd tried to push me through when he first entered my body. Except this time, he was the prisoner.

"Hand me one of your arrows," Mikha'el told the kid. "Now hold down his arms. This is going to hurt."

Fuck. What? No more…

But my thoughts were cut off by the searing pain digging into my chest as Mikha'el used the tip of one of Clint's empyrean steel arrows to carve a sigil onto my bare chest. My entire body arched, but Clint did his best to hold me down.

Mikha'el's voice rang with authority as he chanted, "*Eprecare Deum pacis, ut conterat Mammon sub pedibus nostris, ne ultra valeat captivos tenere homines, et Ecclesiae nocere.*"

Mammon's consciousness was pushed into the cell, writhing and shrieking as Mikha'el shackled it with his words and closed the door shut.

I collapsed to the floor, gasping for air, while Mikha'el and Clint still held me down.

"Jax, are you with me?" the archangel asked.

Vision blurred, I simply stared up at him, unable to find my voice.

"Jax, I need you to tell me it's you."

Little by little, sensation returned to my body, and I could feel my fingers, my hands. I wiggled my toes and took a deep breath. The pain lancing my body was gone, even the burning on my chest had dissipated. Finally, I nodded. "It's me." But for how long? Though Mammon was in that mental cell, I felt him pushing against the barrier.

"Kate…" I said. "Is she okay?"

Mikha'el helped me stand, though a bit forcefully. "Yes. But we must hurry. The sicarii are here, and I don't think they only came for the baby."

I wobbled on my feet and had to brace myself against the wall. "Talia… I need to find her. She has Luke."

"Have you any idea what you've done?" he chided. Though I knew what he was referring to, I had hoped he would save this conversation for later.

"I know. It was dumb, but I had no other choice," I said, checking over the areas where I'd been shot or clawed, but mended flesh now covered all the wounds. The sigil Mikha'el had carved remained a tender burned scar that would forever mar my chest.

"You had a choice," he said, eyeing me intently. "Death is not the end, Jax."

Still a little off kilter, I wobbled as I tried to square off with the angel. When I'd been bleeding and seconds from death, I might have experienced a moment where doubt almost got the best of me, where I almost gave up, but I didn't. I fought against my impending end, reminded of everything I had to live for. "Dying is not an option," I said. "We both know I was brought back from death for a reason. Kate needs me, as does Luke."

The angel drew close, jabbing a finger into my scarred chest. "Mammon is not a soldier, Jax. He was a Throne, one of the most powerful First Sphere angels. There's a reason Samael gave him a lordship in Hell instead of making him one of his lieutenants. Why he chose to not give him a vessel."

Clint looked between us, confused. "Why?"

"Because if given the chance," I said with a side glance, "Mammon would wield the kind of power that could rival Samael's. It's why I chose him. His ambition for more power is the reason I hoped he'd take the bait."

Clint adjusted the crossbow over his back. "What bait?"

"I never intended to actually give him full control of my body. I needed his power to heal me and give me the strength required to fight against Beleth and his assassins."

Clint's brow creased, a sense of understanding filling his eyes. "And you needed me to find Mikha'el so he could trap him inside you without him being able to take full control…"

"And now you've given it a taste of life," Mikha'el said, his voice rough. His anger toward what I did vibrated off him like a tidal wave, making even the shadows cower deeper into the corners of the courtyard. "He's not going to stay shackled for long. Do you even understand the calamity of what you've done? What's going to happen when he breaks free of the mental prison I put him in?"

"I'm not going to allow that."

"You can't be sure of that. And how do you plan to get rid of him? You think you can just keep dying and coming back?"

I knew my actions were going to come at a high price, but I'd done this for her. For my son.

Hadn't I?

"I'll worry about that when the time comes," I said, unable to waste another minute arguing about it. "What's done is done. Right now, I need to find my son."

"The baby is missing?" Clint asked, twirling the arrow Mikha'el had borrowed to carve into my chest.

"A member of the Devil's Army took him," Mikha'el said.

"I saw a group of armed individuals down the east wing of the dormitories after Chaz and I were rifted here. That could be them. Let's go."

"Wait. Chaz is here, too?" I asked, placing a hand on his shoulder and halting him mid-step.

Clint shifted his gaze toward the archangel. "When you sent the distress call, Remiel rifted both of us here."

"Where's Remiel now?" Mikha'el asked. "He hasn't checked in."

"He rifted us right into the middle of the zombie horde surrounding the church, unfortunately. We got split up. I was able to radio Chaz right before I found you. The Marine is hurt, but he's alive. I don't know where Remiel is, though. Last I saw him, he was facing off with some huge ass motherfucker. Not even sure what kind of demon it was, but definitely not anything I've ever seen before."

Mikha'el and I exchanged looks. There was no way there were more Bladeheads out there, right?

The look in the archangel's eyes wasn't very promising.

"Is everyone okay back home?" I asked, trying not to think of the possibility of more *carniceros* out there.

Clint gulped, his shoulders tensing. "Gavri'el and the half dozen warriors Mikha'el brought were able to take back the inn, but we were ambushed on our way to the sanctuary." Clint looked at Mikha'el and it seemed he was holding back information.

"Something's happened to Gavri'el…" Mikha'el trailed, voicing Clint's silent words. His chest heaved. "I feared as much when she didn't respond to my call."

Unable to look at the archangel, Clint dropped his chin. "The sicarii took her captive after they… um… killed all your warriors. I'm so sorry. We lost many Guardians as well," Clint went on, his words bitter. "Remiel was the only one left, though he was badly wounded. If it weren't for him, and the fact Gavri'el saved my life by anointing me as a Guardian," he raised his half-bionic arm, "we would've never made it to the sanctuary alive."

"So the girls are safe?" I asked, hopeful for some good news.

His eyes lit up. "Yes. We can talk more about it after, but the sanctuary… It's a real place, Jax. Kate was right."

I turned to the archangel, but his gaze was lost. My heart squeezed. I recognized that look of desperation. "Gavri'el must still be alive," I said. "Why else would they take her captive?"

Mikha'el's hand fell to the hilt of his sword. "That's what I'm afraid of… Samael doesn't do anything unless it's calculated."

"We'll find her."

"Finding Luke and protecting Kate is our mission," he said matter-of-factly, as if trying to convince himself that he wasn't worried about finding Gavri'el.

I went to place a hand on his shoulder, but he flinched away, so I dropped my hand back. "Thank you for saving me from Mammon," I said. "For everything you're doing for Kate and Luke."

"I do it for humanity."

"You do it for love, and that's what matters. We'll find Gavri'el, I promise you that."

The archangel found my gaze, and for the first time since I'd met him, something more than otherworldly flashed in the golden depths of his eyes, something that almost felt *human*. He nodded, his way of thanking me, a lowly human, I supposed.

I accepted it.

"Okay, so what's the plan?" the kid asked, bouncing on his heels.

"If the church is surrounded by a horde, then maybe we can assume the sect is still here," I said.

"Unless there's an underground tunnel system, I don't see any other way to get past all those infected," Clint said.

I nodded. "I wouldn't be surprised if such a system exists, so we need to hurry. This church is huge though, so we're going to need to split up."

He shook his head *no*, unhappy with my plan. "This place is full of d'shiad and infected. I'm a Guardian now; I can help you."

"Jax is right, Clint," Mikha'el said. "We're running out of time. We'll be able to cover more ground if we split up."

Clint looked like he wanted to protest against the archangel, but then thought better of it. It was hard arguing with such an imposing creature. I placed a hand on Clint's still-human shoulder and a wave of tenderness filled my body. God, it felt unreal to know he was still alive. I'd never told him, but I actually loved the son of a bitch. He was like a little brother to me, and to see him breathing before me brought tears to my eyes. I wanted to just squeeze his shoulder, but I drew him in for a hug. "When I thought we'd lost you, kid, it cleaved my heart in two. I need you to know that."

He wrapped his arms around me, patting me on the back. "I love you, too, man."

After a brief moment, we broke from the embrace. We both pretended to cough, wanting to hide the emotion curled around our voices. "Though Mammon is mentally shackled," I said, changing the subject, "I can still tap into his power. So, don't worry about me, kid. Let's just worry about finding the woman who took my son."

He agreed, begrudgingly.

"Mikha'el, you take the south wing," I said. "Clint, you take the east. I'll head west."

"What about the north?" Clint asked.

Mikha'el nodded toward the opposite end of the courtyard. "Kate's still inside the cathedral."

"You're certain?" I asked.

"I just asked her."

I cocked my head and crossed my arms. "Forgot about your little *telepathy* trick," I said, unable to ignore the bitter taste of jealousy sitting on my tongue. "She okay?"

A muscle flexed in the archangel's jaw, like he was trying to choose his words carefully.

"Don't lie to me, commander."

"She's fine," he replied curtly. "Nothing she can't handle."

A spring tightened in my gut. I wanted to trust his words, but my instinct was to protect her.

Mikha'el took me by the shoulders, rooting his gaze to mine. "Jax, I'd be the first one there, you know that. She's strong, and she's not alone. Hank's with her."

I didn't know if it was the tone of his voice or the calmness in his eyes, but I believed his words. Still, unease ran over my skin like hundreds of fire ants. If anyone could hack through demons, it was Kate—but that didn't mean she couldn't use a little hand. "Clint," I said. "Radio Chaz."

Static crackled as the Marine answered. Clint handed me the radio. "Chaz, it's Jax."

"Cap? Damn good to hear your voice, sir."

"Right back at you, big guy. Listen, we don't have a lot of time here. I need you to find Kate. She's under attack in the cathedral."

"Headed there now, but the halls are clogged with infected. And I'm low on ammo."

"You'll need to make every bullet count. We're going to sweep this entire place until we find my son. I need you to hold down the cathedral with Kate until we get there."

"For how long?"

"For as long as it takes. Copy?"

There was a long pause and my stomach almost bottomed out. "Chaz? Do you copy?"

More silence.

Shit. Had we lost Chaz?

"Roger that, cap. But don't be long. Things ain't looking great back here."

Fuck. Not what I needed to hear.

CHAPTER 20
JAX

Mikha'el reassured me that Kate had things under control, though he wouldn't elaborate on her exact situation. I understood why he chose to keep me in the dark—he wanted me focused on finding Luke—but worrying about Kate wasn't a switch I could just shut off. Every particle in my body kept urging me to go after her. I had to force myself to stay on task—finding the fucking blonde-headed hellion who took my son was priority number one.

Before heading our separate ways, Clint handed me one of his pistols. I told him he probably needed it more than I did, but he insisted. I tucked the gun into the waistband of my jeans, but I had no true intentions of using it unless I absolutely needed it. My desire was to use my bare hands to rip apart the people responsible not only for taking Luke, but for massacring all these people.

The sun's morning rays began to penetrate through the stained-glass windows decorating the simple hallways, but inside this once vibrant stone church, there were still plenty of darkened crevices for shadows to lurk. I stayed close to those areas, slinking down corridors, looking for signs of life, but only death greeted me. So many innocents littered the hallways; my heart cracked to see the indiscriminate manner in which the sect members had killed without any regard for the lives they took.

As I came to an intersection, I heard the familiar wet snarls of infected feasting on flesh.

The rage simmering in my core fanned out to all my extremities, feeding my already boiling anger. My skin grew tight around my body as my transformation took form. But drawing even small amounts of power from Mammon weakened the locks to his mental prison. If I wasn't careful, I could inadvertently free him.

A growl rumbled deep in my chest as I flexed my neck and shoulders. Every strand of roping muscle felt sinewy and vigorous, ready to inflict some serious damage. My nails elongated into black claws that could shred through meat and bone, and my eyesight sharpened to a razor-sharp focus, enabling me to see clearly, even in the gloom-soaked corners.

With my heightened speed, I charged at the two infected hunched over a dead body, their mouths dripping with blood, ripped flesh dangling from their teeth. Hands buried inside the poor man's cavity, they pulled out his entrails, chewing on the bloodied mess like they'd been starving for months.

I didn't even give them a chance to flinch. With a swipe of my clawed hand, I tore off the face of the closest infected, spraying black blood all over the wall. The limp carcass dropped with a hard *thud*. Spinning toward the second creature, I seized it by the neck and lifted it off its meal. It tried to claw at me, but I grabbed its wrist and yanked, ripping the arm right off from the shoulder socket. I flung the torn limb down the corridor like I was launching a football.

Black blood spurted out from the massive wound, but the damn thing kept trying to get free. Laughter bubbled out of me as I watched the armless creature squirm in my grip. Blood-red madness hemorrhaged behind my eyes. I didn't want to simply kill this vile being; I wanted to eviscerate it. I tore its head right off, followed by its second arm. I hollered loudly in a frenzied fury, and I prayed with every pulsing fiber in my body that the whole goddamn church had heard me.

That *Talia* had heard me.

Stepping over the discarded bodies, I ran down the hall when a set of chilling screams pierced the eerie quiet.

Shit. Children.

I followed the noise to a small storage room located at the end of the corridor. I gently parted the door open and grinned, blood-thirst skating over my tongue.

Naked, a tall and bony humanoid figure stood in front of a closet, swiping at the door, trying to break through. More screams erupted from inside the closet as the creature managed to punch through the wood.

"Looking for something?" I growled, bearing my claws.

The creature paused, emitting a strange clicking sound as it turned around. Bald-headed, the creature had no eyes, only holes for nostrils and a large, needle-sharp-teeth filled mouth. It emitted more clicking noises, then lunged at me, its lanky form slow but strong. Long, spindly fingers reached for my neck as the creature leapt, landing on top of me and tackling me to the floor.

The demon opened its massive maw and tried chomping on my head, but I managed to keep its snapping jaws away from my face. I tried punching it, but though frail-looking, its bones were solid and holding it back was using up every ounce of strength I had. Mammon purred inside my mind, his voice taunting, nudging me to tap deeper into his power.

No. If I tried summoning more strength, I risked losing myself to him.

The creature's tongue slithered out and licked my face, and the stench of its breath almost knocked me out. "Fuck!" I screamed as my arms trembled. Then I remembered the pistol. With one more heave, I managed to reach behind my back and grabbed the gun, firing off two shots right into its mouth.

Splintered bone, blood, and demon-flesh chunks splattered all over my face as the creature fell dead over my body.

Shit. Guess I had needed the damn pistol after all.

I slid from under the faceless monster and went to check on the children. When I opened the closet door, two young girls, probably no older than ten, screamed and huddled closer together when they saw my face. Of course, why wouldn't they? Covered in demon guts, I looked like a monster myself. My eyes were likely glowing red, which didn't help.

"I'm not going to hurt you," I said, putting my palms up.

They simply held themselves tighter, their eyes wide and filled with terror, tears streaming down their cheeks. They probably didn't understand a word I said, and I didn't know much Spanish, except for some basic words, but not enough to have a conversation.

"*Mi nombre* is Jax" I said, pointing to my chest, this time willing the deadly power surging through my veins to cool down, hoping at least the glow in my eyes would recede.

One of the girls nodded, her dark hair spilling over her eyes. "M-M-Marisol."

The other girl said softly, "Violeta."

I thought about leaving them in the closet and barricading the door, hoping that someone would find them, eventually. But that someone could be a hellhound, an infected, or another of the bony demons. The poor girls trembled, and I didn't have the heart to leave them behind.

I knelt and tried my best to say something in Spanish that could possibly make some sense. "Marisol. Violeta. *Vamos. Vamos* with Jax," I said, pointing to myself. "*Sí?*"

Unblinking, they stared at me and for a brief moment, I thought I'd fucked this up. I was running out of time to find Luke, and here I was, trying to remember Spanish 101 I took in high school. I pointed at the door. "*Vamos*."

This time, they nodded. I extended my hand out to them and thankfully, they reached for it. I put my finger to my lips in the universal expression to keep quiet as we exited the storage room. The halls were eerily quiet, which wasn't necessarily a good sign. I kept the girls right behind me as we made our way down to another courtyard. The girls let out little startled whimpers as we passed a few dead bodies. Some had been severely mangled by claws and teeth; it looked like they had been attacked by hellhounds or the infected.

There was no point in asking the girls to shield their eyes. We needed to keep moving, especially since soon, some of these dead bodies would reanimate.

And just as I predicted, when we passed one of the people laying limp on the floor, a hand flew out and grabbed Marisol's ankle. The little girl screamed as the infected tried to take a bite out of her leg. I managed to step on its skull, stomping on it several times until all that remained was a heap of crushed bones and exploded brains.

The creature's hand loosened, and I was able to take the girl up into my arms, but that's when I noticed that the half dozen or so infected still littering the ground began to reanimate. Fuck. There was no way I could take on all these infected on my own, while also protecting the girls. To fight our way through, I would need to summon Mammon's power.

The demon chuckled inside my head.

The first of the infected wobbled to its feet. The female creature still looked very much like her human self, except for her blackened eyes and animalistic snarl. Her body jerked in an odd way before her dead gaze locked with mine and she charged. With Marisol in my arms, I took Violeta by the hand

and ran toward the center of the courtyard to the large orange tree. Putting Violeta against the tree trunk, I let go of her hand and reached for the pistol, firing off several rounds into the infected, finally nailing her right between the eyes.

The creature flew back, landing hard on the floor. The other five were now rising to their feet. I raised Marisol up into the tallest tree branch I could reach, then lifted Violeta into the tree as well. I didn't need to tell them to climb higher; survival was an instinct.

I spun toward the rising corpses. A freshly turned infected was easier to kill than one who'd been fully transformed into a slimy gray abomination. Problem was, there were five of them, and I wasn't sure I had enough bullets left. Taking a few deep breaths, I reluctantly reached into the cauldron bubbling deep in my core. Mammon's power called to me, beckoning for me to open the door to his cage.

Euphoria swam through me. He was much harder to resist than the Horseman who'd been trapped inside me before. I knew how good it would feel to have his full power running through my veins. The thought was exhilarating, but I clenched my jaw hard, refusing to let him tempt me to take more power than required. All I needed was a little boost. I dipped my fingers into the cauldron and let tendrils of Mammon's power spread through my muscles, enough to let me bulldoze through the poor souls who'd turned into the damned.

Once transformed, I craned my neck and grinned like a lunatic.

Time to play.

As the first of the creatures charged at me, I spun out of its way, then punched my fist through its back, fingers digging through liquified flesh until I found the spine. I gripped the vertebrae hard and yanked, startling myself when I saw I held a blood-dripping, severed chain of bones in my hand. I tossed the bones and heaved from the mind-blowing amount of strength I possessed. Astaroth's power was a distant memory. Mammon… he was on a whole different level of potent force, and fuck if it didn't feel like nirvana.

I moved at incalculable speed, tearing heads from torsos, pulling hearts from chests, and outright obliterating the freshly-born infected like they were nothing but meat sacks sent to the butcher block. By the time I was done, I was covered in so much black blood, I looked like I had bathed in tar.

The girls looked down from the tree, their bodies trembling. A reddish filter blurred my vision. It had to be the rage consuming me from within. I could hear my heart thumping a million miles a minute inside my chest, as if it would soon explode. Taking a few deep breaths, I slowed my heart rate to even beats.

There was no way I could continue this mission while also protecting the girls, especially in this condition. When consumed by blood-lust, I could inadvertently hurt them. The morning sun would soon cover the courtyard in light. They were safer in the tree than they were with me. I put my palms up and prayed they would understand me. "*Esperar*," I said, hoping I'd used the proper term for *wait*. "*Esperar, aqui.* Okay?"

The girls nodded. I didn't know how to tell them I would be back for them; I just hoped they'd seen it in my eyes.

I took off down another wing of the school, passing more classrooms that had been converted into dwellings. Amada hadn't been kidding when she said this had not only been the biggest Catholic church in the world, but also one of the biggest boarding schools in the country.

Voices echoed from up ahead, and I slowed my pace, staying low and hidden in the shadows. A small group of people stood in a circle in the middle of the hallway. Dressed in red robes and holding black lit candles, they chanted Latin words that were sadly all too familiar to me. I recognized the individuals as sect worshippers. I hid behind a wall and peered over a corner, and that's when I heard the soft coo of a baby. Anger and fear settled over my chest like a lead ball pressing on my lungs. Laying on the floor on a small blanket, Luke whimpered, lips shaking as if he was cold.

He lay in the middle of a chalk-drawn offering circle inscribed with angelic sigils. Fuckers were marking Luke as an offering to Samael. Since Kate had refused to willingly do the offering, these assholes were using a blood ritual to mark him as his. All they needed now were the four stones to complete the transmutation.

My hands burned as a red, glowing light pulsed right under my skin. Baffled, I stared at the energy crackling between my fingers. I'd never experienced this kind of power with Astaroth. But right now, I didn't care how it manifested, or what it made me capable of doing. Right now, the only thought swimming in my mind was that of total destruction.

I was about to push out of the shadows when a figure stepped into the circle, the flame emitting from the candles in the sec members' hands illuminated the face under the hooded cloak.

Talia. A growl reverberated in my throat.

Holding a silver chalice, she drank what I already knew to be human blood, probably from the individual slumped dead against the wall. "Hear me, O dark lord," she began in an American East Coast accent.

Odd. I thought these members were all Spaniards. That was a damn good cover up if they managed to dupe Amada. But why had these members seeded themselves here?

"We offer you this vessel in honor of our unyielding servitude," she went on. "That this flesh may finally grant you entry into our world. For your love and glory, we praise thee."

"For your love and glory, we praise thee," the rest responded in unison.

Every muscle in my body coiled with the need to cut their throats and drain them of every ounce of their wretched life. My chest inflated as I flexed my red-glowing hands. If I charged at them now, I might not only hurt them, but Luke in the process. Or I risked Talia taking him and running again.

Reeling in the monster wanting to rip from under my skin, I focused on the pulsing energy vibrating in my palms. I had no fucking clue how to use it. I checked the pistol Clint had given me. I had four rounds left, and there were six sect members, including Talia.

"Priestess," a male sect member said. "We need the stones. Without them, we can't summon him through."

"Beleth is working on finding the stones."

"Amada is dead," another sect member added, her voice grave. "You killed her, knowing she was the only one who knew the location of the stones."

"Amada was a nuisance," Talia snapped. "I couldn't wait to be rid of her. Do you understand how irritating it was to take orders from a Guardian? I took pleasure in her death, as I will take pleasure in yours if you don't shut your pie-hole. When together, the power of the stones is magnified. Beleth will be able to track them."

I used the fact they were currently distracted in conversation to blend into the darkness, my body flush against the stone wall as I approached.

"What of the archangel and the woman?"

"They are currently preoccupied doing what they do best, trying to save the poor, helpless souls trapped in this church. Idiots. With a horde of infected, a pack of hellhounds, and a pair of clickers on the hunt, they'll be busy for quite some time. No one is coming for the stupid little baby. Unfortunately, the dreadful thing hasn't shut up since I took him, so hopefully, Beleth shows up with the stones soon."

"And Jax?" the male asked. "I've hated that son of a bitch since I first joined the Army under Edith. Always knew he didn't have the balls to be a Horseman. At least he helped open the gates. Asshole."

Interesting…

"Well, he's dead. I put a bullet in his gut. Probably zombie dinner by now."

They all shared a chuckle. "Fucker got what he deserved," someone chirped.

"Not quite," I said from behind the woman who'd been challenging Talia. "I ain't dead yet." Using my clawed hand, I cut across her neck. Startled, she was no longer able to speak as she clutched her neck, blood oozing from her slashed carotid artery. As she collapsed, I shot her smug neighbor point-blank between the eyes.

Thanks to the speed Mammon afforded me, I was able to reach down to grab Luke before Talia did, then I shot the third sect member in the chest and the fourth in the face.

"You look like you've seen a ghost, priestess," I said as I approached the slack-jawed hellion.

Stepping backward, she went to utter a word, but instinctively, I reached out and the red-glowing energy still pulsating under my skin extended out like a red smoky tendril that wrapped itself around her neck, choking her.

Willing the smoky rope as I would my own hand, I lifted her off the ground and watched her flail and fight against my grip. It was mostly a quiet death. I thought I'd feel crazed satisfaction—that I would squeeze so hard, I'd crack her neck—but all I did was stare, passionless, like she was nothing but an insect crushed in my palm.

When the life from her eyes completely expunged, I let go and dropped her body like a sack of discarded trash. Luke began to wail in my arms. I tried rocking him, tried speaking quietly, but he only screamed louder. He needed Kate. Wrapping him tight in the blanket, I made sure he was nestled close to my chest as I ran down the hallway back toward the courtyard where I'd left the girls.

When I arrived, I came to a screeching halt inside the sunlit courtyard. On the opposite end, and protected by the shadows still hugging the corridor, a set of hellhounds pawed at the ground, growling up at the girls in the tree. Marisol and Violeta had climbed even higher, but I knew if those hellhounds decided to brave the sun, they could leap onto that tree in one breath.

I approached slowly, hoping the beasts would stay focused on the girls while I figured out a point of attack, but I accidentally stepped on a flowerpot, drawing their immediate attention. Shit. The beasts now growled louder, inching ever closer to the edge of the courtyard. Their hide sizzled when they tried testing the sunlight, but they retreated immediately, whimpering. Perhaps they wouldn't brave the sun, but they could certainly wait out the day hours until the shadows claimed the courtyard again.

There was no chance in Hell I would have us wait there that long. We needed an escape route ASAP. The power I'd used to take out the sect members had drained me to the point my knees wobbled. The red energy no longer pulsed through my hands, and I knew that if I were to fight off these beasts barehanded, I'd have to do it with my mortal strength.

The four of us would likely die in that exchange. This meant I would need to summon more of Mammon's power, but I could already feel the door to his mental prison coming off the hinges. One more use of his essence, and I'd get him that much closer to taking full control of my body.

The demon laughed. ***Did you think using my power would be that easy, human? That there would be no consequences for your actions?***

I've been fine so far.

When I break free of this cage, I will consume your soul. There will be nothing left of you inside this body.

Astaroth tried threatening me, too. You know where that got him.

Astaroth left his imprint inside you, human. Where do you think that rage comes from? That darkness that calls to you? Your thirst to kill? It lives in your heart because of him. I only feed it.

Shut the fuck up.

He laughed again, but said nothing else as I struggled to think of a way to fight off these beasts with minimal risk to the children.

Fuck. Fuck. Fuck.

Luke's cries were now ear-piercing, and the sound seemed to drive the hellhounds into a frenzy. I didn't know how much longer the light would keep the beasts trapped in the corridor. It was time to make a run for it. But if I stood little to no chance of outrunning those beasts with my mortal stamina, then the girls had even less of a chance. At least from the way the beasts were roaring, they were more interested in me and Luke than they were the girls.

I hoped.

Without any more bullets, the pistol was useless, so I tossed it and put my palms up to the girls, hoping they understood to stay up in the tree.

Mammon chuckled.

Fucker. He knew my intentions.

God damn him.

He already did.

Ignoring his bait, I stirred the cauldron of his power, reminding myself to only take a drop, enough to outrun these beasts. I closed my eyes, feeling its warmth begging me to dive deep into its bottomless abyss. If I submersed myself entirely, I would be invincible. But this power was utter chaos, and it would burn me up like a paper set aflame. With a gasp, I pulled myself out of the cauldron, and when I opened my eyes, the world was bathed in red.

With zero time to waste, I took off in a sprint down the opposite end of the corridor, immediately getting absorbed by the darkened halls. Holding Luke tightly against my chest, I didn't bother to look back, but I knew the beasts didn't even take a second to decide I was the prey they wanted to chase. Galloping at full speed, their claws scraped against the stone floors and their yelps echoed off the walls.

The stained-glass windows lining the hallways didn't provide enough illumination to deter the beasts, so I did the only thing I could. I concentrated on the pulsing energy I knew lay dormant in my hand until it came to life, then I used short bursts of smoky ribbons as projectiles to shatter the windows. One by one, the glass panes exploded in a kaleidoscope of colors as they fell to the ground. Missing a couple of times, I destroyed chunks of walls instead, debris flying in all directions.

The loud yelps and smell of burning flesh were indication enough that my trick had worked—maybe not at stopping the beasts from coming after me, but it had slowed them down. I kept running, my legs burning with every step. I had no idea in which direction I was headed, but I just kept shattering window after window. Still, even though the beasts had slowed, their roars reached my ears.

They would burn themselves to a crisp just to get to me.

When I turned a corner, I lost my footing trying to avoid a mangled corpse, and I went flying. Curling my body around Luke, I braced myself for the fall. I landed hard on my back and felt things crack, but at least nothing broke and Luke was safe.

But the fall cost us precious seconds, and before I could take my next breath, a hellhound launched itself at us. I closed my eyes and curled my body over Luke again, this time protecting him under me and exposing my back to the beast. But as I lay there curled over Luke, expecting to be shredded by claws and teeth, all I heard was a loud buzz, like when a bug gets zapped by an electric bug trap, except this insect was six hundred pounds of muscle.

Lifting my head, I watched as chunks of hellhound flesh got fried and flung in all directions when the beast bounced off the golden shield domed around me and Luke.

What the hell…?

As quickly as it formed, the dome died, and that's when the second beast rounded the corner, heading right for us. I closed my eyes and wrapped my arms tightly around Luke, expecting the worst, but then I felt a rush of air fly over me.

Gently prying one eye open, I caught a blur of someone jumping over me.

The figure barrel rolled to a stop, and on his knees, fired off his crossbow right into the beast's skull.

The golden-brown shaggy hair and shiny bionic arm gave him away.

Clint jumped back to his feet, a massive grin on his face as the beast's dead body slid all the way to the tip of his combat boots, leaving a trail of blood in its wake. The kid reached out and plucked the arrow from the beast's skull, then cleaned it off on his pants before reloading his crossbow.

I looked down at Luke to make sure he was okay. That's when I noticed the sigils covering his arms were pulsing with a dim white light. Holy shit. Had he done this? Had he somehow sensed danger and erected the protective dome?

"You alright?" the kid asked, helping me up.

"I think so. That was some superhero stunt you pulled. Should I call you Hawkeye from now on?"

He smiled again. "Kid's fine."

"Where are the others?" I asked, worried when I noticed he was by himself.

"I haven't seen anyone. I was running back toward the courtyard to see if I could find you. Looks like you found the baby. What of the sect members?"

"They won't be a problem anymore." Luke let out another wail, and I knew I had to find Kate ASAP. "I'll head to the cathedral. I need you to head down this corridor until you find a courtyard. There are two girls up in a tree. Can you make sure to bring them somewhere safe?"

"You got it."

"And kid…"

"Yeah?"

"Stay safe."

He winked. "Right back at you, man."

With a nod, we parted ways. But as I took off running again, a tortured scream pierced the church, echoing through the walls like a ripple of energy.

Kate…

CHAPTER 21

KATE

Eyes glowing red and fangs bared, the two beasts slinked toward us. Hank mirrored my movements as I slowly took a few steps back, both of us tracking the nightcrawlers' approach. Sword drawn, I tried summoning the shield, but for some reason, I couldn't figure out how the damn thing worked.

Ears perked, Hank growled. The monsters were now about eight feet away. They could easily close that distance with one leap. I did a quick scan of my surroundings. The other set of double doors was across the church. There was no way we could outrun the beasts. The crypt was behind me, but it had been clogged with devoured before.

Shit.

Beleth chuckled, wicked and cold, likely reading the despair on my face. "There's no need for this show of bravery, Katherine. Why fight to save a people already lost? Join us. Help us rebuild a new world, a better world, with Samael as your king."

Because that's just what I wanted right now after being abandoned by our so-called God—another king to bow down to and worship. "Hard pass. Not trading one despot for another."

"Harsh words to speak when referring to your Creator. I was never a blind devotee myself, but I still managed to possess a stout amount of respect for Him. Alas, it is to be expected of your kind, crude and contentious. Hence why I am here, to help wipe your existence from the book of life. You never deserved this world. Makes no sense why Samael cares to keep you alive. Though, I can't assure you my pets will honor his wishes, stubborn little monsters they are."

Some help here, Mike… Things are about to get kinda hairy.

Still looking for Luke. You'll need to hold the cathedral a while longer.

My insides clenched. My baby was still missing, and I was stuck here fighting off these pains in the asses instead of joining the search. *And Jax?*

The archangel didn't respond, but I didn't have a chance to get pissed at him for being so selective with what he shared with me, because Hank lunged for one of the beasts before I could blink. He must have picked up on the minute signals the nightcrawlers gave off right before they attacked. As fierce as Hank was, he was half the size of one of those beasts, and the nightcrawler took a wide swipe with his massive, clawed paw, knocking Hank down.

I screamed, dread and anger firing up a forge inside my chest. I dove in front of the beast right before he pounced on my dog. I put my arm out and infused all my will into summoning the shield, shutting my eyes and bracing for the impact in case I failed. A shockwave rippled through me as the beast bounced off the electrified wall that domed around me and Hank.

The smell of burned hair and flesh filled the church.

He hadn't just bounced off; his body had exploded into hundreds of burnt chunks. The other beast circled us, clawing at the floor. Maintaining the shield took an immense amount of concentration, which consumed my energy. Hank pushed up to his feet, but he kept one paw tucked.

I checked for claw marks and blew a sigh of relief when I saw his wounds mending. The process was slow, though. Hank was now out of commission.

Then the shield flickered and died. Fuck. I definitely needed to learn how to use my power better.

Snarling, the nightcrawler rushed toward us, but I quickly picked up a slab of broken pew wood lying beside me and used it as a makeshift shield. It worked to deter his blow, but the impact sent me flying. I lost the shield during my fall, and the beast roared as if already claiming triumph. The only good thing about my predicament was that the beast was completely focused on me and had forgotten all about Hank. The nightcrawler leapt and landed on top of me, jaw clamping around my shoulder.

I hollered in agony as it shook its head, digging its jagged fangs deeper into my tissue. My world spun in and out of focus from the intense pain as bones broke and muscles tore. Unable to keep my fingers wrapped around the hilt of my sword, my weapon slipped from my hand.

The beast thrashed his head harder, like a dog trying to de-stuff a toy. I punched and kicked, but the demon animal was too strong. I screamed again as a slash ripped across my chest when the nightcrawler pinned me down with its massive paw. Heaven save me. He was about to start pulling flesh from my bones.

I couldn't die like this. God, not like this. Teeth clattering, I clung to this world with every remaining ounce of willpower that remained as darkness tried to wrap its icy fingers around my heart. Then a gunshot rang out, and the next thing I knew, I was covered in warm wetness and the nightcrawler's full weight fell on top of me, forcing the breath from my lungs.

"Take that, motherfucker!" a man roared, firing off another shot that sounded like a cannon. The impact shook the dead creature lying limp on top of me.

But that voice… Why did it sound so familiar?

"Kate!" the man hollered. "You okay?"

Chaz? Could it really be him, or was I hallucinating from the loss of blood?

"Kate!"

I closed my eyes and sighed, sending a silent thank you to my guardian angel, if I even still had one. "I'm… okay," I grunted, the beast's weight expunging the last of the breath inside my lungs.

I tried pushing the nightcrawler off me, but my left arm was useless, plus he was too heavy and with my wavering strength, I couldn't budge the damn thing even a little bit.

"I've had enough of this foolishness," Beleth said, his voice slicing through the small reprieve. I'd forgotten we weren't free of this nightmare just yet. "Finish him, then grab the woman."

Like hell I was going to let these demons take me. I wasn't going anywhere without my family. Lungs screaming for air, all I could do was listen as the sicarius flapped his wings, likely taking flight to aim at the Marine from a higher position. Chaz fired off more cannon-like shots, the sound booming as bullets chewed through plaster and stone. There was zero chance he'd come out on the winning end. Human weapons were a paltry match to angelic empyrean steel.

"Chaz!" I tried screaming, but my voice was too hoarse and barely audible. "Run," I croaked out as another set of jaws came near my face and I screamed again, expecting another nightcrawler had come to finish off the job. Relief eased through my body when I realized Hank had bitten down on my shirt, intending to pull me out from under the beast.

With Hank's aid, I was finally able to slide out, my left shoulder and arm shredded. The wounds had begun to mend, but the nightcrawler had done a good job on me and it would take a while before my whole left side would heal. Across the nave, Chaz's shotgun ran out of bullets as the Marine tried retreating to the double doors on the far side. He dropped the weapon and pulled out his pistol, firing off automatic rounds at the assassin. Everything ricocheted off the angel's armor as if Chaz had been shooting a BB gun. Once out of rounds, Chaz pulled out an army knife and the angel unsheathed his monstrous sword. My insides liquified. I needed to do something or the assassin would make minced meat of the Marine.

Spotting the discarded crossbow from the sicarius I had killed earlier, I limped toward the weapon and, with the last traces of strength I possessed, I heaved the enormous crossbow with my good arm and aimed right at the creature. I fired, but like the fucking supernatural being that he was, he spun around and snatched it right out of thin air like a Marvel superhero, his armor glimmering in the early dawn light penetrating the un-shattered stained-glass windows.

Asshole.

Chaz saw his opening and leapt off a pew right onto the hovering angel, jamming his army blade upward at the base of the skull, thrusting it toward the brain, and cutting off motor control immediately. The angel's eyes went blank, and he crashed to the ground, taking the burly soldier with him before turning to pixie dust. Supernatural or not, the damn thing's brain functioned just like ours.

"Woo-hoo!" I cheered, but in that instant, my joy was replaced with incomprehensible agony as Beleth charged at me and pinned me against a pillar, his sword skewering me right through my mutilated shoulder.

"You belligerent, loathsome woman. I don't know what I'll enjoy more, watching you get flayed alive over and over in perpetuity or simply claiming your life with my blade."

Moaning, I raised my good arm, trying to hold on to his sword for stability so I wouldn't slice myself further, but all that did was anger him more and he pushed deeper. I hollered, tears flowing down my cheeks.

The hellish creature laughed. I didn't know how this magnitude of pain was bearable. I should've been dead, yet my soul kept holding on.

Through my bleary vision I caught movement behind Beleth. Hank was skulking through the shadows. Oh God, no. If Beleth saw him, he'd kill him instantly just to break me further. With a couple of subtle and indistinct finger gestures Beleth failed to notice, I instructed Hank to stay back.

The shepherd silently bared his fangs. He was considering defying my order to protect me. My chest heaved, more tears pouring from my eyes. *Please, buddy. Please listen.*

Hooking a finger through the pendants hanging around my neck, Beleth grinned, oblivious to the dog hunting him. "I believe these belong to me."

Head bobbing, I finally managed to latch my gaze onto his. I held his stare for a few seconds that felt like an eternity. I mustered a grin and uttered, "Then take them and shove them up Samael's ass."

He ripped the chains off, then slapped me hard across the cheek, sending blood flying and maybe even a molar. I bit back my tears. This creature would not get any more from me. He would not own my misery. I lifted my head again, tasting iron on my tongue. "You're not allowed to kill me, are you?" I laughed, nonchalantly keeping an eye on Hank. I very subtly shook my head as my canine postured for an attack.

He lowered to the ground, watching me like a wolf, tail wagging like a pendulum.

"And it's utterly eating you alive to not be able to drive your sword straight through my heart," I went on, spitting blood. "I'm the only woman capable of birthing a demon/angel hybrid. If anything were to happen to my son, the only one able to give your master another vessel is me."

He sneered. "You're willing to test that theory, human?"

"It's not a theory, and you know that."

Wrapping his hand around my throat, he pressed hard enough to cut off my oxygen. "I may not be allowed to kill you *yet*, but Samael never said anything about not hurting you."

Choked coughs spurted from my lips as I struggled to breathe, the beast cackling like a maniac as he watched my eyes bulge. He was about to say something when his body disappeared in a loud *whoosh*, followed by the sound of stone smashing.

Barely conscious, I managed to lift my head and through blurry vision, realized Beleth hadn't actually disappeared. He'd been rammed by Mikha'el into the altar, the table now a pile of ruins.

'Bout time the archangel showed up.

CHAPTER 22
KATE

Rising from the rubble, Mikha'el unfurled his enormous wings, stretching them to the max, majestic and radiant, a clear sign of his dominance and power. Eyes burning bright with a fierce glow, he drew his sword when Beleth emerged from underneath the broken altar.

Snarling, the demon's eyes shimmered with twisted hate for the archangel. Golden blood dripped from his brow, staining his pristine armor. Beleth wiped his forehead, examining his blood-streaked fingers with surprise. "Lucky blow," he said, retrieving twin silver curved blades that were hidden in his gauntlets.

Mikha'el's shrug was barely noticeable. "Not lucky enough. You're still breathing."

Slowly sidestepping away from the ruble, Beleth grinned, but the wickedness of his soul swam deep in his gaze. "Buffoonery was never your strongest virtue, Mikha'el. Though, I must admit, I *was* hoping you'd grace us with your imperial presence, oh holy commander. Been a while since our little quarrel in the stone city. Can't deny I'd been looking forward to a rematch."

Eyes narrowed, the archangel inched closer, postured like a panther about to pounce. "Elated to know you've missed me, Beleth. Alas, I can't say I feel the same about *you*."

While the two angels bickered like two overly refined English professors, I tried pulling out the blade still lodged in my shoulder. With my body still pinned to the pillar by the sword, I had no leverage and only managed to cut myself deeper. Blood gushed from my wound, and I grunted in agony.

Loving your little tryst with Beleth, I said to Mikha'el, *but I do have a gigantic sword stuck in my shoulder and I'm kinda bleeding out.*

Mikha'el's wings flared, and he shot me a brief sideways glance before continuing to stalk toward Beleth. *I'm aware. But Beleth has all four stones. Right now—*

I know. He's more important. But can't you just kick his ass already and get this over with instead of chit-chatting about it?

There was no reply. In a blur of leather and gold, he charged at the Horseman of Death. The clash of Mikha'el's sword against Beleth's blades sent sparks flying in the air. They were moving so blindingly fast, you heard the damage they were inflicting on the church more than saw the two supernatural creatures battling each other, shaking the foundation of the church with each collision. Each blow they exchanged reverberated through the air like shockwaves of unholy fury. Dust and debris cascaded around the room as they crashed against pillars and walls, destroying everything Gaudi had created.

Unable to hold my head up any longer, I dropped my chin and closed my eyes. Breaths running ragged, I struggled to remain conscious.

"Kate. Stay with me." Chaz's voice reached me like a distant echo. "This is going to hurt. I'm sorry…"

He pulled the blade out with one giant heave and my entire body spasmed, pain slicing through every nerve. The sword fell to the floor with a loud *clunk,* and I fell into Chaz's trunk-like arms. "I've got you. I've got you," he soothed as he sat me on the floor and leaned my back against the pillar.

Mikha'el and Beleth's battle raged on around us, and we had to shield ourselves from the falling debris. "I'm gonna pack the wound and apply pressure to keep you from bleeding out."

"How bad is it?" I asked breathlessly.

"Let's just say you better hope those healing properties in your veins start working soon, and fast."

Eyes at half-mast, I asked, "Hank?"

"Right here next to us. We need to get out of this cathedral, or we're gonna end up becoming collateral damage between these two. Can you walk?"

"Only one way to find out. Help me up."

As the Marine leaned in to put an arm under my good shoulder, a loud clash exploded in the room, like a bomb had gone off in the middle of the church, pushing us back down to the floor. When the dust settled, Mikha'el stood above Beleth, one foot pressing into the demon's chest, the creature's armor dented and torn. The archangel aimed the tip of his sword right at the creature's neck as all four pendants dangled from Mikha'el's other hand.

With the stones' power stolen from him, Beleth convulsed, his body contorting into his grotesque Fallen form. His once ethereal features twisted into a monstrous visage, and a low, guttural growl escaped his deformed lips.

"It's over, Beleth," Mikha'el said with authority, his voice booming. "Surrender, and you will be spared death."

But Beleth only laughed, his taunting humor curdling a sickening feeling in my stomach. Something wasn't right here.

"After sentencing us to eternity in Abaddon, you think death scares me, commander?"

"Your crimes could not go unpunished. You knew our laws."

"You think yourself so righteous," Beleth growled. "God's unblemished, golden warrior. But does the human know your part in all this, commander?" He turned to look in my direction, those dark, soulless eyes full of derision, tempting me to doubt Mikha'el, to question his intentions.

I swallowed deeply, instantly hating the fact that he'd done just that—seeded doubt, even if just for one microsecond. Because I couldn't deny the fact that Mikha'el was always so reserved. He'd only share bits of information, never the full story, and only if I questioned him. What could he possibly be hiding?

Never trust the words spewed from the lips of a Fallen, he whispered into my mind.

Then what the hell is he talking about?

Not now.

Of course.

Mikha'el cocked his neck at Beleth. "Your kind never wastes an opportunity to twist the truth."

"My kind? We were cut from the same clay, brother. Perhaps it is you who twists the truth. You're incapable of admitting that your betrayal runs deeper than a festering wound. That you're just as guilty for the sickness devouring this world."

Face tense, Mikha'el pressed his blade closer to the Fallen's neck.

Beleth smirked, eyes twinkling with malice. "You… might want to reconsider killing me, commander."

"Did you not lack fear of death only moments earlier?"

That's when I realized that all this time Beleth had just been buying time. I gasped as I saw what—no, who—rifted into the church, hovering above us. "Mikha'el!" I shouted from across the room. "Look up!"

Wings spread wide, two sicarii gently flapped their wings in the middle of the church, and one held a bound female angel in his arms.

A trembling breath trickled from my lips. Gavri'el…

Mikha'el's gaze shot up and the golden hue that always seemed to emit from his pores dimmed and disappeared. Understanding the threat, he removed his blade from Beleth's neck and took his foot off the creature's chest. Taking a few steps back, he stared in horror.

I'd never seen Mikha'el scared before, and it iced my blood more than the blood loss from my shoulder wound.

Beleth scurried to his feet as the sicarius holding the emissary lowered to the ground, placing Gavri'el on her knees. Hands bound behind her back, her wings looked tattered and broken, and her long white hair was matted with dry, golden blood. Her once creamy and glowy brown skin was now cut and bruised. Her condition either meant the injuries were fresh or she was severely depleted of her power.

Misty, bloodshot eyes stared at Mikha'el, but worst of all was the look of defeat in her gaze, as if she'd already accepted her fate. Mikha'el went so still, he may as well have been turned to stone. "Release her at once," he ordered, finally tearing his gaze away from the angel kneeling before him and sneering at Beleth. "She is the Lord's emissary. To take her captive is beyond any crime you have ever committed."

"Who says I intend to keep her captive?" Beleth grinned, his black-stained teeth accentuating his mocking smile. "And I stopped caring about the laws governing Elysium long ago, commander. It's too late to preach to me about a place I no longer call home."

Snatching everyone's attention, another loud boom shook the cathedral as a bare-chested man covered in black goo barreled through the double doors at the opposite end of the church, directly behind Beleth.

My heart sank, not with angst, but with utter joy, as relief flooded my veins. The man that dashed into the room was Jax… and he held Luke in his arms!

Covered in what I now figured was demon blood and guts, something else seemed off about him, but then again, he'd probably fought through nightcrawlers and sect members alike to find our son. At this point, what did it matter if he looked off—I probably didn't look any better. He was alive and so was Luke, and that's all I truly cared about.

The relief I felt in my chest was enough to fill my weakened lungs with much-needed oxygen. But I needed to wrap my arms around him and Luke to make sure they were real and not just my mind toying with me or my wishful thinking. Wanting to run to them, I stumbled to my feet, but Chaz placed his broad hand on my good shoulder, guiding me back down, the quick slice of his head signaling me not to move. He eyed the fight going on between the angels. I grumbled, but the Marine was right. This was too dangerous. Not to mention that having Luke in a room with Beleth and the sicarii had put my son directly in the enemy's path.

Fuck. I didn't think about that.

When our gazes found each other, Jax looked just as relieved and as horrified as me. We were happy to know neither one of us was dead, but this was the last place we would've hoped for a reunion. I offered him a half-hearted smile, an eyebrow raised, silently letting him know I loved him. I was happy to see him, but this was terrible timing.

He arched his as well, acknowledging the same.

CHAPTER 23

JAX

I barged through the damn double doors without contemplating what I might find on the other side. The instant I heard Kate scream, my instinct had been to find her. So, I ran and ran, determined to unleash all my fury at whoever dared lay a finger on her.

Well, as they say, out of the frying pan and into the fire. A terrible cliché, but perfectly apt for this scenario.

Beleth and Mikha'el seemed to be locked in the middle of their own little fight, and two sicarii stood in the center of the church, looking every bit as terrifying as one would imagine holy assassins were meant to look. Gravri'el was present, and judging from the way she was held down by one of the sicarii—and the fact her wrists were shackled, and an assassin held a blade to her neck—she was likely being used as collateral. This was quite literally the worst possible situation I could have stumbled upon, and I'd just made matters worse. Way worse.

Faces scrunched, everyone turned to look at me as if I'd been a rude theatergoer who'd walked in late to a Broadway show and interrupted everything.

When I spotted Kate, the room felt like it dropped several degrees, horror icing over my skin. She looked like she'd been put through a meat grinder. I was glad she was alive, but I swore she was teetering on a precipice, about to nosedive into death. Despite her condition, she offered me a small, almost tender smile, though she still managed to scold me with her gaze, reminding me I should have checked to make sure the coast was clear before storming into the cathedral.

I know, angel. I know.

We couldn't have picked a worst moment to play hero rescues damsel in distress, though it looked like Chaz had beaten me to the whole saving the damsel part. Thank God for that.

"Don't mind me, folks," I said. "Feel free to return to your regular programming. I'm just gonna step outside for a moment while you guys resolve your little squabble."

As I took a step toward the door, Beleth shouted, "Seize him. Don't let him get away with that child."

One of the sicarii quickly rifted from the middle of the church to the back door, blocking my exit. Instinctively wanting to protect Luke, I reached into the cauldron of Mammon's power and dipped my fingers. "Get out of my way or I will shred that pretty face right off your head," I roared at the assassin, my voice heavily distorted.

I regretted my actions immediately. Some type of force wrapped around my body, compelling me to turn around. When my gaze met Beleth's red glowing eyes, my gut twisted into a knot.

"How fortuitous," Beleth chirped with an exaggerated, joyish bounce to his voice, clapping his hands like some cartoonish villain in a spy movie. "Seems Mikha'el isn't the only one harboring secrets. I have to admit, this is exuberantly thrilling. Mammon, is that you, brother? Do come out and let these folks make your acquaintance."

Fuck. Exactly what I'd feared. He'd sensed the demon trapped inside me. My impulsiveness had handed Luke and me over to him on a golden platter. I tried fighting his compulsion, but Beleth was too strong, and as one of Samael's lieutenants, he had authority over all the other demons, including Mammon. He called to him, making the demon stir inside me, more confidently now, as if it knew this moment would come. Mammon chuckled softly inside my mind.

You will regret summoning me.

Could it be that this last bit of power I took had done me in? Fuck. I couldn't give two shits about what these bastards would do to me, but I knew what they had planned for Luke, and every cell in my body burned with rage.

"If you touch my son—"

"Silence, you perfidious human. Your insolence led to all this unnecessary hindrance. You've enraged the unholy army, Jackson Constantine. And now Samael will claim your soul. Come forward and deliver his vessel to me."

"No!" Kate roared, the pain coating her voice slicing my heart in half.

Speaking words in their ancient angelic tongue, Beleth broke the lock of Mammon's prison. Instantly, I felt his mind flood my consciousness, but there was only room for one of us, and his power was mightier than my will. Head feeling like it was about to explode, I fell to my knees, still cradling Luke to my chest. He began to cry, and Kate released another wail that crumpled me.

"Stop this," Mikha'el growled. "Send Mammon back to Hell. If it's a sacrifice you require, take me."

"And grant this traitor mercy?" Beleth spat. "Why would I do such a thing? He deserves an eternity in the Hall of Solitude. And don't fret, commander; you're not escaping *your* fate. We've reserved a special and unique kind of punishment for you."

Forcing myself to look up, I caught as Mikha'el took a step toward me, but Beleth yanked him back with five simple words. "Try it, and Gavri'el dies."

Mikha'el met the demon's gaze, a muscle twitching in his jaw. "Touch her, and I will rip your soul in half."

"So violent," Beleth mused. "You're in no position to be making threats. Though, I'm glad you're finally embracing your dark side." Then the Horseman of Death turned toward me. "Mammon, darling, come out to play."

I curled in on myself as a wave of rippling torment ran through every nerve ending. Mammon was trying to occupy every ounce of my body, and it felt like someone was tearing off my skin in order to grow a new one.

Kate screamed again, "Jax, please. You can fight it. I believe in you."

But I could no longer fight against Beleth's compulsion. Through Mammon, he had complete control of my body now. With Luke in my arms, all I could do was watch from my mental prison as Mammon walked us to the center of the church. He made us glance at Kate, and the absolute terror in her eyes was devastating. Chaz kept holding her back, though she fought him with every ounce of strength she had left.

I sent the big guy a silent thank you. This could only end worse if she tried to intervene.

Mammon handed Luke over to Beleth, who dropped the small blanket Luke had been wrapped in, revealing his naked body as he held him up under the arms. Talia had undressed him and even removed his diaper for the offering. The poor little guy looked like he was freezing. He wailed, his screams the sort of sound that would send any mother into a boiling frenzy, and it thrust me into a pit of despair.

"Please," Kate hollered. "He is cold and hungry. He needs me!"

"This child no longer belongs to you, Daughter of Eve. He's been marked. And he will have no use for you soon." Beleth examined my son's small body—from the sigils on his arms, to the wing stubs on his back.

"A perfect specimen," Beleth said, turning toward me. "You may have betrayed us, but in the end, you played your part well. Regrettably for you, Samael does not believe in forgiveness." He nodded toward the sicarius, who came behind me and manacled my wrists. "But death will not be your sentence."

Holding Luke in one arm, he extended his other hand toward me, drawing sigils in the air until something deep in my core began to bubble, rising up my esophagus like a ball that had been lodged deep in my throat. Suddenly, a plume of black smoke erupted from my mouth, amassing into a large, disembodied dark substance that hovered in the air.

Mammon.

Weakened, I slumped to my knees. I was out of my mental prison, once again in control of my own faculties, but barely able to hold myself upright. The power I'd felt in my blood had been all his. Without it, I was nothing but a useless meat sack.

Beleth looked up at the floating, faceless entity. "Brother, return to Abaddon. Bring news of our victory. Tell Samael I have acquired the vessel."

Beleth glanced my way, his red gaze roaming over my sagging body. "Let him know I'm also bringing him a special gift. He will be delighted."

I spat at Beleth and tried to climb to my feet, but the sicarius pushed me back down to my knees, then brought his blade to my neck.

"No!" Kate screamed, still being held back by Chaz.

"Fate is immutable, Son of Adam. Fighting it is… ineffectual."

Mammon's disembodied essence swirled like a churning storm until, in a blink of an eye, it disappeared, as if sucked through a black hole.

Mikha'el's jaw was set so tight, he looked like he could crush bone with his teeth. He stood like a sentinel, vice-gripping his empyrean sword as Beleth took a step toward him. "Now, hand over the stones, commander."

"If I hand you the stones now, all of this will be for nothing."

Circling the archangel as if he held no fear of what the holy warrior could do to him, Beleth began, "Your commitment to never failing a mission is commendable. But your conviction to help these grotesque mortal beings still perplexes me. The war is over, Mikha'el. You fought well. Let that be your recompense. Surely The Lord God will find a way to reward you for your efforts, if He ever resurfaces to right the wrongs He's made against His people. *Our* people."

Mikha'el kept the pendants close to his body, refusing to capitulate. Faster than I could breathe, the archangel raised his sword and swung it toward Beleth's head, stopping right before hacking it off. "Let me make myself crystal clear. I will never hand over the stones. So do me a favor and relate the following message to your master: Tell him Mikha'el says to go fuck himself."

Eyeing the blade, Beleth remained still as a marble statue, lips curling into a sinister smile. "I… was expecting you'd say that. In fact, I was hoping you would."

The sicarius holding down Gavri'el pushed her forward so she was even closer to Mikha'el, her face tilted upward. Beleth took advantage of the distraction to swivel away from Mikha'el's sword.

The assassin placed the edge of his blade at the base of the emissary's neck and Beleth leaned down by her head, and said, "Go on, darling. Say your final goodbyes."

"What are you doing, Beleth?" Mikha'el asked, a current of worry riding his voice.

"You see, commander, out of everything an angel could fear, nothing is more terrifying than the severing of a soul-bond."

"Stop this. Gavri'el is innocent."

Beleth cocked his head. "You know that's far from true. You took something that wasn't yours, and she gave you something she had no right to give you." He grabbed her hair and forcefully pulled her head back. "Isn't that right, emissary? Or should I call you *whore,* instead?"

"You reprehensible demon," Mikha'el bellowed.

Beleth's red eyes glowed bright. "The stones, commander. Or she loses her head."

A loud grunt snatched my attention to the back of the room, and all I saw was Chaz holding his nose, blood gushing like a broken dam. Kate was on her feet and running—more like limping—toward the center of the room. Seemed she'd elbowed the Marine in the nose to get out of his grip.

Angel, no!

Mikha'el must have sensed her intentions and quickly erected a force field around us, blocking her out. Unlike the crypt when she'd been able to walk through the force field, this time she bounced off like a ball, and I gasped as I watched her get launched backward. Thankfully, Chaz had run up behind her and broke her fall. That didn't stop her from darting back to her feet and storming toward the shield, though.

"Mikha'el… if you give him the stones," she sobbed from the other side, unable to finish what we already knew she wanted to say.

If he gave Beleth the stones, it was in fact Game Over. Samael would have everything he needed to not only be reborn, but to escape Hell. My body trembled. I did not know what his past with Gavri'el was, but clearly, they meant something important to each other. Otherwise, why would Beleth threaten him with her death? Fear wrapped itself around my throat. I understood the look in Mikha'el's eyes. I understood it because it spoke of the love he felt for her, a love that mirrored my own for Kate and my son. The kind of love that makes you do stupid things.

The kind of love that would drive you to betray those you cared about. That would make you wage wars you couldn't win. The type of love you would kill for.

He loved Gavri'el more than life itself, and I could already see his spirit shattering at the thought of her death.

"Mikha'el…" I breathed, "Think this through. This is bigger than her. It's about humanity." But even as the words left my lips, I knew they were empty. They carried no conviction because in his shoes, I would've already handed the stones over to Beleth.

"Give me the stones, Mikha'el," Beleth shouted, losing patience. "I swear to you, she will die!"

Mikha'el succumbed to his torment and tears rolled down his face. "She's your sister," he said, eyes narrowed with utter disappointment at Beleth.

"She means nothing to me now."

Heaving, Mikha'el lowered to his knees, staring up at Beleth with imploring eyes. "I beseech you, brother. Don't do this, please. Take me. Bring me to Samael so he may take my heart with his bare hands, but spare Gavri'el."

"The almighty Mikha'el on his knees, begging for his lover's life. If only God were here to witness how low His revered warrior has fallen."

"Samael would never want this," Mikha'el continued to implore. "Despite everything that happened, he would never want you to use her like this. He'll never forgive you if you kill her."

"I'll let you in on a little secret, commander…" He stepped toward the archangel and leaned down, his thin, crusted lips peeling back in a dark smile. "It was Samael who ordered her execution. Now, hand over the stones. I won't ask you again."

Hands trembling, Mikha'el looked down at the pendants gripped tightly in his hand as if contemplating taking the deal. My heart thumped a million miles a second, waiting to see what he would do. Then, with tears in his eyes, he peered over to where Gavri'el kneeled. Shock. Grief. His entire soul was laid naked for her to see. He shook his head as if he was having a silent conversation with her. Perhaps they were.

Terror flooded his eyes as he very subtly nodded his head.

"For love," Gavri'el whispered, breaking her silence.

"For love," Mikha'el repeated.

Whatever the choice, the decision had been made. I held my breath, expecting the worst.

Mikha'el roared, lunging forward with his sword. Gavri'el sprung to her legs at the same time. Kate shouted for him in the background, joining Mikha'el's woeful cry as the archangel plunged his sword straight through the emissary's heart.

Filled with marrow-splintering sorrow, his piercing bellows shook the walls, shattering what remained of the stained-glass windows. Dawn light filled the room, accompanying the burst of celestial light that erupted from Gavri'el's body. A shockwave rippled through the cathedral, and I was thrust backward, along with the sicarius holding me down.

Then, I was gone.

CHAPTER 24

KATE

After Gavri'el's death and the near complete destruction of the cathedral, Mikha'el retreated to the sacristy and locked himself in the small room. He erected a shield and wouldn't even open the door for me. I tried not to take it personally. After all, he'd lost someone he'd loved.

I had suffered a loss too, though my grief was different because I refused to believe Jax and Luke were dead. They were missing. And I didn't believe that because of wishful thinking, but because I genuinely *felt* them. Not to mention the fact that when Gavri'el died, the blinding light that erupted from her should've eviscerated every demonic creature or fallen angel in the light's path, yet we only found the empyrean sword of the sicarius who was about to kill her if Mikha'el hadn't taken her life instead.

We didn't find Beleth's curved blades or any weapons from the second assassin, the one who'd held Jax. Which meant they managed to rift before the light burned them to ash.

It was how I knew deep in my heart they were still alive. I just had no idea where Beleth had taken them, though I could only surmise he'd either taken them to his lair or maybe to Hell itself. Who knew? That's why I needed Mikha'el, but the angelic commander had locked me out of his mind as well.

I stood outside the sacristy door and went to reach for the knob for the tenth time today, holding my breath in anticipation of the…

Zap.

"Ouch." I pulled back, shaking my fingers as if I hadn't known how much it would sting. "You can't stay in there forever, Mikha'el." I braced my hands against the doorframe, something bordering impatience beginning to simmer. "Please. I need you. I don't want to do this alone."

I waited for a minute without success.

"Kate." Clint approached from the ruined cathedral with Hank at his heels. His hair was a shaggy mess, and his clothes were caked in black and red blood, which meant he hadn't had a chance to change since arriving. Eyes bloodshot and haggard, he looked just how I felt. "You're needed in the infirmary," he said flatly.

Tucking strands of loose hair behind my ears, I puffed out a long breath. Despite being fully healed by now, my muscles felt sore and I had not slept well the last couple of nights. Who could? After everything that went down, my mind couldn't find peace. I was functioning on two hours of sleep, if that, and could hardly keep my eyes open. "More infected?"

"A man and his young son. We found them in the tunnel. They're in bad shape, but I think we can save them in time. But we gotta hurry."

I nodded and quickly followed him across the sunlit nave. Along with several other survivors, we'd cleared a path through the rubble, though the room was still highly unstable. Luckily, I was the only one who really came this way as I kept trying to get Mikha'el to open the damn sacristy door.

I sprint-walked a few paces behind the young Guardian. With his back stern and strapped with his empyrean crossbow, Clint took long, fast strides like a soldier on a mission. Hank kept up with him, tail swinging low, though he periodically looked back as if checking I was still there.

Not going anywhere, buddy.

As tired as I was, physically and emotionally, seeing those two trotting along tugged a small smile at the corners of my lips. I still couldn't believe the kid was alive. He'd been like a little brother, and seeing him as anything other than family wasn't even possible anymore.

And as hard as it was to lose those you loved to this forsaken wasteland, family was what kept us going—though it was also what made us more afraid. Alone, I had nothing to lose, but I also had nothing to fight for. Now, I had everything to lose. But I wouldn't change that for anything. Fear was a survival instinct; it's what kept us alive, kept us fighting.

What saddened me most was seeing the usual joyous teen be so solemn and reserved. Since learning of Gavri'el's death and Jax's disappearance, he'd kept to himself. Couldn't blame him. The emissary had saved his life and Jax was his hero. The day following the church debacle, Clint told me the story about how Gavri'el had not only healed him, but she'd anointed him as a Guardian, repairing his shoulder and arm using empyrean steel, and gifting him the crossbow the assassin had used to shoot him. Luckily for him, the assassin had missed his heart—I wanted to believe he'd missed on purpose. That perhaps Samael had not succeeded in corrupting everyone, but maybe I was just trying to find hope amongst all this destruction.

Or maybe I just missed Clint's jokes and the way he would always tease Chaz. Even Hank knew something was wrong. Kid always played with him, but now he barely got a belly rub. Still, for the last two days, the shepherd hadn't left his side.

Hank was a great sidekick when fighting zombies and demons, but at the end of the day, he was still a regular dog and a wonderful companion, whose nose nuzzles and cuddles could heal any broken heart. I didn't mind sharing his affection if it could bring joy back into the kid's eyes.

Our footsteps echoed down the corridors as we rounded another corner, and I saw all the windows Jax had apparently shattered trying to slow down the pair of nightcrawlers that were after him and Luke. My insides tightened just thinking of the terror that must have been coursing through Jax's blood, though Clint had mentioned he'd seen Jax and Luke protected by some type of energy shield—which sounded very familiar to what Mikha'el and I were able to conjure.

Clint explained how he'd found Jax clinging to life, and that if he'd not summoned Mammon and bound him to his soul, Jax would have died. I didn't know how to feel about that, really. On the one hand, I was relieved he'd found a way to stay alive, but on the other hand, he'd sold himself to another demon. After what happened with Astaroth, why would he want to bind himself to such darkness again?

Then again, I knew how he felt regarding his mortality. After having a taste of invincibility, going back to being a regular human really wounded his pride, his ego. He didn't think himself capable of protecting me and Luke, and I could understand why those feelings could drive a man to make desperate decisions, but the risks had been immense. If it hadn't been for that demon trapped inside him, Beleth wouldn't have been able to compel Jax to hand Luke over, but if he hadn't used the demon's power, Jax wouldn't have found Luke or saved him from Talia's clutches.

It was like an inescapable vicious circle which made one phrase ring inside my head, something Beleth had told Jax: Fate is immutable, fighting it is ineffectual. I used to think fate was what we made, but it seemed that, no matter the choice Jax had made, Luke would always end up in Samael's hands, whether it was because Talia handed him over or Jax did.

I didn't know what to make of that, other than this war between Earth, Heaven, and Hell was far from over. Gavri'el had told me my son was the key to saving humanity, and I was not about to let this one defeat rob me of that hope. If Luke was destined for something more, I had to believe that falling into Beleth's hands was part of the plan.

And that was enough to fuel my determination to find him.

Plus, we still had the creation stones. Without them, Samael would not be able to complete his transformation, and he would not be able to leave his prison. Which meant the humans were still in the game.

My other consolation was, if Beleth had in fact taken Luke to Hell, Samael wouldn't harm my son. He was probably making sure his precious vessel was being cared for exceptionally well. I wouldn't doubt it if he had him heavily guarded, too. Who I worried about was Jax. Something in my gut told me he was alive, though barely. And if anything Beleth said was true, the chances Jax was being tortured were high.

My blood ran arctic at the thought. More of a reason why I needed Mikha'el to step out of his self-created prison soon and angel-up.

I wanted to be sympathetic to his pain. Gavri'el was dead and I couldn't imagine how devastating that loss was to him, especially when he'd been the one to drive his sword through her heart, but many people had lost a loved one that night, too. Spouses, children, friends. Everyone's soul was broken, including mine. The emotional wreckage I felt inside my chest from not having my newborn in my arms or from knowing Jax was likely being tortured was more than I could bear.

I'd given birth to a miracle child, and not because he was some chosen savior, but because I was once told by countless doctors that I could never conceive, that I was barren. He'd been everything I ever wished for, yet I barely got to hold him. He was ripped from my arms before he'd even been a day old.

That alone was eroding me from the inside out, not to mention the fact that, regardless of how well Samael might be caring for him, nothing could replace a mother. Luke needed me and to not be there for him—to feed him or soothe him—had me wanting to tear out my heart.

But I couldn't afford to lock myself in a room and cry myself to sleep. None of us could. As harsh as it sounded, life had to go on; we couldn't afford to dwell in our misery. Not in this world we lived in. This new world ate those who stopped fighting. And I would be damned if I ever stopped fighting for my family. I would scour every corner of this decimated planet, and I would travel to the depths of Hell for my son.

So, I would give the archangel one more night to lick his wounds, but after that, I would figure this shit out on my own.

We rounded a few more corners and passed a couple of courtyards on the way. Clint pointed at the orange tree where the two girls he'd brought to safety had been hiding. He told me the story about the little sisters. Thanks to Father Ortega, Clint had learned considerable Spanish back in New York, and he had been able to communicate with the survivors of the attack, including the girls. Apparently, they told him Jax had rescued them from some weird ass demon, a horde of zombies, and a pack of nightcrawlers. Turned out they were Ofelia's daughters, the midwife who helped deliver Luke. They'd gotten separated during the attack. Ofelia survived by hiding inside a broken fridge in the kitchen. Their reunion was a much-needed celebration amongst all the death.

After the events inside the cathedral, Clint, Chaz, and a few surviving Guardians cleared the rest of the church and dormitories of any lingering devoured, nightcrawlers, and a couple of those bony, eyeless creatures. I'd had to rest until my shoulder healed and wasn't able to aid in the demon-expunging efforts. However, I was glad I missed running into what the church survivors called *Sin-Ojos*, which Clint said simply translated into one without eyes. It sounded cooler and creepier in Spanish.

Then came the really hard part, burning the bodies of the deceased. I commended the people who volunteered for that job. People lost family, children. To have to throw their bodies into a mass pile outside the church to then set it aflame—I wouldn't have had the heart or guts to do it. Not to mention the smell of burnt flesh still lingered in the air, a dark, constant reminder of those we lost.

Diana had been one of those people who sadly lost her life during the attack. According to Clint, the poor young doctor who'd helped me through the delivery had been hard to identify. It didn't look like they found much of her. They were able to finally figure out who the body belonged to because of the lab coat.

The Guardians suffered mass casualties as well, and on the previous night, they held a separate vigil for their fallen comrades, especially their leader, Amada. The tough task of appointing a new leader would take place in the coming days, if not sooner. I hoped for the latter. This church remained a bastion of hope for these people, and they needed a good defender.

Despite all the destruction caused by the attack, a large portion of the facility remained functional, minus the cathedral itself. Their center of worship had been decimated, but these survivors were resilient people. They turned one of the courtyards into a makeshift church, and with the absence of a priest, they appointed Pastor Antonia Morales as their new spiritual leader.

Seeing this community come together in this time of need was refreshing, and definitely bolstered my hope for humanity. There had to be pockets of survivors like these all around the globe, people just trying to make it through the day, fighting for the chance to see another sunrise.

Of one thing I was certain: Where there is darkness, light shines the brightest. And I planned to hold on to that light for as long as I could.

Before we entered the infirmary, we dropped Hank off with a bunch of kids who were playing a game of marbles. He'd grown quite fond of them in the last couple of days—no doubt the fact they had a hearty supply of apple slices to offer him as treats had something to do with it.

When we pushed through the entrance of the infirmary, I was immediately greeted by the sharp smell of dried blood, disinfectant, and sterilized medical tools. Thankfully for these folks, Diana had taken it upon herself to train some people in basic first aid. Some even knew how to draw blood, check for vitals, and how to administer the proper doses of medication, though their supplies were meager and putting together a supply-run team had been relegated to top priority.

About a dozen people lay in gurneys, most of them still recovering from their wounds. Though our theory that my blood could be a cure for the infection had never been tested on humans, we decided to try, anyway. What else were we supposed to do? Watching people mourn their loved ones before they were even dead and knowing what they would turn into was one of the harshest things one could ever witness.

If there was a chance my blood could save people from experiencing that nightmare, why wouldn't we try it? What did we have to lose? So, we drew my blood and injected it directly into people's bodies. Only those people who were bitten but hadn't yet fully turned showed promise of recovery. Unfortunately, there were times we missed the injection window. Those who succumbed to the infection and received the blood infusion burned from the inside out until they were nothing but cinders and ash. Just like Father Ortega had warned.

We knew our treatment tactic went against everything we knew about science and vaccines. Our past knowledge told us you couldn't just inject people with other people's blood and expect a cure.

But we weren't dealing with an Earth-born virus, so we needed to consider an unconventional cure. Problem was, as much as I would've loved to donate my blood to save humanity, I didn't have enough of it for everyone. In order to provide this cure to what remained of the human population around the globe, we would need someone to figure out which properties in my blood were combating the virus, then mass produce it into a true vaccine or treatment.

But first, we needed to send the fuckers who brought this infection into our world back to Hell.

Clint ushered me to a separate area in the back where those who had been infected but hadn't yet turned were being monitored. For their safety and ours, their hands and ankles were strapped to the gurneys. A man and his young son lay on parallel gurneys, their faces pale. Their breaths ran ragged and their skin was already glistening with a cold sweat, and the tremors had kicked in as well. We didn't have much time.

"Let's go," I said, gesturing to the newly appointed medical head tech, Marina.

The young woman's brown eyes were rimmed with dark circles. No one had gotten any sleep around here, but that didn't slow her down. She worked with the speed and seamless efficacy of a nurse in an emergency room. Jumping straight into action, she prepped my arm to draw blood and quickly collected the gold-speckled liquid into a vial, then a second.

Another technician stepped in and took one of the vials, then both of them darted to the man and his son, their arms already prepared to receive the injections. We all seemed to hold our breaths as we waited to see if the blood would take any effect.

The young child, probably no older than six, started to show signs of improvement first. His breathing slowed and color began to slowly return to his skin. Marina checked his pupils and, with a long sigh, she lifted her gaze to mine. Despite her fatigue, a sparkle of light shone in her eyes. The child's sclera had lightened back to white, and his pupils were no longer dilated.

Thank goodness. We'd made it just in time.

When we all shifted our attention to his father, we were about to breathe a sigh of relief when his breaths slowed, but then the man turned to look at his son and what we thought was going to be a smile transformed into a snarl. Marina immediately wheeled the child's gurney away and shielded him from seeing what was about to happen.

I closed my eyes, not wanting to witness it, either.

We'd missed the damn fucking injection window again, and now the boy's father was about to incinerate himself. I wanted to scream at the top of my lungs. I hated losing people, hated the fact this boy had lost his father because of this senseless virus. I clenched my fists. Samael needed to pay for this—for all the pain, for all the tears.

When the creature's remains were carted away and Marina had escorted the child to the main patient area to finish recouping, I asked Clint if we knew of any family among the survivors. According to Clint, the man and the boy had been alone when they first arrived at the church as refugees. The child had no one and would now join the countless orphans living at the church.

I forcefully wiped the wetness beading at the corners of my eyes. Tears weren't going to solve our problems. What happened today with that man was going to keep happening every day, unless we did something soon. With every breath in my lungs, I promised I would fight until there were no more orphans because of this unjust war.

Pulling myself together before heading back to the sacristy to try my last attempt of the day to get Mikha'el to open the door, I went to leave when Clint pulled me aside.

"What's on your mind?" I asked. "I know things haven't been easy around here, so if you need a break…"

He shook his head, a lock of brown hair falling over his tired green eyes. "Nah, I'm good. Promise. It was just… I got to thinking, I know we're hoping to someday, somehow turn your blood into some kind of cure or treatment or something, but have you thought maybe we could also use it as a weapon, kind of like the holy water-infused bullets? Except, instead of just deterring or slowing down the demons and infected, these bullets could literally incinerate them. Could be a game changer."

I cocked my head and stared at him in wonder. Why hadn't I thought of that? Placing a hand on his shoulder, I squeezed gently. "Sounds brilliant, Clint. It may be a while though before we can figure out how to mass-produce that. But you know what, I'm not above dipping some ammo in my blood, as gross as that sounds. As long as it kills those sonsabitches, I'm game." I winked, offering him a playful smile.

A twinkle brightened his eyes and my heart warmed, seeing a glimpse of the old Clint peeking through. All of a sudden, his gaze widened as something caught his attention behind me. When I spun to see what was so interesting, my jaw dropped.

Mikha'el stood at the entrance of the infirmary, his leather armor tattered and still coated in angel blood. Shadows darkened his eyes, and his usual golden luminous skin was pale as snow. Everyone seemed to stop breathing, all eyes trained on the archangel in utter fascination. Despite his tousled appearance, he was still magnificent, especially since he'd not spirited his wings away.

When our gazes met, his lips twitched slightly, and I knew he was glad to see me, too.

Fly with me? he asked softly in my mind.

Well, there was something people didn't ask you every day.

CHAPTER 25
KATE

I was pretty certain Mikha'el could have rifted us to wherever he wanted to take me. Sure, flying was cool, but after rifting across the world, choosing to fly was like having a smartphone but deciding to write a letter instead of sending a text—though these days, communicating long distance via cell phones was a thing of the past. In any case, it didn't make sense to fly us over Barcelona instead of using the wormhole.

Okay, so yeah, the last time we rifted I puked my brains out, and I went into labor, but he'd had to rift two adults, plus a dog. This time, it was just me, and I wasn't pregnant anymore. And frankly, I'd take a little nausea over flying above a crippled city consumed by hunger and death.

But given how mercurial the heavenly creature could be, I decided not to question him and trusted he had a legitimate reason for taking the extra time to fly me across the city when my son and Jax had literally been kidnapped by the Horseman of Death and we had a church full of survivors who needed our help.

All I could do was pray he wouldn't lose his grip and that I wouldn't puke my lunch into the blasting wind. At the speed we were flying, both of us would've been covered in mildly digested grits and diluted coffee.

As a little girl, I always wondered what it would feel like to be Lois Lane while Superman took her in his arms and flew her over Metropolis. Guess clinging to the arms of an archangel as he flew me over a decimated Barcelona was probably the closest I'd ever get to knowing what it would be like to be the smart and fearless journalist.

Who knew my first time touring this city would be soaring through the sky with God's mightiest warrior, the still picturesque yet demon-infested cityscape dwarfing below us. The streets were laid out like a mosaic, showcasing the rich history and modernity that coexisted in the once-vibrant city. The warm, late afternoon Mediterranean sun bathed the buildings in a golden glow, making them appear even more enchanting from above—if one could ignore the countless smoking piles of dead bodies littered across every neighborhood.

As we glided higher, we approached the majestic hills that surrounded Barcelona. *There,* he said into my mind as he pointed at the white dome that came into view. The arm wrapped around my waist felt like a bar made of iron, but my instinct was to hold on so tight, my nails dug into his leather armor.

Nestled atop one of these hills was our apparent destination, the iconic Fabra Observatory. Erected near the top of Tibidabo, the highest hill in the city, it had been one of the oldest functioning astronomical observatories in the world, offering breathtaking views not just of the galaxy, but of the entire Catalonian city and the Mediterranean Sea.

The observatory, with its distinctive dome and viewing towers, stood proudly against the backdrop of the red and purplish twilight sky. I only wished I could've appreciated the magic of the moment, but it was hard to get lost in this unique bird's-eye view of a city I knew ran rampant with flesh-eating zombies, demon dogs, and all sorts of other hellish creatures. People were dying down there, and here I was, flying to an observatory that was no longer even working.

We circled the gleaming white dome several times to make sure it was free of any roaming infected. In the meantime, Mikha'el rattled off details about the landmarks surrounding the area, including the fact the observatory used to house powerful telescopes that had observed the cosmos for over a century, offering unparalleled views of the planets and moons and… honestly, I wasn't paying much attention. None of this mattered anymore.

I was so happy he'd finally decided to brave the world again and that he was out of that sacristy, he could have flown me to a landfill and I wouldn't have given two shits. On any other day, I may have been thrilled to be getting this aerial view of the Spanish city, but I couldn't ignore the acidic choler burning through my stomach. We should've been back at the church assembling a team and going after Beleth, not out here wasting time, playing tour guide and tourist.

Still, despite what Beleth may have insinuated about the commander, my trust in the archangel had not waned. So, I bit my tongue and locked my jaw so tight, it hurt. Surely, he had a reason for this nonsense.

Mikha'el grumbled something unintelligible when he didn't get the response he was hoping for from me. I mentally rolled my eyes and swore his hold around my waist loosened. He could be touchy, but really, what did he have to tell me that he couldn't have told me back at the church?

Patience, Daughter of Eve.

I pursed my lips. I hated that after everything we'd been through, he still used formalities. *My patience has been long gone, commander.* I made sure my tone communicated my sentiment.

He said nothing, but the sudden drop in altitude might have been his reply.

Ass.

Finally satisfied that the area was free of any ghouls, he descended slowly, lowering me onto the teak walkway that, about two years ago, would've been bustling with tourists strolling along the paths, enjoying the sun-setting beauty and tranquility the observatory offered once upon a time.

You're still rolling your eyes.

You couldn't have seen that.

I didn't need to. Your cynicism practically oozes from your pores.

I nudged him with my elbow.

Wobbling on my feet as he set me down, I felt a bit disoriented, but Mikha'el helped to steady me before letting me go. I walked toward the edge of the walkway that overlooked the city, the Mediterranean Sea gleaming in the distance. Warm wind whipped against my face, swirling more strands of my hair loose.

Below, the once lush greenery of adorning vegetation surrounding the grounds was now a tangle of overgrown plants and weeds, many of which were dead and decaying. Still, I couldn't deny the view was anything but astonishing.

A deep gulp of refreshing air filled my lungs, and I finally allowed myself a second to marvel at the landscape's natural charm. Stars, what I wouldn't have given to travel back in time so I could appreciate the true glory of this place. So I could experience what it was like to come here with your family, to show your children the majesty of the world from up top this hill, all while savoring a melty vanilla ice cream cone. Now, the eerie quiet didn't offer tranquility; it only served as a reminder of everything we'd lost.

Mikha'el joined me at the edge of the walkway, both of us looking off into the distance, past the crumbling, burnt city and at the twinkling sea instead. The setting sun behind us provided a prismatic explosion of warm colors that blanketed the entire sky.

I didn't know why, but it was like my heart couldn't take all that beauty. Maybe because it was a reminder that life went on, despite all the horror still going on around us. It didn't matter that millions of people had died and countless others were out there alone, starving, struggling to make it through the day.

The sun would continue to rise and set. The moon would continue to go through her phases. The stars would continue to shine.

It made everything we were fighting for seem so insignificant. Humanity was a speck of sand blown in the wind, and the universe could not care any less.

I was overwhelmed with so much sorrow and anger and despair that everything I'd been holding back for the last two days just came crashing like an avalanche through an evergreen forest, destroying everything in its path.

Feeling sick to my stomach, I couldn't fight the nausea, and I vomited over the side of the walkway into the overgrown brush below until all I puked was bile. Seemed any type of angelic mode of transportation induced retching.

Wiping my mouth with the sleeve of my shirt, I sat on the teak ledge and didn't bother looking at Mikha'el. I just kept staring at the mocking blue sea in the distance. Tears blurred my vision, distorting the fucking serene landscape. "Why did you bring me here?" I asked, not masking the ire riding my voice.

"Because I… needed to remind myself of my purpose. But mostly, I didn't want to be alone."

I didn't wipe the tears rolling down my cheek. "I knocked on your door for hours on end for the last two days. Did it ever occur to you that maybe *I* didn't want to be alone?"

He sat on the ledge, his wings spirited away, his large thigh brushing against mine. "I owe you a myriad of apologies."

I turned toward him, ready to lash out, but as angry as I wanted to be at him for ignoring me the last two days and for bringing me halfway across Barcelona to see a blasted observatory, I couldn't.

I couldn't because, before me sat a broken angel. This wasn't the same warrior I'd seen plow through walls and slice through demons. This was someone who had lost their world. Not a soldier who had lost a battle, but someone who had lost the reason his heart beat.

This pain I could understand. Right now, he needed me more than I needed him. "Tell me about her."

A small smile pulled at his lips as he looked over the trees and toward the sea. "She was more beautiful than the loveliest sunset you've ever seen. More radiant than the largest star, yet as soft and warm as a late summer night breeze. Gavri'el was everything I ever wanted, and everything I should have never taken."

"Why do you say that?"

He breathed deeply as his mind swam with thoughts. Perhaps he wasn't sure if he wanted to or if he should even share that information with me, but I hoped he would. I hoped that after everything we'd experienced together, he'd see me as more than just his charge, but as a friend.

"Gavri'el's heart wasn't mine to claim," he confessed, breaking the silence. "She gave her heart to Samael long before the seraphim ever fell. More importantly, as leader of God's Heavenly Army, I'd taken an oath of abstinence. By renouncing my right to a mate, I ensured my loyalty would always belong to the Father and no other. It was the oath all my warriors took, yet I… broke mine."

"Is this why Beleth said you're partly responsible for this war? Is Samael doing this to punish you for taking his mate?"

He ran a hand through his dark, messy mane. "Revenge motivates him, but it's not his driving force. Still, I didn't insert a wedge between them. Though I loved her from the first moment I saw her, we didn't fall into each other's arms until after the Fall. I imagine when he found out, it added to his hatred for me, but that's not why he declared himself my enemy.

"He and I were close friends since our creation, but when the time came to cast him out, I led his capture. I shackled his wrists, I locked the gates. As his close friend and ally, he never imagined I would follow God's orders, not when I knew why he'd disobeyed, why he'd rebelled against our creator."

"He knew you were God's commander. What else did he expect? Plus, he hated humanity, and you didn't share his sentiment."

"There were many reasons he felt God's love for humanity was unwarranted, but one of his primary grievances with God was the fact He gave your kind the ability to bear children with whomever you pleased, whenever you pleased."

A fierce gust of wind blew and I shivered, rubbing my arms together. "That's not entirely true. Conception is not as simple as penis in vagina."

He side-eyed me. "Crimes committed by or constraints placed on your people by your own people are not what troubled him, nor were anomalies caused by nature. At the onset of creation, God did not put any limitations on human reproduction. But He did put them on angel folk, and that's what Samael resented."

"That's not our fault."

"It isn't. But Samael saw things differently, especially when his relationship with Gavrie'l was not approved by God due to her being a lower-caste angel. While some of us were created through the Song of Breath, all of us were given the privilege to procreate sexually—provided we followed the caste rules. Samael and Gavri'el broke the rule, thus God withheld their ability to conceive a child. Something that, despite understanding His reasoning, broke Gavri'el's heart."

"Let me guess? Samael could not tolerate watching Gavri'el's devastation, and it fueled his hatred for humans even more."

"Yes. But that wasn't the transgression that earned him his banishment. Determined to prove to God he didn't need His approval or power to create life, he not only stole the Song of Breath—the holy melody used by God to bind the power of the elements in order to create life—but he used it to create a life form not ordained by God."

I scoffed. "I don't mean to side with Samael, but I'm not sure why him creating a life without God's approval matters. What's the big deal if God didn't ordain it? God just didn't like that Samael proved He wasn't the only one who could create life."

Mikha'el turned to face me, his golden eyes darkening, his sharp jaw tight. "What he did was blasphemous. And, regardless of how any of us felt regarding God's rules, because I can't say that our people were happy with all the laws governing Elysium, Samael had no authority to corrupt creation. That's why he was stripped of his power, of his beauty. Why he was imprisoned."

"Because he dared fight against oppression?"

Mikha'el's brow creased, and for a brief second, I thought the sun had either set or been eclipsed by clouds. "Oppression? He was a prince amongst the angels. He had everything any living creature could ever want and more. If anything, he suffered from extreme opulence. He wasn't thrown out because he stole the song, or because he defied his creator. God is not that petty. He was cast out because what he created wasn't a child, it was an abomination. The first demon. He bastardized the power of creation, and that's when God saw Samael's true flaw. The absolute danger he posed.

"Though the song creates life, it does so based on the will and spirit of the creator.

Samael would have you believe he stole the song for love. For Gavri'el. That he did it for his people. But his creation spoke for itself. He did it out of spite, out of pride… out of hatred. And if he'd not been punished for it, he would've infected even more angels with his corrosive thinking."

"But why were those constraints put on your people to begin with?"

"The history of our people is long, Kate. Perhaps one day, I'll share it with you, but what matters is that every race—every realm—has rules that govern them for a reason. I don't question them because I am not the one who created them. My wisdom runs shallow compared to God's."

"But that doesn't make it right. Just because you create something, doesn't mean you can abuse it or do whatever you please with it."

"Perhaps you're right. But this is what separates my kind from yours. It's what makes your kind so fearsome. Your free thinking. Maybe that's been the point all along—to see what would happen in a realm not given the rules."

"Or this is all just a stupid game, and humans are the pawns. And all of this pain and suffering is for nothing but God's entertainment."

He pushed up to his feet, wings spread and fluttering. "No, Kate. Not nothing. It's for love. Look out there," he said, pointing to the mountains, then to the sea. "God gave you this world because He loved you. Because He wanted you to know beauty and happiness. But without pain, there can be no joy. It's that balance that keeps you going. What keeps you fighting? Love is what keeps *me* fighting." His eyes misted over as he placed a hand over his heart.

I jumped to my feet and stepped closer. "If you fight for love, then why didn't you give Beleth the stones to save Gavri'el?" I regretted the words the instant I said them, but it was too late to take them back.

His breath seemed to seize, as if I had just slapped him. Hooding his gaze, he looked back across the city, strands of his hair swirling in the wind. "I wanted to give him the stones," he said. "I would have if Gavri'el hadn't stopped me."

I swallowed hard, speechless.

He spirited his wings away and sat back down, shoulders slouched, chest caved. "You probably wanted to hear that my love for humanity was greater than my love for Gavri'el. That I chose a selfless sacrifice over my own wants and needs. But the truth is, the only reason I didn't hand over the stones was because Gavri'el already knew her fate. Her gift of foresight had warned her that the moment would come to pass.

"She knew Samael would sanction her execution and that I would hand over the stones. But she also knew that Beleth would've still killed her. I told her the sicarius would die before his sword ever touched her flesh, but she said her fate was to die and mine was to protect this world. So she ordered me to be the one to kill her instead. She wanted to deny Samael the pleasure of being the one responsible for her death."

I'd seen that wordless exchange between them, but it had been so brief, I didn't give it much thought. Now it all made sense. I sat next to him, placing a hand on his shoulder. "Mikha'el, I don't know what to say."

"The moment I chose her over God was the moment I Fell. I failed God. Failed my mission." He seeded his gaze in mine. "Failed you."

"I know what it's like to love somebody so hard that you'd do anything to save them. You don't need to apologize for that."

"Kate, I've fallen so low, the longevity of my atonement will outlast your sun's life-giving energy."

"God's going to punish you for loving someone?"

He took my hand in his. "If enduring God's wrath was my only worry, I would've been on my knees before Him already, though it's not as if I know where He is. What worries me is what I did to you, and what that means for this world."

"I'm no one to talk about self-flagellation, but everyone makes mistakes. So, you're not perfect. Big freaking deal. I've fucked up plenty of times. Mistakes are what make us human."

"What makes *you* human, Kate. I'm an angel, the rules are different. Gavri'el and I... We were more than mates, we were soul-bonded. It's when we give each other a sliver of our essence and entwine it with the other. It's a bond you can only make once, and it's only breakable by death. Unless killed, we are immortal; thus, in sharing our souls, we made an oath to be together until the end of time. To lose your soul-bonded mate is to live in painful solitude for eternity."

I hung on every word he said, trying to understand the depth of his sorrow, of his guilt.

"I was so afraid to be without her," he went on, "I was willing to break my oath to God—my promise to protect humanity at any cost—all to save my soul-bonded mate."

I sighed. A part of my heart broke when he admitted he would've handed over the stones. But who was I to say I wouldn't have done the same? That none of us would've? "For Jax. For Luke. I would have sacrificed the universe. So don't feel bad about what you wanted to do. You are not above choosing those you love."

"Except Gavri'el did the noble thing. She chose to break the soul bond to save humanity. She did what I was sworn to do, yet couldn't. That's the reason God makes warriors take the oath of abstinence. I should've lost my helm long ago and been banished for what I did."

"Don't say that."

"Kate, how can I confidently protect your people after I was so easily tempted? After I was willing to give up the stones for her?" He lifted my chin and let me see deep into his eyes, showing me all his wounds. "How could you ever trust me again?"

I placed a hand on his warm cheek and wiped the small tear that had trickled down his face. "I trust you because you're my friend. And I don't need you to swear an oath to me for me to value your friendship. You fucked up; everyone does at one point or another. It's what we do after that matters. There will be time to figure out how you can atone for your *sins,* but right now, I just need you to be a friend back."

Smiling, he nodded, slowly taking my hand in his and lowering it from his cheek. "I wish you could see yourself as I see you, as I've always seen your kind. The evolution of your people. All the different species and races that came before what you now call humans… before God perfected his creation."

"Everything about us is the opposite of perfection."

"And that is why you are special. The peoples of other realms were born with their gifts—grand intelligence, physical superiority, depthless empathy, and the advantage of all knowledge. No one has had to earn their right at the table. No one has had to fight to exist. You've risen from nothing on your own, with minimal interference from us or the other peoples of the galaxies. If given the opportunity, your kind will achieve things no other race has ever been able to achieve. It is why you are revered. Thus, I am honored to be called your friend, Kate."

If there ever existed a moment I wanted to sit down and unpack everything this creature had just said, it was this moment right here. He held all the answers to every question about the universe humans had ever had—but I couldn't ask a single question because we had people to rescue and a world to save.

"One day, I want to come back here to this same mountaintop, to this very spot, and I want to buy us vanilla ice cream cones. Then, I want you to tell me all the secrets of the universe while we watch the sun set and lick melted ice cream off our fingers, is that cool?"

"Very cool," he said with a toothy grin, and I don't think I ever saw him smile so hard.

When we'd arrived at the observatory, he told me he needed to come here because he needed to be reminded of his purpose, but it seemed I needed to be reminded of mine.

The veil was ripped from our eyes the moment the gates opened and Hell broke loose. The truth of God's existence was thrown in our faces like a slap across the cheek, and we were not even given a chance to process what had just happened to us. As a society, we were thrust into the deep end of the pool and told to swim. Except, none of us knew how, and it wasn't a pool but an ocean.

Many of us drowned, but a lot of us survived. We learned to swim and now we're helping others get out of the rough seas and onto shores. We did not perish. That's *our* superpower. But survival will not be our story. Mikha'el mentioned that other races owned a seat at the table; meanwhile, humans had been fighting to exist since we were placed on this planet to evolve. Well, the human race would no longer be treated like guinea pigs or experiments on a petri dish. We would no longer be treated like children at the kids' table.

I now understood my purpose. It wasn't just to rescue Jax and Luke from Samael, or to stop him from escaping his prison, but to bring true light to the darkness. To finally uncover the whole truth and let humans be rulers of their own destiny.

I could have asked Mikha'el to rift us back to *La Sagrada Familia*, but I decided to accept the small gift he'd given me by flying me to the observatory. He showed me the raw beauty of the world. A beauty that existed independent of humanity. One that was unchanging and everlasting, highlighted by the power of our burning star.

Mikha'el had shown me the sun because, for more than a millennium, it had been a symbol of hope. So he flew us back before it would fully set behind the mountains, making sure we took in every ounce of its warmth.

Sure, the road ahead was unknown and covered in shadows, but at least, for this moment in time, I would bask in the light. Afterward, I would descend into Hell and defeat the Seraphim of the First Sphere and his Fallen knights, but I wouldn't do it alone. I had my friends, I had my dog, and I had my sword.

I knew this war was far from over, but I was ready to fight until the new dawn came. After all, I was a woman. I was a mother. And the cursed demons who took my family were going to hear my roar.

Kate, Jax, and their friends will return in the next installment of the Hell's Angel Series. In the meantime, follow the author on social media or subscribe to her newsletter for updates on the next book.

Read on for a special bonus chapter.

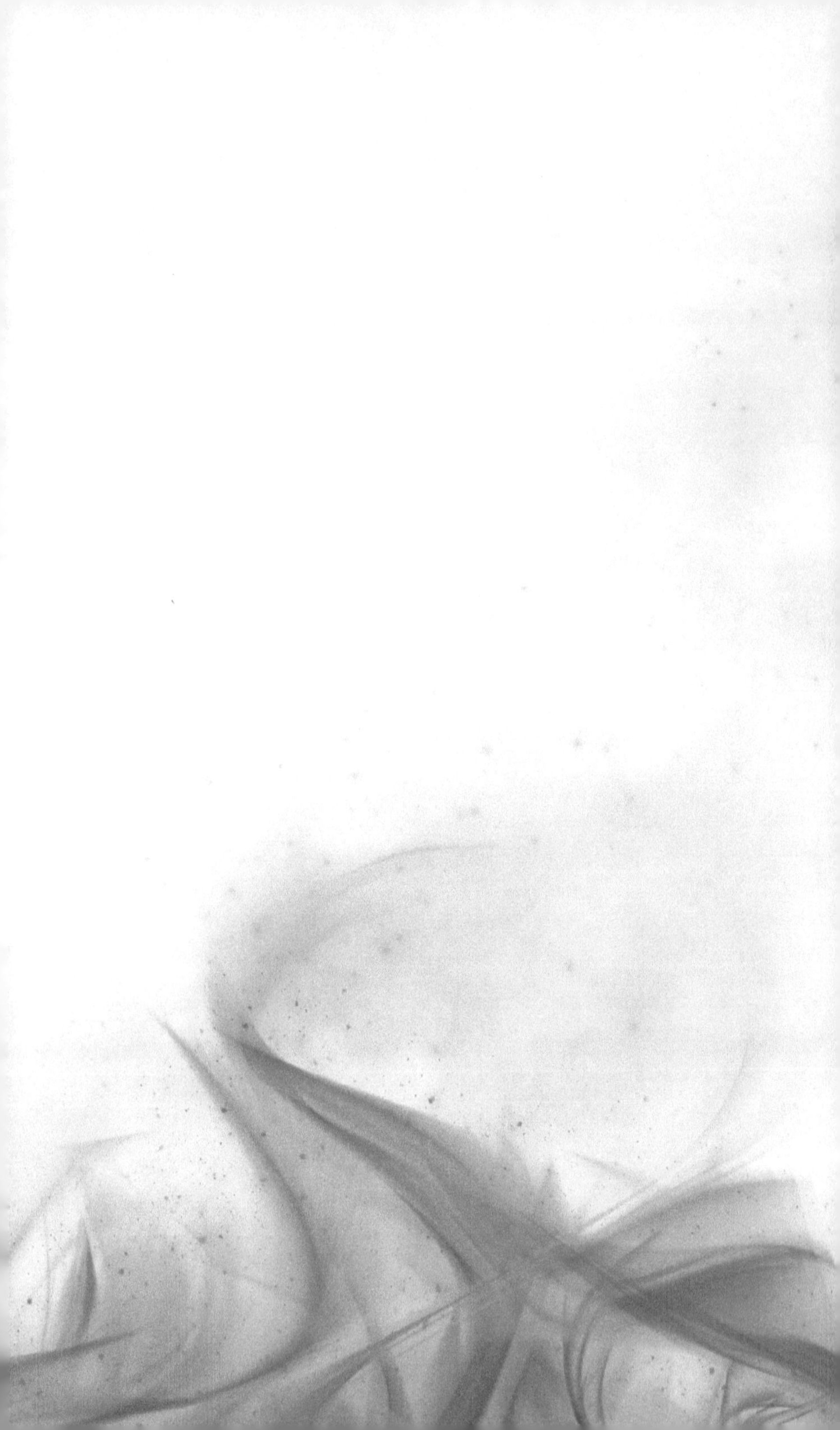

BONUS CHAPTER
BEFORE THE FALL
SAMAEL

Perched atop Apollyon, my Aurelian Starsteed, I galloped on the sandy shores of the Vermillean Sea, headed toward Elysium, Heaven's capital city, which was built into the very rock of Halcion Summit. Gleaming under the divine rays of Luminora, our home star, the citadel's crystal spires rose high into the cerulean sky, their peaks adorned with the sapphire and gold royal standard of God's mighty kingdom.

The banners snapped in the wind as loud trumpets *boomed* from the center of the city. The royal guard was likely already announcing the commencement of today's celebration—the return of our highest-ranking warrior, Archangel Mikha'el, and the Sovereign Vanguard, the decorated commander's formidable legion of elite warriors, known throughout the realms for their unmatched skill, valor, and unwavering loyalty.

Today marked yet another triumph for the archangel of the Third Sphere, protector of all the realms, loyal servant of the Lord God—my *doting* Father—and my most trusted and faithful friend. The legendary celestial hero was revered through the vast expanse of space as a holy defender of the vulnerable and meek. To me, he was just Mikha'el, and even though I loved him like a brother cast from the same clay, some days I detested the vainglorious, pietistic sycophant.

In my Father's eyes, the warrior could do no wrong, and that was because the archangel seldom—rather, *never*—strayed beyond the artfully crafted boundaries of our people's laws. I couldn't even convince him to experiment with the mind-expanding properties of the resplendium flower native to Theraluna, an infant realm still in its early stages of evolution.

Saints forbid the archangel was ever not primed for battle. Still, we'd been friends since the Lord God breathed us into existence, and I couldn't miss the elaborate welcome my Father had prepared in his honor.

I can fly us into the citadel undetected, Apollyon whispered in my mind.

I patted my steed's neck, her lion head's helmet glimmering. Adorned in a luminous, golden coat that shimmered like Luminora's rays, her kind were majestic creatures that exuded an otherworldly radiance. Their mane and tail flowed like streams of stardust, capturing the essence of the cosmic world. Their eyes were said to mirror the vastness of the universe, granting them an unparalleled understanding of the mysteries of creation.

But their greatest gift was their wisdom and deep connection to the angelic realm. With their ability to sense the intentions and emotions of angels, coupled with their ability to express loyalty and love, they shared a unique connection with their rider, one that transcended the spoken word.

Not today, my friend, I told her, letting her feel my appreciation for her suggestion. Flying or rifting was forbidden in Elysium by any angel or beast, except for avian creatures or the Sovereign Vanguard. Even with Apollyon's iridescent wings capable of dissimulation, I couldn't risk it. That's not to say I'd never done it myself; I wasn't above breaking the rules. Incontrovertibly, defying my Father's laws was my greatest virtue. As a Seraphim of the First Sphere, I out-ranked Mikha'el and all his warriors, and refused to let my Father clip my wings.

Nevertheless, today was a day I couldn't draw attention to myself. I needed all eyes on the golden warrior.

Apollyon huffed, annoyed by my response. Always the thrill seeker.

Without flight, we will arrive late for the opening ceremony. Your Father will be disappointed... and so will Gavri'el.

So they would, but I had more important matters on my mind than arriving late to Mikha'el's garish jubilee. With a pull of the reins, I urged Apollyon to run faster, not because I desired to arrive at the citadel any quicker, but simply because I reveled in the feel of the sea's cool spray, my long, platinum hair flapping behind me.

I laughed as the wind whipped against my skin. Today was a day to truly celebrate indeed.

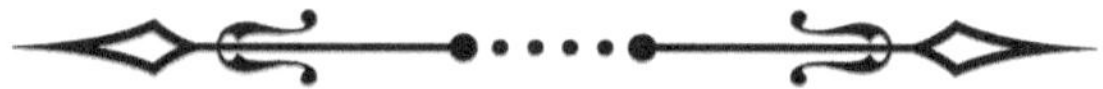

As I expected, angel folk from all three spheres had flocked to the capital city to celebrate Mikha'el's latest victory. He'd been sent by my Father to assist our ally, Queen Loriana Evengale from Aetheria, the realm of the Elementals. For several ethereal arcs or revolutions around their home star, their people had been fighting against the Shadowborn giants from Nethralis. The monsters were a parasitic tribe of nomadic conquerors who harvested worlds until nothing was left but dead rock.

The queen had refused our help for quite some time, but she finally acquiesced. Mikha'el had been gone for almost half an arc before leading the final charge that defeated the Nethralians, decimating them to the point where they no longer posed a threat to any other realm. If it hadn't been for him and the Sovereign Vanguard, Aetheria would have fallen. The queen had been grateful, though I suspected her matriarchal kingdom had been less than pleased that a male archangel knight had stolen the victory.

And now the streets of Elysium were filled with angel children dressed as Vanguard knights, pretending to be Mikha'el and his legion, fighting against the Shadowborn giants. The sounds of flutes and harps floated in the air as townsfolk danced and sang. The aroma of roasted meats, freshly baked breads, caramelized fruits, and fermented grapes permeated the air. My stomach grumbled. I couldn't remember the last time I'd eaten; I'd been so preoccupied with my scrolls and manuscripts. Snatching a fire-grilled poultry leg from a fledgling's hand, I ripped into the flesh and feasted as Apollyon's hooves clomped on the stone passageways that wound around the city.

The child's mother would buy him another.

Galloping uphill toward Etzbakadel, God's magnificent stone and crystal palace, we arrived at the golden gates just as I finished licking the leg bone clean. I chucked the bone, sliding off Apollyon's saddle, and handed the reins over to one of the waiting stable hands. "Make sure she's fed and watered.

Thank you, mitrah, she said, using her kind's word for 'friend.' *Be blessed.*

Rest. I'll be back after I speak with Gavri'el.

The palace corridors were empty of the lords and ladies of my Father's court. Everyone was likely gathered in the great hall, enjoying the early feast—a feast that would be followed by yet another feast once Luminora set and Levaniris rose to grace us with her platinum light. The evening would culminate in a dance ball that would last until dawn.

Normally, I'd be in charge of hosting the palace's debauched affairs, but I'd not been offered the honor of handling the festivities, thus, I held little interest in partaking. Golden eyes glittering, Gavri'el made it a point to remind me in her softest, yet most commanding, voice that not making an appearance would cast a shadow over my friend.

Gavri'el was a Virtue of the Second Sphere and my Father's emissary. He trusted her more than He trusted those closest to His throne. More than the Powers… more than me. Her close relationship with my Father was what brought me close to her. It had been many lifetimes since we first met, but my love for her still burned with the power of a thousand shining stars.

There was nothing she could ask of me that I could refuse. I possessed little power against her wishes, but that wasn't the reason I decided to attend Mikha'el's fete. My absence would trigger the rumormongers to spread their filthy lies, accusing me of jealousy and contempt.

I would rather bend the knee to the human realm than let Mikha'el think I envied him.

Wishing to remain inconspicuous, I chose to use the servants' doors instead of entering through the main entrance. Seemed I'd arrived later than I'd thought. The feast was over, and my Father was no longer in attendance. He was not one to linger long at these events, but I also suspected my absence hadn't helped His sullen mood.

Everyone else stood around the room, milling about, gossiping, politicking, all while sipping wine and ale. Snatching a goblet from a servant's tray, I spotted one of my courtiers leaning against the wall across the immense wood dining table that was littered with mountains of food trays still half-full.

"Chemoth," I crooned, sidling up beside him and taking a sip of my wine as I interrupted his spirited conversation with one of the seraphim females of our court. "Melandriel, looking lovely as ever."

Smiling coyly, she said. "Sam, I thought you might preclude us from your presence today."

I placed an excessively dramatic hand over my heart. "And miss all the fun? Never. Do you mind if I borrow my friend for a moment?" I asked, pulling him away before she could answer.

"This better be important. She was about to tell me how I can—"

"I found it," I said, interrupting whatever lewd comment he was about to make.

"Come again?"

"Naeshma Khartel."

His eyes bulged and he grabbed me by the forearm, dragging me deeper into an alcove nearby. "The breath forge?"

I nodded, lips twitching, thrill riding my veins.

He adjusted the high collar of his silk embroidered, burgundy velvet overcoat. "Do the others know?"

"You're the first."

"What an honor," he feigned gratitude as he leaned his back against the wall and crossed his arms.

Roaming the crowd, a tightness coiled around my lungs when I couldn't find Gavri'el. Astaroth, a high member of my court, and one of my most trusted confidants, spotted me across the hall, his gaze snagging on mine. The tall, broad-shouldered seraphim, with hair the color of molten lava and eyes to match, winked at me as he whispered something to his male companion, both of them sharing an intimate laugh.

I stretched my neck and sipped from my goblet. Acknowledging my silent cue, he bid his lover goodbye and ambled toward us. Unlike everyone else in the room who had spirited their wings away out of respect for the mighty Mikha'el, Astaroth chose to showcase his resplendent red wings, trimmed in gold and sapphire. Dressed equally florid, he drew every eye in the room, female and male alike. His dimpled chin and sensual lips made him a sight to behold.

"How splendorous," Chemoth huffed. "The peacock approaches."

"Behave," I warned.

"Samael," Astaroth drawled in his soft baritone. "Pleased to see you've decided to join your menial subjects."

"By now you should know that unless I'm hosting, these gatherings are for the plebs."

"Chemoth," Astaroth said with a mocking bow. "You've been awfully avoidant."

"What part of modest and plain did you not understand?" Chemoth snapped, gritting his teeth. "You'll be lucky not to be thrown in the cells for displaying your wings."

Astaroth's eyes glittered, his face a canvas of utter aloofness. "Brother, the guard has far more important things to be troubled by than my wings. Besides, Mikha'el himself remarked on their luminescent plumage."

Chemoth shook his head. "You gaudy buffoon. Do you have any idea what's at stake here? Can you, for once in your damned saint's indulgent life, take anything seriously?"

I understood Chemoth's irritation with Astaroth. I'd asked them to be ready to take leave at a moment's notice, should I succeed in finding the location of the breath forge, a place known only to my Father. The place where all life was birthed into existence.

There was zero room for mistakes.

Never one to be involved in politics or anything related to court matters, the dazzling seraph held a reputation as the handsome philanderer who was always primed for merriment and pleasure. If there was ever a time I needed him to drop the theatrics, it was today.

Astaroth lifted the side of his gold and red overcoat, revealing the empyrean sword secured at his waist. Sneering at Chemoth, his flamboyant and playful demeanor became vapors. The molten lava of his eyes churned with the promise of rage and violence. This was the Astaroth I knew.

"I understood quite well what was expected of me," he gritted at Chemoth, red wings fluttering. He then met my gaze. "My liege, everything you requested is in order. My men are at your disposal, should you need them."

I offered him a curt nod. "And Malphas?"

"At the gallery." Astaroth sighed. "You know, he's quite the bore. He prefers solitude over good company."

"He's not a fan of all this wastefulness, more like," Chemoth said, gesturing to all the uneaten food sprawled on the table.

"Get word to him," I said to them both. "And Beleth. We move tonight. Don't forget the amulets."

Astaroth smiled, patting his chest. "It's safe. I promise."

Chemoth couldn't be bothered to crease his lips, though he patted his chest as well, signaling his amulet was also tucked and safe.

Good. Now I needed to find Gavri'el.

"She's on the eastern veranda," Astaroth called out as he watched me squeeze through the crowd, my eyes darting around the room.

I turned to look at him, annoyed he knew I couldn't simply reach her through mind channeling. It was a gift granted by the Spirit when two angels were soul-bonded. Gavri'el and I hadn't been able to complete the ritual—*rather*, she'd refused to until the Lord God blessed our union. Something that, despite His love for me and respect for her, He'd spurned to do.

Not many knew we were not soul-bonded, so I curled my lips at him in a snarl.

She's with Mikha'el, he mouthed, a sardonic smile tracing a line across his lips, those glittering eyes alight with fire. He loved to play the role of aloof lecher, but that gaze spoke of wolfish cunning and deadly rampage. I'd chosen him well, though he still rankled me.

But perhaps what enraged me more was the fact that he knew how deeply his words would cut.

Gavri'el's friendship with Mikha'el shouldn't have troubled me, but the burning sensation eating at my heart was hard to ignore. I exited through the side entrance and headed toward the eastern veranda, my steps quicker than I would've liked. I was a bit too eager to get there, and my impatient steps broadcasted my intentions to anyone with half a brain to figure out what they were.

As I rounded the corner toward the veranda, the turquoise sea gleaming in the distance beyond the cliffs of Halcion, I couldn't help the deep gasp of air that inflated my lungs. Cosmic stars, I could never tire of Gavri'el's unmatched beauty. She couldn't see me from my vantage point, but I had a full view of her side profile. Her long, white hair was plaited down to her waist in a loose braid, wispy strands of her hair gently swaying in the sea breeze.

Dressed in a long, flowing gown, encrusted with aquamarith gemstones that shimmered in crystal blue-green colors, she looked like she'd stepped from the depths of Marinithra, home of the Oceanic Elysians. Leaning over the rail, a bright smile illuminated her soft, brown skin. I took a second to appreciate the warmth that spread over my chest at the sight of her. She had no idea how my entire universe revolved around that smile.

A smile conjured by the hulking archangel beside her.

The warmth stirring in my chest chilled to ice.

Mikha'el stood beside Gavri'el, his shoulder brushing hers as he leaned over the veranda, pointing at something in the distance, their shared laugh too intimate, too coquettish for a celibacy oath-bound warrior and an emissary already committed to another.

Smearing an ice-crusted smile on my face, I ambled toward them, each step painfully slow as I forced myself to seem unperturbed by their lack of decorum, pretending I'd stumbled upon their balcony tryst by mere accident. "Gavri'el, Mikha'el? What a pleasant surprise to find you both here."

Mikha'el jumped to attention quicker than would be expected of someone not caught doing anything wrong. A wide grin split his face, his sharp jaw seeming more angular. "Brother, I knew you'd come." Taking me into a full, loving embrace, he welcomed me like I knew he would, with genuine joy and affection.

Damn saints. Some days, I truly despised how intoxicatingly gracious and chivalrous he was. I echoed his hug, patting him on the back before pulling away, my gaze always on Gavri'el. The jovial spark in her smile snuffed to one plastered out of courtesy. Her disappointment at seeing me felt like a spear shot through my heart. "Darling," I said, sliding a gentle hand across her lower back and brushing a tender kiss over her cheek, disguising the ache at my core. "Stunning as ever."

Her golden gaze softened over me, somehow putting me at ease. "Elated that you were able to make it, my love. Though you missed the feast."

"And what a feast the Lord God prepared for the Vanguard," Mikha'el chirped. "An amazing welcome home."

"Well, let's put it frankly. The feast was in *your* honor, brother."

Dressed in the sapphire and gold formal royal guard uniform, Mikha'el looked exquisitely dashing. Archangels were typically larger and broader than other angels, as most were warriors or guardians, and Mikha'el's impending physical form was undoubtedly built exceptionally well for war.

I squared my shoulders and straightened my back as I looked up to meet his luminous golden gaze. His black mane was neatly tied at the nape and his skin was poreless and dewy.

The warrior looked as refined as an aristocrat making his rounds through court. One would be hard-pressed to envision him covered in the blood of his enemies, though I knew how ferocious and wholly frightening he looked dressed in war armor and brandishing Emrandael, his treasured sword.

There was no question why the Lord had chosen him to lead His holy army.

Eyeing his uniform, I said, "I notice your wings are spirited away, commander. Today is your day to shine. You should have them out on full display for the entire realm to marvel at your glory."

He chuckled. "You mock me. But you know these flashy affairs make me uncomfortable. I have no desire to be the center of attention."

Of course he wouldn't.

I smiled. "Well, I'm happy to have you back home. You've been missed."

"Likewise, brother. Let's go riding soon. I have much to tell you."

Because listening to his war stories and adventures was exactly what I wanted to do in my spare time. "Apollyon would be delighted to run with Bayardon."

He clasped my shoulder with his massive hand. "It's settled, then."

"Commander," one of Mikha'el's warriors called from across the veranda, "Lord Lemendrael wishes a word."

Mikha'el nodded, then turned to me and Gavri'el. "Apologies. Duty calls. I prefer the battlefield over court business, but you know how things are…"

"Of course," Gavri'el said, smiling sweetly. "It was lovely catching up."

He returned her smile, and I hated that they shared something I wasn't privy to. "See you both tonight at the grand gala?" he asked, eyes hopeful, but solely trained on my beloved.

"We wouldn't miss it," Gavri'el said, answering for the both of us.

With a pat on my back, he wished me farewell and was swallowed into the sea of courtiers.

Gavri'el's gaze followed his exit until he was gone from view.

"You're quite fond of him," I said, calling her attention.

She spun toward me, her eyes twinkling. "No more than you. He *is* your best friend."

"Indeed, he is. Here," I said, pulling a small box wrapped in crimson paper from inside my black overcoat pocket. "I've brought you a gift." Her eyes widened as I placed it in her hand. "Go on. Open it."

Gently uncoiling the black silk ribbon, her breath hitched in anticipation. Once she opened the package, she gasped. "Samael… it's stunning."

I took the necklace from the box and asked her to turn around so I could clasp it around her neck. When she turned to face me again, her eyes flashed with excitement, that ravishing smile obliterating the gloom from my heart. The smooth opaline rock embedded in the pendant shimmered as the light from our home star hit its surface. "I found it buried in a riverbed on Theraluna and it reminded me of you. Pure. Lustrous. Beautiful."

Her smile flattened as she looked into my eyes. "Samael, it's gorgeous. Thank you. You know that one of the things I love most about you is your curiosity—your sense of adventure. Your desire for knowledge and to push against the boundaries."

"But…? I know one is coming."

"Samael, the covenant of our people. God has forbidden us from visiting infant realms."

I hung my head. "Of course. The Lord God. Creator of Heaven and all the worlds. Our Father. He must know best." I lifted a misty gaze to hers. The rejection of my gift was like thorns slicing across my skin. "But when have the rules stopped me from doing what I want, from exploring the cosmos?"

"It's for their protection, and ours. You shouldn't have taken this from there."

She went to unclasp the necklace, but I placed my hand over hers. "No. Keep it. I want you to wear it, at least for tonight."

Suddenly, her eyes glossed over, turning milky white. She was being hit with a vision. Her gift of foresight was one of the reasons God had chosen her as His emissary. It lasted but a few breaths before she emerged, eyes blinking fast as she gathered her senses.

Looking at me as if she was seeing me for the first time, she said, "You're not planning on coming tonight."

I couldn't help the smile that tugged on my lips. "You seem disappointed."

She took a step back, something like fear flashing in her eyes. "Of course I am. Why wouldn't I be?"

I swiped a tendril of her soft hair behind her ear. "I have business I must attend to, but I will do my best to come, if only for the last dance of the ball. You'll save it for me, yes?"

Her breath rose. "Don't do this, Samael. Please. I beg you. Come to the ball with me. Let's forget our sorrows and enjoy one night of pure delight."

Swallowing deeply, I almost took her offer. But there were far greater dreams to reach. "Everything I do, I do for love, Gavri'el. I do it for *you*. If anything, carry that in your heart."

Her lips parted, but her words died on her tongue when her gaze rose above my shoulders. She sneered, a gesture seldom seen on her face.

"What is it?" I asked.

"Beleth. Seems he's searching for you."

"You two need to get over your differences."

"Tell *him* that." Her gaze met mine once again, the gold in her pupils swirling like liquid starlight. "My love for you expands the galaxies. I will be waiting for you at the ball tonight, Samael." She placed her soft lips over mine. "Don't break my heart."

With that, she took off swiftly, like a breeze blowing through blades of grass.

"She won't forgive you," Beleth said from behind me as she disappeared through the crowd.

"You don't know that," I replied, leaning against the rail and looking out to sea.

He followed suit. "She's my sister; I know her better than you."

"Doubtful. But even if at first she doesn't understand, in time she will. She'll know I did this all for her."

"Are you?"

I straightened and turned to face him. "Am I what?"

His blue-green gaze reflected the undulating waves of the gentle sea. His was a mirrored visage of his sister, minus the eyes. "Doing this *only* for her?"

"For her, *and* for our people. Are you not tired of not being free? Of living only to serve the other realms as God sees fit? We deserve more, certainly more than the wretched creatures He's chosen for Earth."

Beleth's cruel and wary smile widened. "I've a bloodlust for revolution, so you know I support your goals, but what you plan to do will have irreversible consequences. You will be changing the course of countless worlds. Change does come at a high price, my liege, regardless of its morality or noble cause. Are you prepared to bear the cost?"

He meant Gavri'el.

I knew her heart. I knew what she desired most in this world, and I was prepared to lose her if it meant granting her wish. "It's too late to change my mind. Everything has been set into motion."

"Are you sure these replicas will work?" he asked, palming the pendant hanging around his neck.

"They aren't replicas. They are complete renderings of the original creation stones. I went to great lengths to have them forged."

"Well, then, given this might be the last night I will be a free subject able to roam the halls of the palace, I will make the best of my time and join the celebrations. You should, too." He patted me on the shoulder. "I will await your orders."

Leaning my arms over the veranda, I took in the beauty of my realm from atop the summit. If I'd known this would be the last time I would gaze upon Elysium bathed in Luminora's rays, or the last time I would see Gavri'el's gentle face, I may have reconsidered my plans to betray my Father.

Alas, I was destined to Fall.

ACKNOWLEDGEMENTS

Writing Descension was quite the journey. I'd certainly not expected to take the voyage on my own. While it was sad to part ways with Victoria for this project, the experience was bitter sweet. One of the reasons we chose to co-author Afterworld was to cut the writing time in half. When the decision was made that it was in the best interest of the series to part ways, I was nervous I would not be able to make the deadline.

Well, this year I learned that it is possible for me to write a book in less than a year, which was a huge achievement. My first solo novel took six years from inception to publication, and my second one took two years. Still, I wouldn't have been able to complete Descension on my own without the support of my family and friends.

A special thank you to my trio: Jack, Christina, and Monica. You three are the Three Musketeers to my D'Artagnan. You make this journey called womanhood possible. Your support, daily meme and reel shares, and Tuesday wine nights, keep me sane and confident that I can juggle being a wife, mother, and an author—while also working a full-time job.

A huge thank you to my husband for being such a sport and taking on the job of unofficial narrator when I needed someone to read back Jax and Samae'ls chapters. His voice acting is incredible. Perhaps I should try to convince him to become a voice actor…

I'd also like to thank my kiddos for their patience and their contribution to this novel. They have become big fantasy readers and are dying to read this series. Alas, they are only twelve. However, they are the creative minds behind Bladehead aka El Carnicero and the Sin Ojos demons. Wanting to be a part of the writing process, they got to work and designed these monsters. I'm so proud of them and thankful they think what I do is cool.

Last but not least, as always, I'd like to thank my reader group: Liv's Wicked Tribe. It feels great to have a group of loyal fans who look forward to your books. You are the reason I spend countless nights behind a computer screen imagining these worlds and bringing these characters to life.

I can't wait to bring you the conclusion to the Hell's Angel series, though I can't promise that I'm ready to leave this universe behind just yet…

With love,
Liv

ABOUT THE AUTHOR

REAL LOVE AS IT IS. MESSY. COMPLICATED.
AND SINFULLY ADDICTIVE.

Olivia Boothe is a contemporary romance and fantasy author.
Born in Colombia and raised in New Jersey since the age of eight, Olivia always dreamed of becoming a storyteller. Now, she enjoys crafting novels with deep, layered plots because romance is not just about the first kiss and the happily ever after, it's about everything in between.

In addition to writing, Olivia loves reading across all genres, binge watching her favorite TV shows, and hanging out on Tuesday nights with her girlfriends for wine, snacks, and junk-TV therapy. Olivia lives in Northern New Jersey with her hubby, three boys, and a mini Aussie named Rosie.

To read more from Olivia, visit her website and follow her on social media

www.oliviaboothe.com
TikTok: @oliviaboothebooks
Instagram: @authoroliviaboothe
Facebook: @authoroliviaboothe

TABLE OF CONTENTS